PRAISE FOR BOOK ONE IN THE
FALLEN SIREN SERIES

Cursed

"One entertaining and fast-paced read. Best of all? Zack, the wildly sexy werewolf FBI agent! What better crime-fighting partner could a girl have?"
— Jennifer Ashley, *New York Times* bestselling author of *Tiger Magic*

"*Cursed* is the perfect blend of magic, mystery, and romance. Emma and Zack are strong, noble characters who are trying to overcome their dark pasts, and their quests for redemption will make your heart hurt. This is a series you need to read now."
— Sandy Williams, author of the Shadow Reader series

"A promising new writing collaboration.... After delivering a hefty helping of danger and drama, Harper then sets the groundwork for more fast-paced adventures."
— *RT Book Reviews* (4 stars)

"Authors Samantha Sommersby and Jeanne C. Stein (the writing team that is S. J. Harper) have created something wonderful with the Fallen Siren series." — Wit and Sin

"I love the story, I love the world, I love the concept, and I lov~~e the characters.~~" — Fangs for the Fantasy

"A ... and contemporary
UF ... hing Book Reviews

D1021839

Also by S. J. Harper

Cursed

RECKONING

A FALLEN SIREN NOVEL

S. J. HARPER

A ROC BOOK

ROC
Published by the Penguin Group
Penguin Group (USA) LLC, 375 Hudson Street,
New York, New York 10014

USA | Canada | UK | Ireland | Australia | New Zealand | India | South Africa | China
penguin.com
A Penguin Random House Company

First published by Roc, an imprint of New American Library,
a division of Penguin Group (USA) LLC

First Printing, October 2014

 REGISTERED TRADEMARK — MARCA REGISTRADA

ISBN 978-0-425-26330-3

Printed in the United States of America
10 9 8 7 6 5 4 3 2 1

To the readers who stepped into our world and welcomed Emma and Zack into your hearts. We thank you.

ACKNOWLEDGMENTS

Writing can be a very solitary experience. Like Emma and Zack, we've become a terrific team. But we haven't done it alone. We want to give special recognition to Aaron, Angie, Mario, Warren, and Jeff of the Pearl Street Critique Group. Phil, Jeannette, and Steve for being good to Jeanne and to one another. Bill, Beverly, Max, and Daren for being there day in and day out for Sam. The S. J. Harper street team for believing in us from the get-go and for their tireless enthusiasm. Editor Jessica Wade and the Penguin team for their expertise. The media relations department of the San Diego Police Department and the FBI's office of public affairs for answering all of our questions. Any mistakes within this work are our own.

Siren *noun* 1. One of three sisters ejected from Mount Olympus by Zeus and cursed by Demeter for failing to prevent Hades from kidnapping Persephone. 2. An immortal goddess bound to earth who, in search of her own salvation, saves others from peril. 3. A beautiful and powerful seductress, capable of infiltrating the minds of others in order to extract truth or exert influence.

CHAPTER 1

What we're doing is wrong on so many levels. That's what I tell myself as I wake, my body aching in all the right places. In just a few short months, we've fallen into the kind of pattern I'd normally think of as dangerous. But somehow, when I'm with him, I feel safe.

My mind drifts as I watch the flutter of curtains. The morning sunshine pours into the bedroom from the balcony. Have I ever had a steady lover so possessive, so creative, so ... demanding? His hand on my hip comes to life, fingertips skimming downward across the curve of my buttocks. He inches closer to me, spooning his body against mine. Nothing separates us under the sheets—it's skin on skin. Fingers slide between my thighs. I'm wet. It seems lately, in his presence, I'm perpetually this way. I just can't help myself. A Siren is a Siren. A sexual creature, born of Gaia. I'm one of three, cursed by Demeter thousands of years ago for failing to protect Persephone. It's for this I atone, for this I pay. It's the reason I search for the missing and avoid love at all costs. The first brings me closer to the promise of redemption. Forgetting the latter? Finding real love? That promises nothing but ruin and death.

"Good morning," I whisper.

He lifts one of my legs. His long, thick shaft slides between them. I feel the warmth of his smile as he replies, "It's about to get even better."

The rumble of his rich baritone, still rough from sleep, along with the promise of what's to come, makes me smile. But the sense of contentment is fleeting. The first few bars of "Bad Moon Rising" blare from my phone. Liz, my best friend, and quite possibly the most powerful witch this side of the Mississippi, added the ringtone to my cell five months ago and I haven't been able to change it. She assigned it to Zack, my partner, a dark, rugged werewolf who was formerly, and quite secretly, a badass black ops assassin. Now, like me, he spends his days working for the FBI and searching for the missing.

I feel Kallistos' irritation at the interruption. I pat his hand. "Hold that thought," I say, then reach for my phone.

"Zack. It's early. What's up?"

"Jimmy. He wants to see us right away and apparently you haven't been answering your texts."

I glance at the clock on the nightstand. It's just past seven on a Monday and I've managed to piss off the boss. "Why didn't he just call me?"

"He did. Twice."

"Damn it! I must have slept through it."

Or Kallistos had taken it upon himself to set my cell to silent. *Again.* Thanks to Liz's spell, and much to Kallistos' chagrin, Zack's calls ring through regardless. Liz knows how close Zack and I came to disaster. This is her special way of reminding me of the ever-present danger. She's also the main reason I'm sharing the vampire King's bed now. She encouraged him and pushed me like a veritable yenta. After countless protests they wore me down. I decided to give the no-strings-attached-relationship proposal a trial run.

Kallistos has retreated to the other side of the bed. I'd like to think out of guilt, but I know better.

I momentarily mute the call. "Stop silencing my phone," I scold.

His clear blue eyes give nothing away. "You don't get enough rest." His tone is matter-of-fact. No argument. No apology. Not ever. Admittedly, it's one of the downsides of dating a vampire King with more than a millennium under his belt—one that I'll eventually have to address if our arrangement continues. Eventually. But not today.

"You don't get to make decisions for me," I counter.

He answers my rising ire with a disarming smile. "You need coffee, Emma. I'll call down."

I unmute the phone, turning my attention back to Zack. "How much time do I have?"

"The briefing was scheduled for seven thirty. Reminding Jimmy it was Labor Day got us a reprieve until eight."

I brace myself, knowing I shouldn't ask, but do anyway. "Did you and Sarah have plans?"

My question about Sarah, the she-wolf who shares Zack's beach house, is met with the expected pause. Zack doesn't say much about his private life. His reluctance doesn't have anything to do with our history. As far as he's concerned, we have no history; there's never been anything personal between us at all. Thanks to Liz's super-duper spell casting, Zack's memories of those times have been erased. Not all of them, of course; only the ones indicating there had ever been any physical intimacy between us. Our casework history, secrets shared about our natures and pasts—that's all remained intact. But remembrances of our one, glorious night in Charleston and the fact we became lovers after his move here to San Diego a year later? Gone.

Kallistos climbs out of bed and heads for the balcony. "Maybe the four of us can do something together later," he murmurs on the way.

I throw a pillow at him, but miss by a mile. By the time it hits the floor he's outside and, thanks to a little pink pill called Protectus, appreciating the early-morning sun like only someone who's spent more than a thousand years in darkness could—face tilted up, eyes closed. Kallistos is responsible for the creation of Protectus, part medical miracle and part magic. It's been around for a couple decades now, along with the Blood Emporiums he created.

Most Emporiums are located in the backs of businesses catering to those who pursue alternative lifestyles—tattoo shops and heavy-metal clubs. For vampires they offer fresh blood from paid donors who, for the most part, have no idea where the blood ends up or who is paying for it. Would-be vampires and goths simply believe they are indulging in a fantasy. They never see the real vampires who come to buy their blood bags and the drugs that allow them to function during the day.

I watch my lover breathe deeply of the ocean air. Appreciate the way shadow and light play across his body, which is hard, lean, and eternally young.

"I was going to make my famous London broil," Zack finally volunteers. "But, duty calls. Right, *partner*?"

Zack has a way of saying the word *partner* like it really means something. And it does. A lump forms in my throat. Our reasons may be different, but the mission is the same. Zack understands me better than any partner I've had.

I nod. "Yes. Duty calls."

"I'll let Jimmy know we're on our way in."

"I'll meet you at the office in forty-five minutes." As I hang up, I silently recite the same words I do every time I go out on a new case. *Redemption could be one rescue away.*

Kallistos is beside me with a robe. "No time for breakfast, I suppose."

I wave him off and begin to hunt for my clothes. "I have to go. As it is, I barely have enough time to get home, shower, and change. Can you help me find my other shoe?"

I crouch down to check under the bed.

"If you kept some things here—"

"I'm not moving in," I tell him for the hundredth time as I climb to my feet. My eyes fall to the large saltwater aquarium across from the bed. My black patent pump is dangling off of an outcropping of orange coral.

Kallistos follows my line of sight. "Oops."

"Oops?"

In response he opens the closet, pulls out a hanging bag, then tosses it onto the bed. Two shopping bags follow.

"What's this?" I ask.

"Emergency clothes. By the time you get out of the shower, breakfast will be here. You now have time."

I quickly rummage through the bags. He's thought of

everything—shoes, stockings, undergarments, classic black pantsuit, and a dove gray poplin shirt with French cuffs. "You're dressing me now?"

"Sorry, no. You're going to have to put those on yourself." Kallistos picks up the phone and asks for room service.

I make a beeline for the bathroom, new black lace bra and matching panties in hand. I don't get very far. His arm snakes around my waist as I pass, pulling me close. "I'll happily take them off tonight, though," he murmurs into my ear.

Twenty minutes later I emerge from the Hotel Palomar—to-go coffee cup in one hand, fresh croissant in the other. My car—a standard-issue black Suburban—is waiting in front. I tip the valet and get in. A quick check in the rearview mirror assures me that the glamour I pay Liz for, the one that furnishes me with the wholesome, plain-Jane facade I've become so accustomed to seeing, is firmly in place. My skin is fair and unblemished. I don't wear makeup. No mascara. No lip gloss. Nothing. This morning, my long dark hair is pulled back and twisted into a sensible chignon. I drop the coffee into the cup holder, toss the croissant onto the dash where I'll be able to easily reach it, then throw the car into gear and pull into traffic.

I have fifteen minutes. Within five I'm pulling onto the 163 heading north. I switch over to the 8 West, then go north on the 15. It's a little warmer than usual in San Diego, eighty-five degrees. Not a cloud in the sky, and due to the holiday, the traffic is light. I work on my croissant and coffee while listening to the morning news. The

Padres are, miraculously, still in good standing. Due to a last-minute donation from the Gates Foundation, several local after-school programs that were believed to have been doomed will be reopening tomorrow. And the wildfire that began Sunday morning in the Cuyamaca Mountains is now under control.

Just another perfect day in paradise.

As I approach the exit to Aero Drive, I see Sarah's silver BMW just up ahead. The top is down and Zack is behind the wheel. His dark brown hair, which he manages to keep slightly longer than regulation, is blowing straight back. Sarah, forever perfectly coiffed, is wearing a red silk scarf around her head. Its ends trail behind her, reminding me of the days when barnstorming and open-cockpit flying were all the rage.

When we stop at the light, Zack catches a glimpse of me in the rearview mirror. He doesn't turn around, just lifts his hand into the air. I do the same. Sarah pivots in her seat. She slides her dark designer glasses halfway down the bridge of her nose so that she can give me a proper glare. One of the first things Sarah Marie Louis did after following Zack out here from South Carolina was to pull me aside and stake her claim. Zack had described what they had back in South Carolina as casual. For Sarah, it had been anything but. She was in love with him. She is still in love with him.

I understand that. So am I.

The light turns green and I follow Zack into the parking lot of the FBI field office. He pulls into the drive by the front door. I park at the end of a row of other black Suburbans. By the time I reach the entrance, Sarah is in the driver's seat.

"What? No kiss good-bye?" I ask Zack as she drives off. "Did someone wake up on the wrong side of the bed?"

Zack shoves his hands in his pockets. "The moon was full last night," he reminds me. "This someone spent the night locked in his cage. Alone."

Although I'm dying to know where Sarah spent the night, how she rode out the inevitable changeling time, I resist the urge to question Zack further. My patience pays off.

"She's thinking about joining a pack. She ran with them last night." He gives me a sideways glance. "I don't have to ask who you spent the night with. You reek of vampire and sex."

I dramatically roll my eyes before heading for the entrance. "I just showered."

He beats me to the door and opens it for me. "You need to use stronger soap. And spend less time with His Royal Undead. I don't know what you see in him."

I push the call button for the elevator. *When I'm with him, it's easier to avoid thinking about you.* The thought, like so many others, goes unsaid. I plaster a practiced smile on my face, the one meant to convey that Kallistos is my world. "You haven't seen him naked."

"A fact that saddens me deeply. It's number three on my bucket list, you know."

The elevator doors open and we step inside. Just as they are about to close, another agent joins us. The familiar banter, laced with the kind of innuendo that I'll later play over and over again in my head, comes to a full stop. Zack and I move to opposite ends of the elevator. We face forward. Zack makes small talk with the other agent. I've worked in the same office with the guy for more than a year, and right now I can't remember his name.

But I remember every moment spent with Zack.

That's all part of my punishment, part of my penance. A cold chill creeps up my spine. I can almost feel Demeter watching.

Satisfied?

A shiver passes through me.

Agent What's-His-Name crosses his arms protectively in front of himself. "Whoa, think they overdid it a bit with the AC this morning."

I know the drop in temperature has nothing to do with the building's air-conditioning. It has everything to do with Demeter. Ever present. Ever watching. Ever ensuring that I am suffering.

I steal a glance at Zack, but quickly force myself to look away. I'll always remember but he'll never know what we had. What we lost. And I know that this morning, Demeter is smiling down upon us, pleased with herself, full of smug indignation and self-righteous conceit.

CHAPTER 2

Day One: Monday, September 2

The office is quiet as we make our way from the elevator through the maze of cubicles that makes up the FBI San Diego field office. Thoughts of Demeter fade as Zack and I exchange nervous looks. In spite of the holiday, half a dozen agents are already at work, either with a phone receiver to an ear or at a computer, fingers flying over the keyboards. What's missing is the banter that usually accompanies agents at work like this. The muted atmosphere is unsettling.

Zack tilts his head toward the far wall. "Something is very wrong."

Deputy Director Johnson's office, which is walled with floor-to-ceiling windows, is the middle of three that look onto the general work area. The door is closed, but the blinds that are usually drawn are open, giving Johnson a clear view of the agents in the bullpen and us a clear view of him. Our normally unflappable bulldog of a boss is pacing, cell phone to his ear. The second he sees us, he disconnects and stiffly motions us inside.

"And it's personal," Zack mutters under his breath.

"Personal?" My question goes unanswered.

Zack holds the door open, allowing me to pass through first.

Normally I would attribute the gallant door-opening gesture to his old-world Southern charm. But when I see the look on Johnson's face, I realize it might be more self-preservation than good manners that prompted Zack's gentlemanly behavior. Johnson's steely eyed glare skewers me.

"Monroe, is your cell phone broken?" He moves to his desk and drops heavily into his chair before looking up at me expectantly, his face a rigid mask of irritation. "Well?"

"No, sir."

"Did you lose it, maybe, or leave it at a friend's?"

"No. Sir."

"Then why the fuck haven't you checked your messages?"

I do a mental shuffle, trying to come up with an excuse when I know I have none. "Sorry, sir," I say at last. "The truth is, the ringer was muted and I didn't realize it."

Zack steps to my side. "It is a holiday, sir."

"When I want your opinion, Armstrong, I'll damn well ask for it!"

Johnson's outburst silences anything else Zack might have contemplated saying in my defense. I throw him a sideways glance. He's staring straight ahead, the picture of composure, the ultimate professional, like a good soldier patiently awaiting his next order. Only the telltale tic in his jaw provides an indication of his level of annoyance.

Jimmy called us in to tell us something. Either he doesn't know how to start, or he just plain doesn't want to. Zack suspects it's personal. So, maybe it's a bit of both.

The testosterone standoff is getting us nowhere. I decide to change tactics. "For the record, I'm sorry I didn't answer when you called." Risking another angry outburst, I approach, asking softly, "What's going on, Jimmy?"

For a moment he says nothing. Then his shoulders suddenly slump. He passes a hand over his face, releases a breath, and slouches back in his chair. "Sorry, Monroe, Armstrong. I had a rough night and my morning hasn't been much better." He motions to the chairs in front of his desk. "Have a seat."

Zack takes the one to the right, I the one to the left. Johnson begins by sorting through some papers on the desk. After a moment he pulls two from the pile and hands them to me first.

"The girl on the left is Hannah Clemons. The girl on the right, Sylvia Roberts. Both sixteen."

I glance at the pictures. They look like school photos, the kind of head shot you'd find in a typical yearbook. Both girls are blond and blue-eyed. They are wearing identical white blouses, Peter Pan collars lying neatly on top of navy blue cardigans. Their smiles radiate the confidence that comes with being young and pretty. I hand the pictures to Zack as Johnson hands another to me.

"This is Julie Simmons. Eighteen."

Another blonde. Same uniform. She's as pretty as the other two, but with a shadow of something—distrust, disillusionment—that makes her smile less open, more cautious, guarded.

Zack takes the third picture from my outstretched

hand. Johnson allows him a moment to scan it before speaking.

"All three are missing. No one seems to have seen Hannah Clemons since school got out on Friday. The Roberts girl has been missing since Saturday. Julie Simmons has been missing a little over twelve hours."

"Three girls missing in three days from the same school. Which one?" I ask.

"Point Loma Academy. It's a private school. The locals are handing the case to us because with three girls now gone, they are thinking serial kidnapper, maybe serial killer, and they have no leads. They've kept the cases quiet, hoping to avoid hysteria. Being a long weekend, it's been fairly easy to do. The first two girls were friends, so they weren't entirely sure of foul play. But now that a third girl is missing, they are looking at the case differently. The pressure is on to go public. Someone may be targeting the school, and some high-profile parents have kids who go the Academy."

"Any ransom demands made?" Zack asks.

Johnson shakes his head. "No. None of the kids are from families who could afford to pay much even if a ransom demand was made."

"But they could afford private school?" I ask. "Correct me if I'm wrong, but I thought the Academy was pretty pricey."

"You're not wrong," says Johnson. "All three of these girls were scholarship recipients."

Zack pulls his notepad from the inside pocket of his jacket. "Well, we've got another connection, then. Could this be a prank of some kind? A bunch of rich kids ganging up on those who are less privileged?"

Johnson passes Zack another sheet of paper. "According to Principal Robinson's statement, the identities of the scholarship recipients are kept in strict confidence. We've been asked to keep it that way."

"I'm surprised." Zack's tone is sharply critical. "I'd think letting the parents who put money in his pocket know it's been only scholarship students targeted would soothe some minds."

I shake my head at Zack's sarcasm. "Are there any other scholarship recipients?" I ask.

Johnson glances down at his phone. "One other. My niece, Rain. Julie Simmons is a friend of hers. A very good friend. She called me when she heard that Julie was missing."

Zack and I exchange glances. I didn't know whether to attribute it to his keen sense of hearing or instinct, but he was right. It is personal for Johnson.

"So you made a call to the local police to offer assistance," Zack interjects.

Johnson nods. "We would have ended up with the case anyway."

"Undoubtedly," I agree. "Your niece?"

"Is safe at home waiting by the phone for news from me. Rain doesn't know about the other two girls, or about the scholarship connection."

"Which could be more coincidence than connection," I add.

"Until we're sure, I've got a friend watching my niece's home. I want you two to start working the case immediately. Before any other girls go missing." He sweeps a hand in the direction of the outer office. "I secured the necessary warrants. Agents Billings, Garcia, and Garner are gathering the background information you'll need on the girls and their families. The others are consolidating information we have from the local police. They'll have reports for you tomorrow morning. In the meantime, I suggest you make first contact with Julie's parents."

He slides a piece of paper across the desk. "The address. They're expecting you."

Zack holds up his hands. "Shouldn't we wait until we have the police reports, at least? We're going in cold."

Johnson looks up as if surprised both by Zack's question and the fact that we're still in his office. "Exactly right. I want you to look at this case from a fresh perspective. As if you are the first on the scene." A pause. He looks down at his desk and then up again. He picks up the paper he'd placed on the corner of the desk and shakes it. "Did I not make myself clear?"

"Crystal." I grab it from his hand, snatch up the three photographs, then give Zack a nudge. We've been given our marching orders. We'll have time to study the evidence and ask questions later. Right now Johnson needs some space.

Zack waits until we've exited the elevator and are heading across the parking lot before speaking. "What do you think?"

"I think Johnson's afraid for his niece."

"Ever met her?"

"No," I reply absently, looking for the Simmonses' address as we go.

Since I still have my car keys, I steer Zack toward the end of the first row. I've found the address. I recognize the street. "Point Loma Academy isn't far from the Simmonses'. If I'm not mistaken, the school's only a five-minute walk or so from this address."

"Maybe we can swing by on the way, check it out. What else do you know about the Academy?"

"Not much, really. I attended a fund-raiser there a year or two ago." What I don't add is that my date was an agent from a different division whose kid attended the school. Unfortunately, his ex-wife decided to check herself out of rehab and show up for the fund-raiser, too. Unexpectedly, and very drunk. Not a pleasant experience. For me, or the agent who not too long after accepted a transfer and moved to the East Coast with his daughter.

I've already made my way to the driver's side, leaving Zack no choice but to ride shotgun. I can hear him complaining under his breath. "Sure. Why don't you drive?"

I smile and give him just enough time to get settled in the passenger seat before shifting into gear and pulling out of the lot.

The FBI building is located right on the I-15S interstate, which is what I head for. It's not even midmorning yet and it's hot enough in the SUV to crank up the air-conditioning. Zack hasn't said another word. His jaw is tight, his shoulders bunched. I have to wonder whether it's the job that's got him in this mood or something else. Disappointment that he's not spending the day with Sarah? Being the professional that I am, I push that notion aside and ask, "How do you want to handle the interview?"

He stares straight ahead. "You heard Johnson. We'll handle it like we're the first on the scene. We should be prepared to take some flak for making them repeat what they've already told the first officers, but if they're concerned about their daughter, they'll cooperate."

"*If* they're concerned? Since when did you become Glass-Half-Empty Guy?"

I momentarily cast aside concern about his uncharacteristic moodiness and concentrate on the drive.

My memory was correct. We take the Nimitz Boulevard exit to get to Ocean Beach. On the way to the Simmonses' apartment, we go right past the school on West Point Loma that all three missing girls attend. I pull over and we take a look.

Point Loma Academy is a sprawling two-story stucco building set back from the road, surrounded by a well-manicured lawn and ensconced behind a high stone wall. A wrought-iron gate opens to a circular drive that leads from the street to the building entrance. A digital sign at the foot of the drive flashes upcoming events and boasts of recent sports victories. No students are around because of the Labor Day holiday. No cars in the adjacent parking lot. The entire campus looks deserted. High-end surveillance cameras are evident not only at the gate and main entrance, but in other key areas as far as my eyes can see, a sad testament to the fact that security is not only necessary but mandatory on school campuses nowadays.

Zack comments first. "You sure this is a high school? Looks more like Fort Knox."

"High-profile students, remember?" I point toward one of the cameras. "Anyone targeting students here probably spent time on or around campus, don't you think?"

"I'll call Garner. We need to get someone assigned to reviewing recent footage."

I nod.

Zack makes the call.

I pull out and after five minutes and a couple more right turns, we've arrived at the address printed in Johnson's neat flowing script.

Zack glances from the paper to the building and shoots me an inquisitive look. "This is it?"

I understand his confusion. The building we're looking at is an apartment, two stories of chipping plaster fronted by a lawn in a losing battle against a vicious army of weeds. The parking lot is marked by deeply pitted asphalt and broken berms. A battered car by the entrance is balanced on four concrete blocks, its wheels gone.

"One look at this place and anyone would be able to figure out the Simmons girl is on a scholarship," Zack says. I nod my agreement.

We trudge across the lawn to a gate set into a chain-link fence. The hinges squeal as we push it open and make our way to a row of mailboxes against a far wall. The Simmonses' mailbox is marked *2B* in red Magic Marker.

The stairway to the second floor is a series of concrete steps, the banister an afterthought of rough, unpainted wood probably attached to avoid a code violation.

As soon as I place my hand on it, I wish I hadn't.

"Damn it!"

A sizable splinter is lodged in my index finger.

Zack reaches out. "Let me see."

I place my hand, palm up, in his. He's unimpressed. With barely a glance, he plucks out the sliver and lets it fall to the ground. "Good as new. Let's go."

"It's bleeding. Not everyone has super-duper speedy-quick healing powers, you know," I remind him. Demeter didn't want to make it easy for me. I'll heal from anything, but I do it the old-fashioned way, like a human, with time and pain.

"I could lick it," he offers.

His tone doesn't possess even the slightest hint of innuendo. A Were's saliva contains properties that ward off infection and hasten healing. Nonetheless, suddenly I'm not thinking about my hand. I'm thinking of a night last spring. Of a warm fire and cool sheets. Of a soft touch and a hard body. Of the feel of Zack's tongue and mouth.

I snatch my hand back and start once again up the stairs. "You're right, I'm fine."

I don't make it far. "Emma?"

I square my shoulders and turn around. My mind races as I struggle to maintain a neutral expression and at the same time formulate a plausible explanation for the arousal that Zack's heightened senses no doubt detected before I did.

"I'm sorry if that sounded out of line. It wasn't . . ."

"Of course not!"

"We're good?"

"Totally!" I nod as if nothing happened. As if I don't know that he knows. Then we head up to 2B.

Zack raps on the front door with his knuckles. We stand back a few feet so anyone looking out the peephole can see us clearly. I'm prepared to hold up my credentials and explain who we are, but before I have my badge out, the door swings wide-open to reveal a girl of about five. She smiles up at us with a gap-toothed grin.

"Goldie said not to bug her. Not for nothing," she announces. "So you better go away." Her small frame is swallowed up by a pink chenille robe at least five times too big for her.

"Who's Goldie?" Zack asks.

"Not supposed to talk to strangers," she replies, taking a step back.

Zack produces his badge. "We're . . . like policemen."

"*Like* policemen? Where's your uniform?"

In an effort to save Zack from being bested by the five-year-old, I bend down low so my face is almost even with hers and ask the question he should have asked. "Are your parents here?"

"Nope," she replies. "Goldie's watching me."

"Only *not*," Zack mutters.

"We'd really like to talk to them about your sister. How much longer do you think Goldie's going to be?" I ask.

Her face scrunches up in concentration. "She went in to take her medicine one *Dora* and three *SpongeBob*s ago." One glance back at the television and we've lost her. "I like this one," she says, as she climbs back onto the sofa. "Have you seen it?"

"Sounds like an invitation to me. After you, Agent Monroe."

Just as Zack steps over the threshold, a door off the living room opens. "Gracie?" a female voice rasps. "Who are you talking to?"

The woman, presumably Goldie, is tall, drug-addict scrawny with a sallow, shrunken face and hair the color and texture of straw. She's barefoot, dressed in jeans and a flannel shirt. Despite the heat, a worn cardigan is pulled tightly across her chest. She glares at the child. "What have I told you about answering the door?"

Gracie shrinks back.

Zack and I produce our badges and quickly dispense with introductions. Instantaneously, Goldie's manner shifts. Her tone softens. "Yes. What can I do for you?"

Zack steps forward. I can almost see his nose twitch as his werewolf senses go on alert. If she's holding drugs in the apartment, he'll know. He narrows his eyes at the woman. "You are . . . ?"

"The babysitter," she replies, omitting her name. We let it go, for now.

Gracie has moved so that she is standing by my side. "Where are Mr. and Mrs. Simmons?" I ask, placing a gentle hand on top of the little girl's head.

"Out."

"When will they be back?"

The woman looks away, watching Zack as he surveys the apartment. His eyes land on the room she just left. When he starts toward it, Goldie yelps, "You can't go in there. Actually, you shouldn't even be in here. This is private property. And . . . and you have to have a warrant. And you don't."

"Exigent circumstances," Zack snaps back. "You have pinpoint pupils and a very bad habit. We have a child here who could be in danger."

"Please!" she pleads. "Gracie's fine. Aren't you, Gracie?" The woman worries at the hem of her secondhand-store sweater, twisting the fabric until it shreds and comes apart in her hands. She barely notices. Her attention is on Zack. She lowers her voice. "Look, I'm trying to stay clean. Honest. I can't afford to get busted."

Voices drift into the apartment from the parking lot below.

Goldie begins to babble, edging around Zack and moving toward the door at the back of the room. "Hey, listen—they're back! How about I just get my purse and get out of here?"

But Zack steps in front of her. "If you go into that bedroom, I'll want to look in that purse, and if I find something illegal, we're going to have to arrest you. How about you just get out of here."

She hesitates only a moment. She may be high, but not so high that she doesn't recognize she's being given a choice. She turns, glances at Gracie, then up to me. Without another word to either of us, she's out the front door.

I take Gracie's hand and lead her to the couch. "Is she a neighbor?" I ask her.

Gracie nods. "She lives downstairs."

I hear the fall of Goldie's footsteps on the stairs as she makes her descent.

"Does she stay with you often?"

"Not so much. She has a boyfriend now."

An apartment door below us slams shut.

Zack, who had disappeared into the bedroom, returns, holding a purse. He places it on an end table near the couch. "You can give Goldie back her purse the next time you see her," he says. He moves around the couch so he's standing next to me and surreptitiously slides something out of his pocket just far enough for me to see what it is. Goldie's drug kit.

Gracie toys with the robe's belt.

"That's a very pretty robe."

She lifts her shoulders in an elaborate shrug. "This is Julie's robe. She misappeared. My parents went to find her and bring her home."

I put my hand over hers. "Gracie, did your parents hear from Julie? Is that why they left?"

Before Gracie can reply, the front door swings open. Gracie jumps up from the couch and runs to greet the man and woman who stop abruptly on the doorstep when they see Zack and me.

"Who are you?" the man asks, more fear than challenge in his tone.

I show him my badge. "Mr. and Mrs. Simmons? I'm Special Agent Monroe of the FBI. This is Agent Armstrong. We're here about your daughter."

CHAPTER 3

The woman bends down and gathers Gracie into her arms. "FBI?" She hugs the little girl to her chest and turns wide eyes to us. "You found Julie? Where is she? Is she all right?"

Mr. Simmons places a hand on his wife's shoulder. "Let the agents speak, Angie." He takes Gracie from his wife's arms and brings her to the couch. "Want to watch more cartoons?"

Gracie nods enthusiastically. Her father hands her the remote, then motions for us to follow him. Once in the kitchen, we all take seats around a small, round table. Mr. Simmons reaches for his wife's hand. Her eyes are brimming with tears. They sit quietly without fidgeting, both sad-faced and stoic, the American Gothic in cotton shirts and jeans.

I break the silence. "Mr. and Mrs. Simmons, the FBI has been asked to take over your daughter's case. I know we'll be asking questions you've already covered with the local police, but it's important we go over the information again."

"Sometimes," Zack interjects, "with time, something

comes to light that may have been forgotten during the first interview."

They exhibit no suspect reactions. No nervous side glances, no indication that they are upset by the idea of another interview. Their attention is riveted, their expressions hopeful.

Zack continues. "But before we start, there's something you should know about Goldie. She wasn't watching your daughter. Gracie answered the door and let us in. Goldie had told her not to bother her. There's no easy way to say this. She's a heroin addict and she was using. It's fortunate you returned when you did. I know the last thing you need right now is another child in jeopardy."

Shock and anger play across the Simmonses' faces. It's clear these folks are at the end of their tether. After recommending they do nothing about Goldie save ensure she's never relied upon again for babysitting and promising we'll be making referrals to law enforcement, we start in, alternating questions. When was the last time they saw Julie? How did she seem? Was she upset about anything? How was she doing in school? Did she have a boyfriend?

The answers are clear and straightforward. They saw Julie last when she left to go to the local library. She had some research to do for a school project and some books to return. She seemed fine, although she was running a little late and worried about making it before closing. She didn't want to incur a fine. She was doing well in school, hoped to win a scholarship to Stanford to study marine biology. No, she didn't have a boyfriend.

Zack has been jotting answers on a small notepad. He

looks up. "Had anything happened at home that might have upset her?"

That question brings the first physical reaction from the pair. They exchange looks. Mrs. Simmons clears her throat. "One thing." She looks at her husband and he nods. She clears her throat again. "A few days ago, we found out Julie had gotten a tattoo. What do they call it? A tramp stamp."

"My Julie's no tramp. She's a good girl!" Mr. Simmons assures us. "I don't know what she was thinking."

"And you confronted Julie about the tattoo?" I ask.

Mrs. Simmons nods. "She reminded us that she was eighteen and could legally make her own decisions. She was right about that, of course, but it didn't keep her father and me from being upset. Julie has always been such a levelheaded girl."

Mr. Simmons chimes back in. "We had words, but by dinnertime we had all calmed down. She even hugged her mother and I before bedtime. All was forgiven."

Mrs. Simmons nods. "Never go to bed angry—that's what my mother always said. What's done is done."

"Wish my parents were that understanding about my teenage screwups," Zack interjects.

Mr. Simmons says, "Well, we knew who was *really* to blame for the tattoo."

I lean toward him. "Who?"

"Rain Johnson." He spits the name. "She's trouble, that one. I told the police they should question her. Have you seen that girl? One look at her and you can tell she's trouble."

I see Zack's eyes widen at the mention of Deputy Director Johnson's niece, but neither he nor I make any comment. Instead, I ask, "Why do you say that, Mr. Simmons?"

"We never had any problem with Julie until the two of them became friends. Then Julie became very secretive about the things they did together."

I nod in understanding. "Teenage girls do like to have their privacy."

"It was more than that. Shortly after they started hanging out, Julie came home past curfew with liquor on her breath. We thought she was studying at the library. Turns out Rain brought her to a party. We grounded her, of course. And we told her she couldn't see Rain outside of school. If we could have, we'd have barred her from having anything to do with the girl even *at* school, but that would have been impossible." He shakes his head. "We should have watched her more closely." His breath catches. "And we never should have let her walk to the library alone."

Mrs. Simmons reaches out and gives her husband's forearm a gentle squeeze. "Julie's walked to the library hundreds of times alone," she reminds him before turning to us. "It had gotten better. She's a smart girl. She's a *good* girl. It was only that once with the party. She wouldn't run away. She wouldn't worry us. . . . You *have* to find her."

My stomach wrenches as the poor woman dissolves into tears. Her husband offers her a clean handkerchief and words of reassurance that seem to comfort her despite being totally meaningless. No matter how many cases I've worked, this part is always the hardest.

"We'll do our very best," I say.

Zack jots a final note and slips the pad and pen into his jacket pocket. "Think we could see Julie's room?" he asks.

Mrs. Simmons rises immediately from her chair. "Oh yes. I'll show you. The police didn't seem very interested in it. Julie shares the room with her sister but we haven't touched her things."

She leads us back through a hallway to a door that opens into a small bedroom. The walls are painted pale yellow with a border of daisies. There are two beds, one made, one still rumpled, two chests of drawers, a small desk, and a bookcase along the wall under a window. Mrs. Simmons points to the bed on the right—the one made up with a bedspread of daisies that matches the wallpaper border. "That's Julie's."

We thank her and ask if we can have a few minutes alone in the room.

"I'll be in the kitchen. Would you like coffee when you're finished?"

Zack says yes immediately. I know it's more to ensure we have privacy than because he needs the caffeine. Mrs. Simmons leaves us. Zack and I pull out pairs of latex gloves and get to work.

The first thing we do is open the laptop that's sitting on the desk. The screen comes to life, displaying Julie's San Diego County Library account page. Zack hits the refresh button and the "Log-in expired" message displays. Fortunately, she stored her ID and password; one more click and we can see that fines have begun to accrue.

"She never made it to the library," says Zack. Then he closes the device and begins to unplug it. "Let's ask if we can take it. Billings might find something worthwhile on the hard drive."

I nod in agreement. Zack begins to rummage through the desk. I turn my attention to the dresser closest to Julie's bed, opening and closing each drawer. Nothing unusual, just neatly stacked piles of under things, T-shirts, sleepwear. I pass my hand under each drawer. Nothing here, either. I draw a penlight from my bag and get down on my knees and check under the dresser and bed. Nothing again.

Zack has been looking through the closet. One side is lined with Julie's school uniforms, slacks and jeans, blouses. Shoes are lined up on the bottom. He picks up each shoe, shakes it, puts it back in its place.

I'm just about to turn to Gracie's dresser when her small hand touches mine. I'd been so intent on what I doing, I hadn't realized she'd entered the room. "I'm looking for anything that might tell us where Julie is," I explain, smiling down at Gracie. "Do you mind if I look in your dresser?"

She shakes her head.

With Gracie glued to my side, I do the same check I did before. Her eyes follow my every move. I find nothing. Zack has moved on to the bookcase. It's the only thing we haven't searched. I wait. Gracie, now bored with this game, is perched on her bed.

Zack sighs. "Nothing."

We've finished our respective searches and, save the possibility that we might find something of value on the laptop, we've come up empty.

"You're way cold," Gracie says.

"Cold?" asks Zack.

"Not anywhere near it."

I sit down alongside her. "Near what?"

The little girl raises a finger to her lips and in a hushed, almost imperceptible whisper says, "Julie's special hiding place. Would you like to see it?"

Out of the mouths of babes. "We would."

She tiptoes to the bedroom door, closes it, and gets down on her hands and knees in front of the furnace register near the foot of her bed. Little fingers pry at the grate covering the vent. In a moment, it falls free. "Look in here," she says triumphantly. "Julie didn't think I ever saw her but I did."

I want to hug the child. Instead I kneel down beside her and pass my hand inside. At first, I don't feel anything. I reach deeper. My fingertips brush something. I look up at Zack. "Something's in there, a bag, I think. But I can't quite reach it."

Zack doesn't question, just slips off his suit coat, tossing it on the nearby bed before crouching down next to me. He rolls up his shirtsleeve, then reaches inside. I hear the crinkling of plastic as he grabs hold of the bag.

We climb to our feet. I brush the dust from the knees of my slacks. I'm eager to see the contents. "What is it?"

Zack pulls out what looks to be a checkbook and an envelope.

Gracie scrambles up beside me.

Zack has opened the checkbook. He gives a low whistle and hands it to me. "Fifty-two hundred dollars deposited weekly, two hundred dollars at a time, for the last six months." He opens the envelope next, and fans four one-hundred dollar bills. "The next deposit?"

The door opens. Mrs. Simmons knocks discreetly on the jam. "Is Gracie bothering you?" Mrs. Simmons asks.

We turn in time to see the little girl dance out. "I helped. Right?"

"She did." I point to the furnace register. "We found something. Maybe we could go back to the kitchen?"

"And we'd like to take Julie's laptop with us, so we can examine it more thoroughly," Zack adds.

"Of course."

When Gracie is once more ensconced in front of the television, this time with a bowl of Cheerios, the four of us take our places at the kitchen table. I slide the checkbook across the table to Mr. and Mrs. Simmons. "Ever seen this before?"

The astonishment reflected on their openmouthed faces answers more clearly than any words.

"Why was Julie hiding someone's checkbook?" Mrs. Simmons' eyes zero in on the balance. She gasps. "Harry, there's fifty-two hundred dollars here!"

Before Mr. Simmons has a chance to reply, Zack opens the envelope and spreads the bills in front of them. "The account is in Julie's name. And we found this."

Mrs. Simmons presses a hand to her mouth. "I don't understand."

"Mr. Simmons?" Zack asks.

His lips tremble. "This doesn't make sense." He rises from his chair, agitated, pacing. "How could Julie possibly get this much money?"

There are a few obvious answers. None a parent ever wants to consider. "We've seen a lot of drug use in this neighborhood," Zack says. "A high demand for everything from marijuana to—"

Mrs. Simmons gasps. "Julie dealing drugs? Never! She was against drugs."

"You did mention she once came home with alcohol on her breath," I add quietly. "Maybe she was experimenting with other things."

"No." The reply is heated, adamant, and immediate. "Not Julie." Mrs. Simmons and her husband stare at each other, but it's a look that lasts only a heartbeat.

Zack clears his throat, then asks the next tough one. "Do you know if Julie was sexually active?"

"We're Catholic, Agent Armstrong," Mr. Simmons replies, tight-lipped, as if that's all the answer necessary.

Mrs. Simmons snatches up the passbook. "She was holding the money for someone else," she blurts. "I know it. And I know who it is. It's that Johnson girl. Go ask her. Find out what she dragged my Julie into. This is her fault." Her voice rises to a wail. "Julie has so many friends, we've never understood why she gives that girl the time of day. Talk to Rain Johnson. I guarantee you, she's the reason our Julie is gone."

CHAPTER 4

We have only a few follow-up questions for Julie's parents. They do not recognize the other two missing girls. Julie is indeed attending the Academy on an academic scholarship, a scholarship that would surely be threatened by rumors of illegal activity.

We assure them we will exercise discretion when dealing with the school unless we find proof Julie is involved in something illegal. Zack slips the checkbook and envelope into evidence bags along with the laptop and gives the parents a receipt. Then we take our leave.

When we're back in the car, our eyes meet. His are troubled. I'm sure mine are, too. I release a breath. "What are we going to say to Johnson?"

Zack places the evidence bag containing the cash in the glove compartment and locks it. He stashes the one with the laptop under his seat. "Do we have a choice? We have to ask him to bring his niece in for an interview."

He grabs his cell and dials the office. The call lasts less than a minute. "Johnson left for a lunch meeting." He returns the phone to his jacket pocket. "He won't be back until around two. I told his assistant to have him call us when he returns."

Lunch. "Hungry?"

"Have you ever known me not to be hungry?"

I smile. Never. Must be the wolf genes.

The hot September sun beats into the car. "We've got time," Zack adds. "Want to head for the beach? Find something near the pier?"

Since we're already close to Ocean Beach and it's a blissful ten degrees cooler here than inland, I'm game. "I know just the place."

I drive straight to Poma's and manage to score a parking place right across the street. The Italian deli located on the corner of Niagara and Bacon has been an OB fixture for nearly fifty years. Their meatball subs are amazing. If *I* can smell them a block away, Zack must be salivating.

"Order whatever you want. I'm buying," Zack says as he opens the door.

His sour mood seems to have lifted. Perhaps it's the salt air and promise of crashing waves. He admitted to me once that he moved to the beach partly due to nostalgia, memories of growing up in Hilton Head, and partly because the ocean soothes him.

A memory of my own—a long walk on the beach—washes over me. It wasn't that long ago we'd walked hand in hand along the ocean's edge, sharing secrets and stealing slow, burning kisses. Once inside Poma's, I push those thoughts and feelings aside.

The small storefront is packed with beachgoers of all shapes and sizes. A raucous group of young men follows us inside. Zack scents the air. He's subtle, but I notice and understand. They don't. They're stoned and too busy cutting up and looking for something to satisfy the cravings brought on by their binge. One grabs a twelve-pack of Pacifico from the enormous cooler. Another dives into a large bag of chips. The old man behind the counter gives the guy stuffing chips into his mouth the hairy eyeball.

"I've told you boys before. You don't eat until *after* you pay!" he yells.

"Keep your pants on, Pops. You know we're good for it."

"Good for nothing, is more like it." The man turns his attention to Zack. "What can I get you?"

"Meatball sub, toasted, and a Limonata," I chime in.

Zack removes his jacket, giving the punks behind him a good look at his gun and his badge. "Make that two."

They may be stoned out of their minds, but they aren't stupid. They don't bother to wait and order sandwiches. They drop more than enough money to cover the chips and beer on the counter, and then beat it out of the store, leaving their receipt and whatever change they were due behind. Order is returned.

When Zack tries to hand the man a twenty for our lunches, it's refused. "On the house, Officer . . ."

"Armstrong." He drops the twenty into the tip jar along with his card.

The gesture earns us a big smile. "We'll give a shout-out when your order is ready. You're number forty-two." He hands Zack a receipt.

Ten minutes later the two of us are strolling down Niagara toward the pier, subs in a brown paper sack, sipping our Limonatas.

"The kids were stoned."

Zack nods.

I glance up at him. "That's the second time today you've let a bust slide."

Zack touches the side of his nose. "They didn't have drugs on them. My guess is that those clowns smoked most of their stash. Small potatoes. I'll turn Goldie's name over to the DEA. No use getting sidetracked. You've got to pick your battles."

I wonder at his tone—thoughtful, introspective. Is he talking about more than work?

I follow him down the steps to the beach. We find a place on the seawall in the shadow of the pier and sit side by side.

We tear open the wrappers around our sandwiches. The rich marinara and spicy meatball concoctions take concentration to eat without making a mess. We dispense with the pretense of small talk. I know Zack has got to be thinking about the same thing I am. Johnson's niece.

I decide to wait until after we've finished to broach the subject. In between bites, I wipe my mouth with a napkin and hold my sandwich to the side to keep from dripping sauce on my slacks—my brand-new slacks.

Zack isn't as patient. After consuming the first half of his sandwich, he dives in. "How do you think Deputy Director Johnson is going to react when we tell him that we need to speak to his niece?"

"He won't like it—that's for sure." I pause to scrub at my mouth. "But he'll play this by the book. He'll bring her in. Johnson's been at this a long time. He knows the sooner we talk to her, the sooner we can eliminate her as a suspect."

He waits until I've swallowed another bite before pouncing. "Suspect? You think she might be a suspect?"

"I don't know what to think. The Simmonses certainly didn't like her."

We continue to eat. The combination of breeze, salt air, and Zack are a bittersweet balm for my soul. I place my palms on the wall behind me, lean back, and close my eyes. "This is perfect. Let's just hang out here for the rest of the day."

"Crap! This was a brand-new shirt."

A dollop of bright red tomato sauce the size of a Kennedy half-dollar now decorates Zack's chest.

I dismiss his concern. "I'm sure Sarah can get it out. Hand over a napkin."

He does. I put my sandwich aside and use the napkin to sop up the sauce. My cheeks grow hot from the memory of what it was like, being with Zack. I remember the curve of his biceps, his well-muscled chest, the very lickable washboard abs. My mouth is suddenly dry. I shake off the memory before it takes hold and I embarrass myself for the second time today.

"If you think Sarah does laundry, you don't know her very well." He takes the napkin from me and lobs it into a nearby trash can.

"Maybe not, but I do know how to get a tomato stain out. The longer it sets, the worse it's going to be. If you rinse it back through from the underside now, it will be easier to treat later."

An outdoor shower is running just a few feet away.

Zack follows my line of sight, then he hands me his gun and removes his tie and shirt. It doesn't take any more encouragement than that. He hands me the tie and strolls over to the shower.

I sit on the wall and try not to stare. Before starting on the stain, he sticks his head in the stream of cool water. By the time he tosses his hair back to shake off the excess, a blonde in a sky blue bikini is trying to make small talk with her breasts. Zack laughs at something she says, exchanges his soiled shirt for the towel she's offering, and takes a stab at drying his hair. In the meantime, Blondie makes a concerted effort to further ingratiate herself by vigorously rubbing at the stain.

The shirt's been off for less than a minute and already a fan club is forming. I've lost my appetite.

My cell rings. It's Liz. I toss the rest of the sub into the trash can and answer. "Hey."

One word and she knows. "What's wrong?"

Liz recognizes my moods better than anyone.

"You mean besides that fact that I seem to be stuck. Here. Forever. Alone. That I have to walk around wearing some stupid Clark Kent disguise, saving people in hopes that one day the wack job of a goddess who banished me will decide that the good I've done has outweighed the bad?"

"Yeah, besides that."

I smile.

Liz doesn't skip a beat. "You know you're not alone. You have me. And you have Kallistos."

"He keeps asking me to move in."

"Why don't you?"

I frown. Zack is on his way back. "You know why," I tell her.

Zack drapes his wet shirt on the wall, then sits back down and resumes his attack on the meatball and cheese. "Tell Liz I said hi," he says between mouthfuls.

I do, then sign off, promising to call her back later and wondering how much of my conversation he overheard. I don't have to wonder for long.

"So, it's getting serious between you and Tall, Dark, and Pasty?"

"He's not pasty. He's fair. His people were Dorian."

I hand him back his gun and holster.

"Still, centuries without sun. That's got to affect a guy."

I recall what Kallistos looked like this morning, out on the balcony. "I think it really makes him appreciate it now."

"He probably has a vitamin-D deficiency."

"He doesn't have a vitamin-D deficiency."

"That'll lead to brittle bones as he gets older, you know." Zack tosses the wrapper from his sub into the trash.

"He's already older."

"Not to mention dead."

"Undead."

"Whatever." He knocks back the rest of his soda. "Why aren't you moving in with him?"

The question catches me by surprise, the directness of it. "What do you mean?"

"It's a simple question."

My mouth opens, but nothing comes out. I release a

breath. "I guess because I'm not in love with him. Moving in with someone . . . Now, that seems like a really big commitment."

He smiles and reaches for his shirt. "And now we're talking about me and Sarah."

I follow him back up the stairs to the parking lot. "You've been living together for what—five months?"

"Uh-huh."

"She seems happy," I finally say.

Zack keeps walking. Stoic. Silent.

"And you seem . . . happy," I add.

We reach the car and Zack holds out a hand for the keys. He opens the back, throws his shirt inside along with the tie and suit coat, then slams it shut.

"Are you happy, Zack?" I ask. A dangerous question. One I have no right to ask.

I'm standing, my hand on the passenger door to the Suburban. He's on the driver's side, key in the lock.

"I'm not sure I ever will be. Something's missing. I don't even know what it is, but I know I want it back in the worst possible way."

The locks on the car pop. We both climb inside. I look straight ahead, expression neutral. The engine turns over. For a second I think he's going to say more. Then the moment passes and he's grasping the steering wheel and slipping into traffic.

I don't know what to say, so I say nothing. Is he starting to remember? Liz swore to me he wouldn't. Maybe old feelings are beginning to resurface? Maybe they never went away?

We turn onto West Point Loma Boulevard, then take Sunset Cliffs heading toward West Mission Bay Drive. I know exactly where we're going. We're heading back to the scene of the crime, my crime—to the place where I broke every rule. Where I let my guard down. Where I showed my true self. Where I loved Zack and he loved me. And where I, in the space of a moment, both saved and betrayed him.

We're going to Zack's house.

Zack lives in a two-story beach house right on Mission Boulevard. The luxury oceanfront property came fully furnished and decorated. The last time I was inside, Zack had been living here for just a short time. Back then the place looked more like a showroom than a home. It contained nothing personal, nothing that was clearly Zack's—except for the cage where he sleeps during the full moon. I imagine all that's changed now. Sarah strikes me as the kind of woman who would waste no time and spare no expense feathering her nest. The Spartan cage is probably adorned with matching his-and-hers monogrammed silk pillows.

Despite my hopes to the contrary, Sarah's BMW is in the driveway. Behind it is an old, beat-up, red Chevy pickup. Zack parks on the street.

"Looks like you have company."

"Hmm."

"I'll wait in the car."

Zack shoots me a sideways glace.

"What?" I ask.

"Sarah's convinced you don't like her. If you wait in the car—"

"What are we? Back in junior high?"

Zack frowns. "Please, you were never in junior high."

Well, he's got me there.

"What could I possibly have against Sarah?" I ask him, hoping my pants don't catch fire. "Sarah's a long-legged blonde who wears designer clothes and lives on the beach... *with you*. If anything, she's the one who makes other women feel insecure."

"Other women, maybe, but not you. Not really. And she knows it."

Insecure? No. Terrified? Yes. The spell Liz had worked to make Zack forget wasn't originally intended to be far-reaching. The fact that Zack had told Sarah about our night in Charleston was an unexpected complication but not much of a challenge for Liz to rectify. Although her knowledge of the intimacy Zack and I had shared was obliterated, something lingering still remains. Female intuition? The instinct to mark her territory? Whatever it is, it's reason enough to stay clear of the she-wolf.

"Fine."

At the first sign of capitulation, Zack's out the door. He pulls the still-wet shirt out of the trunk, then heads up the driveway. I trail behind like a reluctant puppy that knows it's following its master into a room containing a big, hot mess. Once we get to the front door, being the gentleman he is, Zack holds it open and makes me walk in first.

Sarah is at the far end of the foyer, dressed in a gauzy peasant dress and strappy summer sandals. She looks at me with a sour expression and says nothing. She doesn't have to. Her expression says it all.

I feign indifference and look around. Except for the presence of Sarah and a man I've never met before, the place seems surprisingly unchanged.

"Zack, good to see you again!" the man says.

"Seamus."

The two men shake hands.

"Casual day at the office?" Seamus asks with a grin. His manner is easygoing, his smile infectious.

"I had a run-in with a meatball over lunch," Zack says. "I'm just gonna run upstairs and grab a clean shirt."

"His shirt became a casualty," I add, offering my hand. "Emma Monroe, Zack's partner."

His grasp is firm, his hand calloused and warm.

"Seamus O'Malley. We were just heading out to grab a bite to eat." He glances down at his white T-shirt before stuffing his hands in the pockets of his worn-out blue jeans. "Maybe we should avoid Italian."

In his flip-flops and wire-rimmed glasses, the red-haired, freckle-faced thirtysomething looks unassuming, but he's unmistakably Were. A member of the pack Sarah wants to join, perhaps?

"I have a sneaking suspicion you can hold your own against a meatball," I tell him. "But I do recommend you settle on a place with air-conditioning. It's really heating up." I remove my jacket and toss it over the back of the sofa. "Don't let me hold the two of you up."

"Shall we?" Seamus asks Sarah.

She hesitates.

Zack bounds down the stairs, fresh, starched white shirt in hand. "Thought you two were on your way out." Zack barely spares her a glance as he slips on the shirt and buttons it up.

Sarah heads for the door, pausing only to collect her purse. The cheerful yellow Miche bag perfectly complements her dress and sandals. "Will you be home for dinner?" she asks.

The first words she's uttered since I walked in the door.

Her tone is casual, but the question is not. It seems to catch Zack off guard. His brows furrow. "Probably not. New case."

She nods. I realize how little I've seen of the two of them together, but even so, I recognize the undisguised tension between them.

I want it back in the worst possible way.

I wonder how much of that tension has to do with me.

"Ready?" Zack asks.

My heart is pounding. "I'm just going to use the bathroom before we hit the road," I say, anxious to escape the awkwardness of the moment. I make a beeline for the powder room. Once behind the closed door, I wash my hands, smooth my hair, then give myself a long, hard look in the mirror.

"Keep your eye on the ball, Monroe," I tell myself. "He's just another guy. He's your partner. That's all. That's all it's ever going to be."

Sarah and Seamus have left by the time I return to the living room. Zack is ready to go, too, keys in hand. "Ready?"

I nod. Zack follows me out the door, locks it, and makes for the car. "How does Sarah know Seamus?" I ask, once we're on the interstate.

Zack keeps his eyes on the road but I see his shoulders draw up ever so slightly at the question. When he doesn't answer right away, I feel my own defenses go up.

"Seamus is a Were. I know that much. I figured maybe he's part of that pack you mentioned. But, if you don't want to talk about it, just say so."

Zack releases a breath. "He's not just a member. He's the Alpha."

"He is?" I recall his gently self-effacing manner. "Really? He doesn't seem . . ."

"What?"

"Alpha-y?"

"His leadership style is unconventional. He holds the power of the pack because its members have given it to him. He's earned it, don't get me wrong, just not in the traditional way."

"Does he have a job? No. Don't tell me, let me guess. Organic farmer."

Zack smiles. "Close. He's a Park Ranger at Cuyamaca Rancho State Park."

"That's convenient. Lots of open space."

"He also owns a kind of ranch-slash-commune that borders the park in the Cleveland National Forest."

"Even better."

"Yeah. It's great."

Zack's tone says it's anything *but* great. Suddenly, I wonder whether Sarah wants to do more than connect with a pack. Could she be thinking about wanting to live with them? And planning on taking Zack with her?

We're nearing the office and I'm not sure whether I should ask Zack directly if that's a possibility. He hasn't volunteered very much personal information about his relationship with Sarah, even though he knows everything about Kallistos and me.

I'm still debating with myself when Zack's cell phone chimes to life. It's synced with the car's audio system and once Zack connects the call, Johnson's voice booms out over the speakers.

"Got a message you need to speak with me."

Zack glances at me, takes a breath, and says, "Sir, it

looks like we're going to need to talk with your niece. Can you have her meet us at the office this afternoon?"

"Rain? What's this about, exactly?"

In a few short sentences, Zack recounts what happened at the Simmonses'—what we found in Julie's hiding place and her parents' accusation that Rain is somehow responsible not only for the money, but for Julie's disappearance. He keeps his voice even, his tone detached.

I expect a heated response from Johnson, but it doesn't come. "Deputy Director Johnson? Are you still there?" Zack finally asks.

A soft "Yes." Johnson clears his throat. This time his response comes through loud and clear. "Yes. I'll have Rain at the office in an hour."

The line is cut.

Zack clicks his phone off.

"Well," he says. "I think we're in for an interesting afternoon."

We arrive back at the office thirty minutes before Rain is expected. We spend the time checking with the three agents assigned to do the background checks on the missing girls. They've turned up nothing out of the ordinary—all three families are low to middle income, live in apartments or rentals, but are not heavily in debt. Their children have never been arrested, never been in trouble at their schools, never had complaints filed against them by the property managers of their buildings.

"Squeaky clean," Zack comments.

"Except for Julie Simmons' unreported stash," I counter.

"Except for that."

When Rain comes into the office, she is escorted not by her parents, but by the deputy director. I catch myself staring as he directs the girl into his office and closes the door.

Zack nudges me with an elbow. "*That's* his niece?"

I understand his astonishment. I'm feeling it, too. The girl with Johnson is dressed head to toe in black. Black jacket, black T-shirt, black leggings, big, black clunky boots. Her hair, too, is raven black, pulled straight back from her pale face and secured in a short, wispy ponytail by a leather thong. She's pretty but I doubt that's what most people would notice. The tiny silver bars piercing her nose, upper lip, and one eyebrow compete for attention with a tattoo that wanders from the neckline of her tee to her right earlobe. It's a vine of some kind done in bright green.

When I look at Zack, his eyebrows are raised.

Maybe mine are, too. I don't have time to think about it. Johnson is once again at his window beckoning us to join him.

"Come on, partner," Zack says. "It's showtime."

CHAPTER 5

Rain is seated in the executive swivel chair behind Johnson's desk. She looks neither concerned about nor particularly interested in the reason she has been called in for questioning. She's spinning round and round, studying fingernails lacquered shiny black (what else?) when we walk in.

She doesn't bother to stop and look up until Johnson makes the introductions.

Her eyes, beautiful and as green as the leaves climbing her neck, flit from Zack to me, then back to Zack. She says nothing.

Johnson makes no move to leave the room and he doesn't suggest we go elsewhere. Zack and I claim the visitor chairs so that we are both facing Rain. Johnson maintains his post by the door.

"Did your uncle tell you why we wanted to speak to you?" Zack asks.

A half shrug lifts her shoulders. "No. But I assume it's about Julie."

Zack nods. "Yes. How well do you know her?"

"We've been friends for a while. She's one of the few kids at the Academy that will talk to me."

"You know that she's missing?"

"Yes, but you already know that. I told Uncle Jimmy the whole story. I'm not sure why I'm here."

Zack frowns. "It's important we hear it again from you. Can you tell us about the last time you talked to her?"

She nods. "Right before she was supposed to meet me at the library. We're working on a history project together and she called to say she'd be a little late. She had books she needed to return, and we were going to work on the outline. She never showed. Didn't answer my texts. The library closes at nine. I knew her folks would freak if I called, so I got Johnny to do it."

"Who's Johnny?" I ask.

"He works behind the desk. He's cool. He pretended to have a homework question. Mr. Simmons gave him Julie's cell number and said she was at the library, had left a couple hours ago to work on a school project."

Zack leans forward in his chair. "Then what happened?"

"I kept calling and texting. I didn't know what else to do. I figured maybe she'd caved to her parents' stay-away-from-Rain rule and paired up with someone else. But I knew she wouldn't miss curfew, so after the library closed, Johnny and I drove over and parked in the lot across the street. He called the home phone again. Still no Julie. Her folks were certain she'd be home any minute. We waited and waited. No Julie. After a while, I fell asleep. Johnny woke me up around two when the cops showed up. Then I called Uncle Jimmy. I knew something was very, very wrong."

"Did you know Julie had a checking account?"

She blinks at the change of subject. "Why would I? Lots of people have checking accounts."

"With over five thousand dollars deposited in them?" I ask.

Another blink. "Five *thousand*? No. Have you asked her parents? That'd be my next move. They kept a pretty tight rein on her."

"Her parents knew nothing about the money," Zack cuts in. "They thought perhaps it was yours."

Rain straightens in her chair. Her brow furrows. "Mine?"

"That perhaps she was holding it for you."

"Why would they think that? Where would I get that kind of money?"

"That's what we're trying to find out," Zack says. "Mr. and Mrs. Simmons think you might have talked Julie into doing something illegal."

A flash of anger. "Like what?"

"Like dealing drugs."

Now the anger becomes red-hot. Her hands ball into fists and she leans toward me. "If they think that, they're the ones that are high. Julie isn't into drugs and neither am I. I can't believe her parents. They actually said those things? It's because of the stupid tattoo, isn't it? They blame me for Julie getting a tattoo. I didn't force her, you know. She wanted to get a tattoo and all I did was take her somewhere safe, to someone I knew would do a good job."

I slip the pictures of Hannah Clemons and Sylvia Roberts onto the desk in front of Rain. "What about these girls? Are you friends with them, too?"

She sniffs. "Not hardly. They're cheerleaders."

"You have something against cheerleaders?" Zack asks.

Rain rolls her eyes. "Let's just say we don't have a lot in common. Are they saying shit about me, too? That's nothing new."

I add the photo of Julie and line them up in front of Rain. "No. They're also missing. This now makes three. Three girls missing in three days. You're a smart girl, Rain. We need your help. If you know something, if you are hiding something, please, tell us. We believe these girls have been abducted. Every hour that goes by lessens our chances of finding them."

The anger drains from her. She begins to tremble. "Why would you think I know something?"

"You're Julie's best friend. A girl suddenly falls into something that nets her two hundred, cash, per week? That's something she shares with her BFF."

Rain shakes her head. "I don't know anything about any money. If I knew where Julie was, if I could think of anything, if I *do* think of anything . . ." Her eyes well up with tears. "My first day of school, all anyone did was stare. They judged me because I didn't look like all of *them*. That's why Julie's parents don't like me. That's why they're blaming me. Julie is my friend. That first day, that awful, awful day, she invited me to sit with her for lunch. Then we just laughed as they stared at both of us. If it wasn't for Julie, I would have dropped out." She turns to Johnson. "You can test me right now, a drug test, or a lie detector test. I'm telling the truth, Uncle Jimmy."

Johnson steps forward. "Okay, that's enough. Rain, wait for me outside. I'll take you home."

The girl hurries past us, makes straight for the door, and slams it shut behind her. The tension in the room is thick and oppressive.

"Do you believe her?" Johnson comes around the desk and takes his seat.

"Do you?" Zack asks.

Johnson draws a hand over his face. "I do, but Christ, she's my niece. I *want* to believe her."

"She volunteered for a polygraph," I point out. "We could pursue that, but my gut says she's telling the truth. If she knew something she thought would help, I think she'd tell us. She seemed genuinely surprised by the money. I say we try to follow the money, see if we find any more similar connections between the victims."

"Do it," he says simply. "I'll see about the warrants. And interview the families of the other two missing girls. Rain said she and Julie didn't know them very well, but Rain didn't know Julie had fifty-two hundred dollars stashed away, either. Maybe they weren't as close as she thinks."

He looks at his niece through the glass walls, standing with her back to the office, her posture rigid. "She's a nice kid. She hasn't had a particularly easy life. Her mother is a bit of a flake. I want to believe her. It's up to you now to prove I can."

We watch as he leaves us, approaches his niece, and puts an arm around her shoulders. She leans against his chest a moment; then the two walk toward the elevators.

"So," I say, turning to Zack. "What do *you* think?"

Zack's eyes are still on Johnson and his niece. He's quiet until the two enter the elevator and the doors close. "I think we'd better run those financials on all the girls, Rain included. If we find something, we can always circle back and schedule another interview with her." His gaze is on me now. "A special interview. One without Johnson."

I know what he means, of course. Using my natural talent to ferret out the truth is tempting, but it comes with a price. Demeter frowns on any use of power that might draw attention to an Immortal on earth. Each use of my power risks Demeter's wrath. Finding one of the missing, saving them, tips the scales in my direction. A justified risk for the greater good is tolerated. Necessary, so that I can continue with the mission, so that I can bring another victim home, so that maybe, someday, I can go home.

It's almost five o'clock and all but one of the agents, Garner, has left. We join him at his desk.

He waves his hand at two stacks of reports. "I've compiled the police reports here, in chronological order, and the background information you looked at earlier, here. I'm afraid I didn't find much. I was going to start reviewing the security footage from the campus next."

"You got it already?" asked Zack.

Garner nods. "Came in around twenty minutes ago. If you'd rather I work on something else first, I can. My wife is visiting her folks in New York and I have nothing to go home to except a frozen fillet of fish. She's trying to get me to cut down on red meat."

Zack grins. "Well, as a matter of fact, we could use a little more help. We need financials run on the missing girls. And Johnson's niece, Rain."

Garner raises an eyebrow but turns to his computer.

"Think we can have them in the morning?"

"No problem." Garner's fingers are already working the keyboard. "They'll be on your desks when you get in."

I remember Zack telling Sarah earlier he probably wouldn't be home for dinner. Although it looks now like he could be, he makes no move to leave. Instead, he removes his jacket and loosens his tie. He takes a seat next to Garner. "If we both work on this, we'll get it done faster. When we're finished, I'll spring for steaks at Donovan's, and you can drive me home. Deal?"

"Are you kidding? For a steak, I'll come in early to start reviewing the surveillance."

I touch Zack's shoulder. "I can stay, too."

Garner looks up from his keyboard. "I think we've pretty much got it covered."

"There you go," Zack says. "No need for you to stay late. Besides, you have someone waiting for you. Right?" His tone is teasing, playful, but an unmistakable sadness shadows his eyes.

You could have had someone waiting for you, too.

I've known from the beginning that Zack doesn't love Sarah. But something keeps them together. I guess I was hoping that something would be enough. That Sarah would make him happy.

Obviously, she hasn't.

My cell phone vibrates announcing a new text. *Hot vampire here with cold champagne. Awaiting your arrival. K.* Kallistos may not be perfect, but there's an honesty about our no-strings-attached relationship that's refreshing. We understand each other. We know what we want and accept what we can't have. Kallistos may be complicated, but the arrangement we have isn't. And it's such a damned relief not to have to watch every thought, every action.

Hot vampire here with cold champagne. Awaiting your arrival.

I don't bother to answer Zack. He and Garner are busy chatting away. I just grab my purse and head for the elevator.

Day Two: Tuesday, September 3

I gave up trying to sleep long ago. The sun has yet to rise, but the city below is waking. From my vantage point on the sofa of the penthouse, I can see the outline of buildings. Random windows dotted with light shine like beacons against the dark blanket of the bay beyond.

My laptop sits open on the coffee table in front of me. Three images appear side by side on the screen—Julie Simmons, Hannah Clemons, and Sylvia Roberts. I wonder what kinds of sinister secrets those sunny smiles and sparkling eyes are masking. What I wouldn't give right now to question just one of them.

I pour the last cup of coffee from the pot and walk out onto the balcony. The edges of my silk robe flutter in the predawn breeze. Two hundred dollars per week, per girl. No more. No less. Zack's text confirming Hannah and Sylvia both received and deposited the same amount of money came while Kallistos and I were in the tub. It was around midnight when I noticed the message. Ever since, I've been chomping at the bit for more details. As soon as the sun comes up, I'm going to call Zack.

"Did you get any sleep?"

Kallistos encircles my waist with one arm.

"No." I lean back against him and close my eyes. "I came out to the living room so I wouldn't wake you."

He sweeps my hair aside and kisses my neck. The gesture is tender, not passionate, not possessive. "I'm afraid I've grown used to having you in my bed. I miss you when you aren't. I wish you'd reconsider and move in."

I turn to face him. His chest and feet are bare. The fact that he's wearing pajama bottoms is testament to the fact that we didn't have mind-blowing sex to the point of passing out last night.

"You aren't going soft on me, are you?" I ask him.

He tugs on the tie of my robe until it opens. Then he reaches for my hand and places it over his erection. "Does this feel like I'm going soft?"

"I wasn't referring to your . . . equipment," I say.

Kallistos cradles my head in his hands, then leans down for a kiss. He starts at the corner of my mouth before moving to my lower lip. "I know what you were referring to," he murmurs, his breath warm and inviting. His hand presses firmly over my mound, fingers sliding across the silk of my gown to slip between my legs.

"This is supposed to be a relationship of convenience," I remind him.

He pulls me hard against his body. His hand tangles in my hair at the base of my skull. He grabs hold and forces me to look into his eyes. I see anger, frustration, and something else, something I can't quite identify. Regret?

"I'd find it more convenient to have you here all the time, to be able to fuck you anytime I want."

I push him away and head inside. "Yeah, well, good luck with that."

He follows me inside. "You think you've come to terms with it. But you haven't."

"Come to terms with what?" I've busied myself by gathering up the coffeepot and empty cup. By the time Kallistos answers, I've made it as far as the dining table.

"Not being able to have who you really want. Armstrong."

It's not said in anger or recrimination, but once the words spill from his lips I can't seem to walk any farther.

The delicate china cup begins to rattle against the saucer. I look down. My hand is shaking. He takes the cup from me along with the pot and sets them on the table.

"Talk to me," he says, pulling me back over to the sofa.

"I *can't*. Not about this."

"Are you afraid you're going to hurt my feelings?"

"You have no feelings." As soon as I speak the words, I regret them.

"Don't mistake control for lack of passion. I know the rules. I know how to play the game. I'm not some naive, idealistic boy. I was once. Not anymore." He places my hand over his heart. "I am devoted to you. I will forever remain so. Demeter is the only one who could jeopardize that, and her ability to do so, her power to do so, is extremely restrictive."

"As long as I live without love," I whisper. "As long as I don't give my heart."

Kallistos drops my hand. "Just stick with me, kid."

"You sure that what we have is enough?"

"I am."

I smile. "But what if that changes? You know, I've been told I can be pretty irresistible."

Kallistos gets up, walks over to the bar, and despite the fact that the sun has just risen, he pours himself a drink. "You may be irresistible. But I'm not. At least not where you're concerned." He swallows the scotch, then sets the glass down. "I can walk in the light, but I'm not of it. I've done things, had to do things, will continue to do things. Do you understand?"

I'm not sure I do.

His back is to me. Heaviness bows his shoulders. "I'm not the hero, Emma. I'll never *be* the hero. I can't be redeemed."

Kallistos straightens, draws a breath, continues. "Will you come to me tonight?"

The uncertainty in his voice is wrenching. I nod, then find my voice. "I will."

When I arrive at the office, Zack and Garner are both sitting in front of a large flat-screen monitor, coffee mugs in hand. "Got started early on the surveillance footage?"

"We haven't been at it long," answers Zack. "Coffee's fresh."

"Anyone need a refill?" I ask.

Garner pauses the display. "One's my limit. The wife says caffeine isn't good for my blood pressure. Listen, I'm gonna run to the deli and pick up one of those bacon, egg, and cheese sandwiches. Want anything?"

Zack and I exchange amused looks. Only Garner seems to have missed the irony.

We both mutter, "No, thanks."

"Did you get my text last night?" he asks, following me to the coffee station.

"Yes, but I figured it was too late to call. Fill me in." I pour the last of the pot. It's barely half a cup.

Zack's already pulling out a new coffee filter to start a fresh one. "Not really anything more to report. We found accounts for the other two girls. All three are using a bank close to the school. It looks like deposits were made at a nearby ATM during lunch period. Apparently students of certain academic standing were allowed off campus for lunch."

"What about Agent Billings? Did he turn up anything on Julie's computer yet?"

Zack shakes his head. "He just came in a minute or two before you."

The coffee is now brewing. "So, where do we start?"

"I figured we'd start with Hannah's folks, then swing by right after to connect with Sylvia's. I called last night. They're expecting us."

I dump what's left in my mug into the sink, then give it a quick rinse. "Let's go."

CHAPTER 6

Armed with the knowledge that both Hannah and Sylvia had accounts similar to Julie's, Zack and I head out first to interview Hannah Clemons' mother. Our reports indicate that she and her husband have recently separated. She and Hannah live in Lakeside, a bedroom community in East County. The drive should take no more than twenty-five minutes because by the time we start out, midmorning, we've missed the commuter traffic that often clogs the 52E.

Zack doesn't have much to say. He's driving today and I'm glad. Gives him a chance to pretend he's focusing on the road and me a chance to focus on Kallistos and our conversation from this morning.

My thoughts spin like a kaleidoscope. I'd been certain moving in with Kallistos was wrong. Now bits and pieces of our past conversations replay in my mind and I'm not so sure. I look out the window at the passing landscape. I have to admit, our relationship is working better than any I've had in a long time. Sex is as much a part of his nature as it is mine. We're good together, more than good. He's strong enough that I can let go, completely.

The things he does, the way he can make my body feel. Yes, he is domineering, egotistical, self-assured. But he can also be thoughtful, gentle, caring, especially with those under his protection.

I remember how he looked when he saw the desiccated bodies of the vampires Barbara Pierce had tortured in her death lab. The sorrow in his eyes was real.

The feeling in those same eyes when he looks at me is real.

Not love. But as close to it as either of us is likely to get.

I am devoted to you. I will forever remain so.

Kallistos isn't a man who speaks lightly of commitments.

"Hey, Emma."

Zack's voice brings me back with a start. I look around. We've come to a stop in front of an apartment building. I recognize the name, Maplewood Apartments, as our destination. When I look at Zack, he's raised both eyebrows and is staring at me.

"Where have you been?"

"Thinking."

"Something about the case?"

I shake my head.

"Something personal?"

"Yeah."

"You want to talk about it?" Zack asks.

"No."

He frowns. "I am capable of being Sensitive Listening Guy, you know. I mean, I'm more comfortable being Decisive Action Guy. But for you, Monroe . . ."

I turn away and push my door open. "I'll let you know."

Zack follows me up the hedge-bordered path from the road into the apartment complex. Like most of the lower-income apartment buildings in the county, this one is two stories, stucco and wood, with individual air-conditioning units and outside storage closets. It's been well maintained, no trash or broken glass littering the bushes or walkways. The lawn area is healthy and neatly trimmed. It's quite a contrast to Julie Simmons' home even though the two families are in the same income bracket. Maybe the Simmonses just wanted to live close to Julie's school and they took what they could afford. Rents closer to the beach are always higher.

We stop in front of a cluster of mailboxes marked with numbers only, no tenant names. Zack pulls a copy of the police report from his breast pocket and quickly scans it. "Apartment 1G," he announces.

He and I find the unit in the back corner of the ground floor. We both have our badges out of our pockets when he rings the doorbell.

At first we get no answer. Then Zack rings again and knocks on the doorjamb.

Just when we think we've struck out, the door swings open.

"Yes?"

The woman is short with wide shoulders and hips, long dark hair piled on top of her head in a mass of unruly curls. She's wearing a bright red shift that ends right above her knees and matching flip-flops with rhinestones along the straps. The sparkly theme is repeated on the bridge and earpieces of oversized, black-framed glasses that make her look bug-eyed. She's holding a can of Pledge in one hand and a dust rag in the other.

"Agent Armstrong?" she asks, looking up at Zack. Then her gaze shifts to me.

I step forward. "Mrs. Clemons, I'm Agent Monroe."

"As I explained on the phone, we're here because we've been assigned to your daughter's case. We want to help find Hannah," Zack interjects.

She's already motioning for us to come inside. "I've been a bundle of nerves. Can't sleep. Can't eat." She places the furniture polish and the dust rag on a small table next to the door and removes her glasses. If the smell of the tiny apartment is any indication, Mrs. Clemons has been cleaning nonstop since Hannah turned up missing.

"Shall we sit?" I ask.

She looks toward the sofa in the middle of the room. "Of course. I'm sorry."

Zack and I follow her, taking seats at opposite ends of the small couch while she sits facing us across a coffee table that I could use for a mirror.

Zack sniffs the air. "Apple pie?"

Mrs. Clemons looks surprised. "I just put it into the oven. You can smell it already?"

Zack looks abashed for a moment. He's forgotten his Were sense of smell detects more than the lemon of Pledge and chlorine of bleach.

I jump to his rescue. "I could smell those fresh-cut apples and cinnamon as soon as you opened the door. Besides, apple pie is his hands-down favorite."

She reaches into the pocket of her dress and pulls out a crumpled tissue. "I just put it in the oven a few minutes ago," Mrs. Clemons repeats. "It's Hannah's favorite, too. Please, Agent Armstrong, you have to find my baby."

While Zack promises we'll do our best and buoys hope by talking about the Bureau's clearance rate, I take a moment to look around the place Hannah calls home. Pictures of her crowd the polished surfaces of scattered end tables, allowing us to see the progression from infant to young lady at a glance. On the mantelpiece over a faux fireplace is a larger version of the school picture we have in our folder. Alongside that one is a portrait of Hannah in a cheerleading outfit in front of her school.

She looks happy, well adjusted.

Zack takes out his notebook and pen. "When did you last see Hannah?"

"Friday morning when she left for school. It was like any other morning. I woke her up. We had breakfast together. Waffles. I made her lunch. She packed up her backpack. Then I drove her to school and waved goodbye." The tears start to flow. "I wish she'd never gotten out of that car."

I spy a box of tissues on the counter space that doubles as a breakfast bar and serves to separate the kitchen from the living area. I tilt my head in its direction and Zack picks up my cue.

"What time did you drop her off?" I ask.

"I'm an RN. I work the seven-to-three shift at Sharp Rees-Stealy in Point Loma. So I drop Hannah off at six forty-five every morning and pick her up at three fifteen. Except for days off, of course." She plucks a fresh tissue from the box Zack offers and dabs at her eyes.

"What time does school get out?"

"Two thirty. Hannah usually starts on homework while she waits. She's a good student. She skipped the seventh grade altogether. Don't know where she gets it. She has a 3.85 GPA."

"Was she having problems with anyone at school?" Zack chimes in.

"No."

He sets the tissues on the coffee table and reclaims his seat. "Any problems here at home?"

"Things have been going really well, better than they have in years."

"How so?"

"Hannah's father, Jason, moved out about six months ago. He . . ." She swallows hard, then looks Zack right in the eye. "He would drink too much. And he would beat me. One of the doctors at the hospital caught on. He talked me into going to a support group. After a few weeks, I started to bring Hannah with me. We'd both lived in fear for so long, I thought it would help, and it did. Finally I was able to get a restraining order. He's broken it. Twice."

"Do you know where he lives?" Zack asks.

"He *was* staying in the apartment above his sister's garage in Chula Vista. They had a falling out about a week ago and he moved out. I called her Friday night. I figured he should know—about Hannah. His sister has been trying to track him down."

"We'd like to get your sister-in-law's name and address from you. Has Mr. Clemons made any threats toward Hannah?"

"No. Absolutely not. He's a shit and a deadbeat, but he never hurt Hannah."

"Did Hannah have a boyfriend?"

"She has friends who are boys. No one she's especially

interested in. I'm afraid living in this house has made her a little gun-shy about relationships."

Zack slips three pictures out of a folder. He lays them faceup on the table in front of Mrs. Clemons. "Did Hannah know these girls?"

Mrs. Clemons' eyes quickly skim Rain's picture, and Julie's, but pause at Sylvia's. She picks it up. "Sylvia is in Hannah's cheer squad."

"She's been missing since Saturday."

"What? No!"

"You didn't hear about Sylvia?"

She swallows back a sob, pauses, composes herself. "I haven't listened to the television for three days. Or answered the telephone without screening calls. I've been afraid to. Afraid there would be news of Hannah . . . or that there wouldn't be."

Zack nods that he understands and points to Julie and Rain. "What about these two girls? Do you recognize them?"

She shakes her head. "I don't know them. If they're students at the Academy, Hannah probably does. The school isn't that big. Are they missing, too?"

I tap Julie's photo. "This one is."

"Dear God."

Zack slides a bank statement across the table. "We've found an account in your daughter's name at a local bank in Ocean Beach. Were you aware she had opened it?"

"No. But it doesn't surprise me. She's been saving for college for as long as she's known what it was. First it was change in a little piggy bank. Then she cashed that in and started stashing babysitting money in a shoe box in her closet."

I point to the spreadsheet, run my fingers down a column of numbers. "I think she's been depositing more than babysitting and birthday money. Hannah opened this account last June with an initial deposit of close to fourteen hundred dollars. Since then she's made substantial weekly deposits."

"How substantial?"

"Two hundred per week," Zack says.

Mrs. Clemons rises abruptly, grabs her glasses, and returns to snatch up the spreadsheet. After a moment, she says, "This has to be a mistake. Three thousand dollars? Hannah babysits. But only during the summer. She's too busy with her schoolwork and cheerleading during the school year to work. And no way could she have taken a job without me knowing." She slaps the sheet back down on the table. "It's another Hannah Clemons. It has to be."

I repeat the Social Security number attached to the account. "Is that your daughter's Social Security number?"

"Yes."

Zack hands her a copy of the account application. "Her handwriting?"

Mrs. Clemons nods. Like Julie's parents, she seems baffled.

While Zack collects the photos and bank documents, I ask the next question.

"The deposits occurred throughout the summer. What was Hannah doing then?"

It takes Mrs. Clemons a few moments to regain her composure. She slips her glasses down the bridge of her nose and peers at Zack over the lenses. "Let's see, Hannah spent a week at cheer camp right after school got out. Then she went on a college trip. She was so excited when she came home. She wants to go to Berkeley." Mrs. Clemons pulls another tissue out of the box and wipes her eyes again before continuing. "The rest of the time she did some babysitting for a neighbor's kids downstairs. Nothing that would account for this."

Zack follows up with, "What about socially? What did she do with her spare time?"

"She didn't have that much spare time during the week. But she did things with her fellow cheerleaders on the weekends. Practices, movies, parties. Friday or Saturday nights mostly."

"What about her father? You said he's been out of the house for six months. Has she spent time with him? Could he have given her the money?"

She shakes her head. "First of all, he doesn't have any money. And Hannah hasn't wanted to see him, which is fine with me."

She looks suddenly tired, her face drained of color. The strain she's been under for the past couple days, not to mention the appearance of two FBI agents on her doorstep, is taking its toll. My sympathy goes out to her.

"Just one more thing," I say. "Could we take a look at Hannah's room?"

Her eyes widen in panic. "I dusted her room. Should I not have done that? The police said they were through."

"No worries," I assure her. "We're not crime scene investigators."

"I'm sure the police were thorough," adds Zack. "Sometimes a fresh eye sees things differently."

She sighs. "I was hoping you had new information, but you don't, do you?"

"We have three missing girls now, Mrs. Clemons. Agent Armstrong and I are giving this case our undivided attention. It's our top priority, our only priority right now. We hope to have news soon."

She reaches for my hand and squeezes. "You'll find my Hannah."

Her desperation reminds me of another mother's. I'd almost forgotten those early days, when we were all still searching and hopeful—before the banishment, the curse. When life was simple, idyllic, and love was a promise arriving with the dawn of each new day.

Before Demeter's bitter thirst for vengeance replaced every bit of kindness and warmth she possessed.

The memory prompts me to take the hand of the woman looking at me so expectantly. "We're very good at our jobs, Mrs. Clemons. I believe we'll find her."

Zack snaps his notebook closed. "We'll do our best." His tone is clipped, sharp, directed at me. Then, "Will you show us to Hannah's room?" he asks Mrs. Clemons.

She shows us down the hall to a closed door and stands aside so we can enter. She doesn't wait for us to ask to be left alone. "I'll be in the living room when you're done."

Hannah's room is small but, like the rest of the house, clean and orderly. A twin bed sits along one wall with a dresser opposite, bookcases line a third. Under the window are a desk and chair. The walls have posters tacked up of some of the more popular movies and television shows: *The Vampire Diaries*, *Buffy the Vampire Slayer*, *Twilight*. One is a pinup of an actor who plays a werewolf in a brand-new television series, muscles bulging, smooth, bare chest gleaming. From the corner of my eye, I see Zack surreptitiously give him the once-over—and then shake his head, snapping his gloves on for emphasis. "Werewolf with a waxed chest," he mutters under his breath. "Only in Hollywood."

He turns toward me. "You shouldn't have told Mrs. Clemons we'd find her daughter."

I avoid his eyes, knowing he's right. It was an unprofessional thing to do. Still, I can't help but say, "I do believe we'll find her."

He shakes his head. "What if we don't?"

I don't answer and Zack doesn't press me. He's said his piece and moved on to the task at hand.

His gaze sweeps the room. "I'll take the dresser."

That leaves me the closet. Hannah's wardrobe is arranged by item on the rod: one side holds skirts, blouses, dresses, and jeans. The other, her cheerleading outfits and school uniforms. All the clothes are neatly pressed and smell like fabric softener. I search all of her pockets, feel inside each shoe. Nothing. Nothing of interest in any boxes, nothing out of the ordinary on the shelves.

Zack looks up from the floor where he's stooped to look under the bed and dresser. "You got anything?"

"Yeah, a whole lot of nothing." I glance around the room. "I don't think we're going to get lucky twice."

I pass my hand between the mattress and box spring on the bed. Shake the pillows. I also check the few framed photos on the nightstand.

Zip.

"If she kept a checkbook at home, I'm beginning to

think it's not in her room. And the police reports say the girls' lockers at school had been searched."

Zack nods and climbs to his feet. His eyes go to the desk. It's the only thing left and it's just a flat surface with no drawers. A pile of books, pens, pencils, a backpack, and a notebook have been placed on top. "Johnson said the girls' lockers at school had been emptied. After the local PD went through everything, they returned the items to the parents. I doubt we'll find anything of value." He tosses me the backpack. "You search the backpack and I'll take the rest."

I plop myself on Hannah's bed and empty the contents of the backpack. Nothing but what you'd expect a teenage girl to carry—lip gloss, mascara, a cell phone, earbuds, comb, brush, a pack of gum, and a schedule for cheerleading practice. I hold up the cell. "This has been dumped, right? I think I saw phone records in the police reports."

"Yep. All the girls' cells have been dumped."

I put everything back. Look around the room again. "Zack? I don't see a computer."

He looks around, too. "You're right. What kid doesn't have a computer these days?"

"Maybe the police still have it."

I tug at the bedspread to straighten it, slip off my gloves, and shove them into the pocket of my jacket. "Let's ask Mrs. Clemons."

When we go back to the living room, Mrs. Clemons is standing by the front window, looking out at the courtyard. She turns when she hears us approach. When she sees that we're empty-handed, despair drags at the corners of her eyes and mouth, a sad look of hopelessness that touches my heart.

Softly, Zack asks her whether Hannah had a computer.

"Yes," she replies. Her back stiffens. Her expression becomes stern, as if answering the question strengthens her resolve not to give in to the misery. "I told the police that it was missing. She kept it in her backpack."

Zack asks, "Could Hannah have let someone borrow it?"

"Or lost it?" I add.

She shakes her head. "No. Hannah was extremely protective of her laptop. I'm sorry I didn't think to mention it. I figured you were coordinating monitoring with the police."

Zack pulls his notebook back out. "Monitoring?"

"The computer can be tracked. As soon as I realized it was missing from the backpack, I told the police. They *are* tracking it. Right?"

"We're going to look into that. Mrs. Clemons, could you give Agent Monroe any information you have about the tracking service?" Zack turns to me. "I'm going to call Mrs. Roberts and let her know we're running a little late."

"I have everything written down in my address book. Let me copy it for you," Mrs. Clemons responds.

I follow her into the kitchen. "I'm sorry to make you go over this again."

She finishes writing and presses a slip of paper into the palm of my hand. "Find Hannah."

I drop it into the pocket of my jacket and retrieve a business card. "My office number. On the back is my cell. Call anytime."

She takes the card and stares down at it. Tears roll down her cheeks and splash onto her hands. She doesn't look up as we walk to the door. When I glance back, she still hasn't moved. I close the door quietly behind us.

Hannah, where are you?

CHAPTER 7

"Do you really believe we're going to find these girls?" Zack's tone is quiet, introspective, as he starts the car.

He doesn't want to voice the obvious. Someone took Hannah. She's been gone more than seventy-two hours. No word from her kidnapper. No ransom demand. Nothing.

The odds are not in her favor.

"I want to believe." I turn to look out the window. *These girls, young, blond, innocent. They remind me of her. Persephone.* "I'll call Billings about tracking the laptop."

As Zack starts the car and throws it into reverse, I call the office.

Billings sounds surprised. "There was no mention of a missing computer in the initial report. You said you have some information about it?"

As Zack drives south to El Cajon, I pull the note from my pocket. I give Billings the Web site for the tracking service, as well as a log-in and password. I also ask him to put in a request with Johnson to find Hannah's father.

"I can't believe the PD didn't initiate the trace right away," Zack says when I've disconnected.

I don't answer. I keep seeing the faces of the missing girls . . . so young, so full of promise. What could have happened to them?

Our next stop is the home of Sylvia Roberts. They live in a duplex on South Anza Street, close to downtown El Cajon. A chain-link fence surrounds each of the yards. The one on the right has a German shepherd standing guard. When we pull into the shared driveway, the dog goes bat-shit crazy, baring fangs, barking, and running up and down the length of the fence.

I step out of the car and nod toward the dog. "Does Killer here belong to the Roberts family?"

Zack walks over to the fence, hands stuffed in his pockets. As he approaches, the animal locks eyes with Zack, shrinks back. He lowers his head, whining—snarling beast turned cowardly lion.

"All bark and no bite," I say as the dog slinks back to the porch, tail between its legs, whimpering.

Zack grins at me. "Sometimes having a big, bad wolf on your team comes in handy."

I smile back.

The only light moment so far in an oppressive day.

The entrance to the duplex is through the gate to our left. No dog rushes out to challenge us. As soon as we step onto the porch, the front door opens.

"Are you Agent Armstrong?" A disembodied female voice from behind an opaque screen door calls out the question.

"Yes, ma'am," Zack says, he lifts his badge. "FBI. Agents Armstrong and Monroe."

The screen door is shoved open.

I follow Zack inside, the heavy perfume of incense

hitting us with the force of a blow. I actually see Zack's nose twitch in protest.

Mrs. Roberts is standing to the right of the door, Mr. Roberts beside her. They are both tall, thin, solemn faced. Mrs. Roberts' light brown hair is pulled straight back into a classic French twist. She's dressed in a modest, navy blue A-line skirt that's topped with a matching sweater set. Against the dark backdrop a small gold cross shines on a delicate chain. It's the only jewelry she's wearing other than her wedding band. Low-heeled black leather pumps ensure that she's no taller than her five-foot-sixish husband, who is dwarfed by Zack. Mr. Roberts' hair is close-cropped, graying at the temples. He's wearing khaki slacks that have been starched and pressed with precision, immaculate polo shirt, brown loafers. On the wall to his right is a large crucifix.

Mr. Roberts leads us down the hall. "Abigail, get the agents coffee, will you?"

Zack holds up a hand. "No. Thank you. Please don't go to the trouble. We'll try not to take up too much of your time."

Mrs. Roberts extends her arm, motioning us to go first. Despite the early hour, and the bright morning sun, the living room is dark when we enter. Drapes closed, shades drawn, lights out. My eyes focus on a framed portrait of Sylvia on a nearby table. A half dozen prayer candles surround it. One has gone out.

Mr. Roberts nods toward it as he opens the curtains. "Abigail, will you relight that one, please?"

While she busies herself pouring off the wax and trimming the wick, I notice two cushions on the floor. Two sets of rosary beads, one on the table, and the other on a nearby chair. On the wall above the miniature shrine, a print of the Sacred Heart of Jesus in a rather ornate frame looks down at us.

"I'm sorry," I say. "It looks as if we've interrupted your prayers."

Mr. Roberts takes a seat on the sofa. "We've been taking turns saying the Rosary."

Zack and I take our places on chairs beside each other.

As soon as the candle is relit, Mrs. Roberts joins her husband on the couch. Their expressions are drawn, dark circles smudge their eyes. Where Mrs. Clemens was desperate and frazzled, plagued by the relentless need to do something, this couple is eerily quiet.

Zack begins with words of concern for what the couple is going through and explains that we will likely be asking some of the very same questions the police asked earlier.

Mr. Roberts bows his head in acknowledgment.

I repeat the litany of questions we asked Julie's parents and Hannah's mother for the third time.

Mr. Roberts takes the lead, answering by rote, mostly in monosyllables.

Did Sylvia know Julie or Rain? No.

Did she know Hannah? Yes.

How did she know Hannah? Cheerleading.

Was she having trouble in school? No.

Was she having trouble at home? No.

Did she have a boyfriend? No.

When did they last see Sylvia? The morning she disappeared. She left on foot like she does every Saturday morning to attend catechism. She never returned.

Mrs. Roberts sits still and quiet, her face betraying nothing as she listens to her husband.

That changes, however, when we bring up the subject of the checking account.

Like he did with Mrs. Clemons, Zack produces a spreadsheet of their daughter's account and places it on the table in front of them.

"What is this?" Mr. Roberts asks, taking a pair of readers from his shirt pocket.

"It's a copy of the bank activity for an account in your daughter's name."

"Not possible." Mr. Roberts' reply is automatic, even as his eyes continue to scan the sheet. He reaches the account balance and blinks up at us. "Twenty-two hundred dollars?"

Mrs. Roberts' shoulders jump. "How much?"

Zack turns the sheet so she can see it, too. "The deposits started in mid-June."

Mr. Roberts shakes his head emphatically. "That just can't be."

"She might have earned twelve hundred over the summer. Maybe the bank made a mistake?" Mrs. Roberts suggests.

"We don't think so," replies Zack. "Tell us how your daughter spent the summer?"

Mrs. Roberts answers first. "She started working for the Spirit Group as soon as school got out. The job lasted right up to Labor Day weekend."

"Spirit Group?" I ask. "Is that a religious organization?"

"No. They run cheerleading camps in Julian. Five two-week sessions through the summer. In exchange for her work, she was able to attend the camp for free."

"You said she started working as soon as school was out. Did she do anything else?"

Mr. Roberts nods. "She took a school trip—a week visiting college campuses. Most rising juniors go."

Mrs. Roberts glances down at the bank statement. "This is a mistake." Her tone is adamant. "This money. It has to be a mistake."

"The mistake," Mr. Roberts snaps at his wife, "was letting Hannah be a cheerleader. I told you it was a bad idea from the beginning. She's fallen in with the wrong crowd."

Zack leans forward. "What do you mean, Mr. Roberts?"

"Peer pressure. Someone must have duped or . . . or . . . coerced her into doing something unseemly. She's compromised her principles and now she's in trouble and too afraid to come to us."

"I don't believe that, Stewart." It's Mrs. Roberts' turn to bare her teeth. "Sylvia is smarter and stronger than that, she would never compromise her values. No. She's sick or hurt."

Something squeaks outside. The dog in the yard next door begins to bark.

She tilts her head toward the door and rises abruptly. "Was that our gate?"

Her husband reaches for her hand. "No, dear, it was the one next door."

She turns to Zack and me. "I know Sylvia will have an explanation for this when you find her. Mark my words."

When you find her. Not if.

I find myself admiring her faith.

Zack folds the sheet and slips it back into his pocket. "Do you mind if we have a look at Sylvia's room?"

"The police have been all over it," Mr. Roberts grumbles. "They left it in shambles."

Mrs. Roberts shoots her husband a disapproving look. "Of course you can look at Sylvia's room. It's the first door on the right. I think I'll make that pot of fresh coffee. I could use a cup. Let me know if either of you change your mind."

Zack and I head to Sylvia's room, leaving Mr. Roberts sitting alone on the couch. The sound of the water running in the kitchen drifts down the hall. As soon as we close the bedroom door behind us, Zack says, "Prayers and Pledge. It's been an interesting morning."

I look around Sylvia's room. "Doesn't look like it's in a shambles to me."

"Bet you lunch Mrs. Roberts cleaned it up."

Like that of the other two girls, Sylvia's furniture is plain and functional—bed, dresser, desk. The walls are a cheerful yellow. The bedspread is bright pink and covered with a splash of Gerbera daisies. The color and light in the room are a sharp contrast to the austerity of Sylvia's parents and the rest of the apartment. The only common touch linking the two spaces is the crucifix above the dresser. I make my way over to the desk. A bulletin board hangs above it, covered with candid photos. A framed montage of pictures of Sylvia with the cheerleading team—action photos from school sporting events, group shots from social events, Sylvia alone and . . . Sylvia with Hannah. I point the last one out to Zack.

He nods. "I'll take the closet," he says.

"I'll start here." The top of Sylvia's desk is neat and tidy. There's a stack of textbooks on one corner, and a caddy containing pens, pencils, and paper clips. The drawers are organized, as well. The top one contains a stack of notebooks. I flip through them—Sylvia's class notes in a precise hand. Nothing additional. No doodles. No apparent missing pages. The second drawer holds a variety of magazines—typical fare for a teenage girl. Fashion magazines, a couple of teen mags, a dog-eared copy of *People*. In the bottom drawer I spy a messenger bag.

"Bingo!" I slide an older-model laptop out of the bag and flip open the lid. Pressing the power button yields nothing but the same, a black screen. "Looks like it's out of juice."

"Is there a power cord?" Zack asks.

I check the bag's zippered compartment. "Yes, along with a small external hard drive. I'll bag them."

We quickly complete the rest of the search, turning up nothing of interest. No checkbook, no diary, no secret hiding place. Unless Billings is able to get something off of Sylvia's laptop, the morning's been a bust. Time is slipping past, like water through a sieve. We're no closer to finding these girls now than we were yesterday.

We leave Sylvia's parents with the same promise to be in touch that we've made twice before. When I reach the car, I glance back. Mrs. Roberts is standing at the living room window, watching.

Waiting.

"Lunch?" Zack asks.

"I'd like to get this laptop to Billings," I answer. "It's

about the only thing we've got to show for this morning's work. How about we drop it off, then go grab some burgers?"

"Downtown Hodad's?"

I nod. "Perfect. I'll text Billings and let him know we're bringing in another laptop."

CHAPTER 8

Twenty minutes later, the custody of Sylvia's laptop has safely been transferred to Billings. The computer was, as we suspected, out of power. He's working on Julie's now. It will be a while before he's able to turn his attention to Sylvia's.

Meanwhile, Zack and I decide to grab some lunch. Zack is a carnivore through and through and the burgers at Hodad's are his favorite. Mine, too. Miraculously, we score a parking spot right across the street. I feed the meter as Zack dashes to get a place in line for a table. "We're already next for a table?" I ask Zack as I join him. The line has moved fast and is uncharacteristically short.

He pulls out his phone and checks the time. "I didn't realize it was so late. Looks like we missed the big rush." Just as he's placing it back in his pocket, it rings. "Sorry, I've got to take this. Order me the usual?"

He steps back outside to take the call. I follow the hostess to a table by the window.

It's midafternoon so we have no trouble getting a nice spot by the window. A tall, willowy redhead appears out of nowhere.

"I'm Candy." She drops napkins, silverware, and straws on the table.

"I know. You wait on us all the time."

"Right, you and your . . . boyfriend?"

I shake my head.

"Husband?"

"Partner," I inform her. "Strictly business."

Her already high-wattage smile goes up another notch.

I place our orders—double bacon cheeseburger, rare, for Zack; cheeseburger, medium, for me. A large basket of fries. Two Cokes.

When Zack makes his entrance, Candy's isn't the only head to turn. He's the best-looking man in the place and completely oblivious.

"A smile?" He slips into the seat opposite me. "Haven't seen you wearing one of those in a while. What's the occasion?"

"You amuse me."

"Glad to be of service."

"You have no idea, do you?"

"About?"

I lean forward. "The effect you have on women. The blonde at the beach yesterday? Candy?" *Me?*

"Who's Candy?"

Right on cue, she arrives with our fries and drinks. "Your burgers will be coming right up."

"She would be the young lady who just slipped you her number."

"Huh?"

I tap the edge of the napkin his drink is on. "And you call yourself a special agent."

Zack reaches for the ketchup. "Candy evidently thinks I'm special."

I beat him to it. "Better let me do that. You're wearing a white shirt again."

"Very funny."

I squeeze a pool into the basket and we begin dipping the hot, crispy fries into it. Suddenly I'm starving. "I just realized I got distracted and missed breakfast this morning," I volunteer, licking the salt from my fingertips.

Zack holds up his hands. "Please, spare me the details of your sex life with the King of Darkness. My burger should be coming any minute. I want to enjoy it."

"I missed breakfast because Kal and I were talking. As in having a conversation."

"How progressive of him."

I lean forward. "Why do you dislike him so?"

Zack shakes his head. "It's none of my business."

"Yet you can't seem to leave it alone. Out with it."

Zack snaps his fingers. "Here's Candy." He holds out his hand and takes his plate. In a minute, he's bitten off a mouthful of burger.

I stare at him. The chance to get him to say any more is gone. I settle for raising my own burger to my lips. For the next five minutes Zack is preoccupied with the monstrosity that's his lunch, me with the lack of progress on our case.

When we've finished and the plates are cleared away, Zack and I sit back, nursing our drinks.

"Is any of this coming together for you?" I ask him.

He takes one last slurp. "Not really. Things don't quite fit. I think by now we can say with certainty these are not kidnappings for ransom. Abductions, yes. But what's the motive?"

"Well, we have a definite type. Blond, blue-eyed, pretty. The school connects them all. Scholarships. Hannah and Sylvia are cheerleaders. The school trip." I pause. "Did Julie go on that trip, I wonder?"

"Probably not," Zack grunts. "She's older than Hannah and Sylvia and a senior."

I nod. "And her parents didn't mention it."

"No. They were too busy going off on Rain." He pauses. "The other connecting factor is the money. They were getting payments from someone." He pulls his cell from his pocket. "I'm going to put in a call to the Ocean Beach PD and see if they know anything about the missing computer. I'd like to know if they tried to track it and why it wasn't in the report."

He's got all the local police departments in his cell's contact list and as he's scrolling for the right one, I glance toward the window. A dark-haired, tree trunk of a man stands outside on the sidewalk across the street. He's built like a wrestler—square, heavy chest, thick thighs. At first, I think the guy is just checking out the restaurant.

But as he crosses to approach the door, Zack's head suddenly snaps up. A low growl escapes his throat as he slaps his cell on the table. "Un-fucking-believable."

His eyes flash. It's obvious who has him so suddenly riled.

"You know him?"

Zack doesn't answer. His eyes are glued to man as he walks past the window we're seated in front of and into the restaurant. After weaving his way through the line, he swaggers toward us, exuding badass power. Zack repositions his chair away from the table, back to the window. He doesn't want the table between him—and anything.

I'm instantly on alert. I recognize the man for what he is, a werewolf. A pissed-off werewolf. Zack's hand edges toward the butt of his gun. The instinctual tell is enough to set me even more on edge. My heart races. My pulse quickens. I slowly draw my weapon. Gun hidden underneath the table, I track the wolf's movements.

By the time he reaches us, Zack appears once more composed and in control. His projected sense of calm does me wonders.

That and knowing I have enough firepower to blow a nice big hole in the Were's stomach.

When Zack greets him, his expression is neutral. "Asa."

Asa? My thoughts spin back a few months, to when Sarah first arrived. She was running away from her pack master in South Carolina. A vicious predator. How did Zack describe him? *Asa Wade is the worst kind of wolf.*

Wade's face is leathery from sun and wind. His sharp jawline is further accentuated by a neatly trimmed Van Dyke beard. His most dramatic feature, however, is his eyes. Wide-set, they are the color of a stormy sky, neither blue nor gray. And they're fixed on me.

"Aren't you going to introduce me, Armstrong?"

"Wasn't planning on it," Zack answers, his voice steady and strong. "You are not welcome here."

Asa grabs an empty chair and parks himself at the end of the table. "You are an interesting little thing," he croons, leaning in toward me, tasting my scent. "What are you doing with this big ol' hound dog here?"

I shrug. "Just enjoying watching him mark his territory."

His eyes widen at the realization that I recognize his second nature, but Zack's sharp voice cuts in before he can comment.

"And you're way outside of yours, Asa," Zack says.

Asa locks his eyes on Zack. "You have something of mine. I came to collect." He speaks the words softly, but underneath the velvet is steel.

I smile at Zack. "Isn't this where you do that growly thing and tell him Sarah's yours and he can't have her?"

Zack shakes his head at me. "Sarah isn't anyone's. She's free to choose who she wants." His gaze snaps back to Asa. "And she didn't choose you."

"Sarah swore fealty to the pack, my pack. You left her. She's not your mate. You have no claim on her, boy. None. As Alpha, if I want her, she's mine. It's my right to take whatever female I fucking please. I earned it fair and square."

"Bullshit! The pack Sarah pledged her fealty to was a different one altogether and you damn well know it."

"Tell you what. We can settle the matter the old-fashioned way. If you win, you keep Sarah. If I win, I get both Sarah and this one." He turns his head to look at me. "She isn't Were. But I can easily fix that."

Zack leans forward. "Don't make the mistake of thinking that the reason I didn't challenge you before was because I figured I wouldn't win. I walked away because what you're offering isn't what I want. It's not what Sarah wants. There are plenty of women in that pack who would jump at the chance to be your mate. Sarah isn't one of them."

Asa's grin is menacing. "Yeah, but none of them looked quite so good leashed and collared, riding my cock."

I reach out for Zack's hand, but I'm too late, too slow. He's already risen, squaring off against Asa. The two men, equal in height, are toe-to-toe.

"Let's take it down a notch. Shall we, gentlemen?"

A new voice, quiet yet commanding, startles us all.

Seamus.

Appearing out of nowhere.

"Someone forgot to check in with the local pack master," he says, stepping between the two men. "Bad form, Mr. Wade. I'd say it's a darned good thing we decided to follow you."

Zack takes a step back while Asa drinks in the unassuming Seamus with his freckles, red hair, and glasses.

"Well, Opie, be sure to apologize to him for me," Asa growls, chest puffed out, arms crossed.

Seamus stands his ground, smiling up at the bigger man. "The name's Seamus, and you can tell me how sorry you are yourself."

"You?" Asa bursts into laughter. "You and what army?"

"This isn't your fight, Seamus," Zack says, his voice a growl. "Sarah and I aren't your problem."

His words do no good. Instead of backing down, Seamus ignores Zack and takes a step closer to Asa. "Don't push your luck, Mr. Wade. I have men right outside, should it prove necessary." As if responding to some subliminal signal, a dozen or so Weres are suddenly visible through the window. The men stand just to the left of the door. They could be office workers waiting to get in line for a table, but their fixed stare at Asa Wade makes their real purpose clear.

"You are in my territory, Mr. Wade," Seamus continues. "You have not shown me even the commonest of courtesies by announcing your presence. I could be persuaded to overlook these transgressions, but only if you leave my territory. Tonight."

Asa scans the faces outside. He may be many things, but stupid isn't one of them. Twelve to one is not good odds. "I will go," he says simply. "But you can bet this isn't the last you'll hear from me. You want to play the protocol card? Then, by all means, let's do that. Rules have been broken. Sarah is mine. Armstrong took her away from me. I have a right to exact justice."

Seamus nods. "Yes, you do. And I'll grant you a measure of justice equal to the measure of respect I received. Zack, apologize to Asa for your civil disobedience of his most uncivilized practices."

Zack looks as if he's going to resist, but Seamus nails him with a look that conveys this isn't up for negotiation. "Sarah told me everything. This is what she wants, what's necessary. It's time to move on and that won't be accomplished by shedding more blood."

Grudgingly, Zack gives in. "I apologize."

"Apology accepted," Asa says, grinning. "I will collect Sarah and be on my way."

"No." Seamus utters the one word with finality.

"No?" Asa's face reddens. "You want to avoid bloodshed? I'd be real careful about denying me what is mine."

"This is not up for negotiation," Seamus says. "You mistreated Sarah. She came here because she was afraid of you. She is under my protection now. You're a long way from home, Mr. Wade. If you try to force her to leave, you'll answer to me. More importantly, you'll answer to my pack. And, I should warn you, they're fiercely loyal." He glances once again toward the window and nods. Three men, three big men, separate from the group and step toward the door. "These men will see you to the airport."

Asa wants to resist, to fight. But he knows he's beaten. His glare telegraphs the message: *You win. For now*. He strides stiffly out of the door without a backward glance and is swallowed up as Seamus' men surround him and march him off.

I grin up at Seamus. "You are full of surprises."

Zack is still watching through the window. When Asa is no longer in sight, he swivels around to face Seamus. "Thanks for the heads-up, man."

"Heads-up?" I ask, slipping my Glock back into its holster.

Zack waves Candy over. "The call I received a few minutes ago was from Seamus. Apparently Wade tailed us from the office here. Sounds like he spent much of the morning staking out the house hoping to find Sarah, and when that didn't work, he started to follow us."

"Where is Sarah?" I ask.

Seamus plops himself into Asa's vacated chair and orders a Guinness. "Sarah's safe at the Manchester Grand. We got her out before Wade arrived at Zack's place. After about four hours of sitting on his ass in his car, Wade broke into the house. He found nothing of Sarah's. We made sure of that. So, he decided to move on to Zack himself. He parked in the lot across the street from your building. You two showed up shortly after he arrived."

"How long have you been tailing him?" Zack asks.

"Someone alerted us to his presence last night. I'm not sure how long he's been in town." Seamus takes a sip of his beer, then settles back in the chair. He looks at me. "We've got something serious to discuss, Emma. It involves Asa Wade and Kallistos Kouros."

Zack groans. "What has the Soulless Sovereign done now?"

I ignore Zack's gibe. "We're listening."

Seamus takes another pull from the frosty mug. "Mother's milk," he sighs.

"Seamus." I lean toward him. "What about Kallistos?"

He sits up straighter, places the mug on the table. "Asa didn't travel here by himself."

"Meaning?"

"He accompanied Philippe Lamont, the vampires' Southern King."

"The Southern King is in San Diego?" Zack sounds not only surprised but concerned. He looks at me. "Remember a few months back when I told you the Southern King was against the Blood Emporiums? That it was rumored he was behind the trouble in New Mexico and Arizona? The torched Emporiums? The tortured patrons?"

"Yes," I answer. "Do you think they're trying to negotiate a truce of some kind?"

"I was hoping you could tell us that." Seamus leans back in his chair and smiles sheepishly. "Even Kings have been known to talk in their sleep."

"It's remotely possible this is a diplomatic mission," Zack adds. "But preparations for a visiting dignitary would be hard for anyone in Kallistos' inner circle to miss."

Meaning me. I search my memory but come up with nothing. "I haven't seen or heard anything out of the ordinary. I don't think Kallistos knows he's here."

"I want to know what this visit is about." He turns those greener-than-clover eyes on me. "You can find out for us. Ask Kallistos if he has been in touch with Philippe Lamont."

"And if he hasn't? Seamus, do you really think Lamont would be foolish enough to challenge Kallistos on his own turf?"

"I do." He lets the words drop away and takes another pull of Guinness.

"I lived in Lamont's territory," Zack says. "You're right not to underestimate him. The bastard is ruthless, cunning, and will stop at nothing. He has no conscience, no limits. He glorifies the old ways, views humans as cattle. His influence has been spreading slowly west. He may be consolidating power, hoping to increase the size of his realm. If that is true, Kallistos may well be in danger." Zack glances back and forth between Seamus and me. "And, I hate to say it, but if he loses power and Wade and Lamont take over, all of the supernaturals in the territory will be in danger."

"Not to mention the humans," I add.

Seamus nods. "Kallistos is old and powerful. I'd like to be able to say I'm not worried, but I can't. Because of his progressive views, he's made enemies. And he has vulnerabilities. You, for one."

"Are you suggesting Lamont would use me to get to Kallistos?"

Seamus looks at Zack. "You know Lamont. What do you think?"

"I've met him. I wouldn't exactly say I know him," replies Zack.

The discussion stops when Candy comes to the table to refill our Cokes. As soon as she leaves I ask, "What can you tell me about him?"

Zack shrugs. "Just the rumors. He was turned around 1575, so he's younger than Kallistos. Rumor has it Lamont was a lover of Catherine de Medici. He was instrumental in overseeing the assassination of Admiral Gaspard de Coligny, an event that set off an orgy of killing, resulting in the massacre of tens of thousands of Huguenots all across France. A river of blood was spilled and Lamont bathed joyously in it. If the stories are true, he lost his soul long before he became vampire."

Seamus finishes off the rest of his beer, then stands up. "Maybe I'm overreacting. Maybe when you go home tonight, Kallistos will be hosting a dinner party for the Southern King and his visit is nothing more than a stop on a coastal vacation."

"Doesn't explain why he'd bring Asa Wade with him," Zack interjects.

"Perhaps he needed an extra guard dog." Seamus laughs at his own joke while Zack and I stare at him. "Well, I thought it was funny. Zack, you might want to check on Sarah. She's pretty shaken up. I wanted her to come back to the ranch, where we can protect her, but she didn't want to come without you."

"You want me to convince her?" Zack says.

"Don't you think that's for the best?" Seamus turns and winks at me. "Now, off you go, too, Mata Hari. I'd like a full report by morning." He throws a couple bucks on the table. "For the tip." Then he leaves.

Zack reaches for his wallet. "You get the car, Emma, and I'll get the check. You can drop me off at the hotel. Seamus is right. I need to talk to Sarah, and you need to speak with Kallistos."

"Johnson's going to want a report." *Now that the Were pissing party is over, we still need to find these girls.*

"After I get Sarah settled at the ranch, I'll call and update him. It should take an hour or two at the most. By then, maybe we'll have more info from the Ocean Beach PD about the missing computer."

"Or maybe something from the school's security footage or Julie's hard drive," I add as I fish my keys out of my pocket.

Zack pulls out a couple twenties and calls out to the waitress.

I move to leave, but he reaches for my arm and stops me. "You had your gun out. Would you have shot Wade?"

"Depends."

"On?"

"Whether he tried to hurt you."

CHAPTER 9

When I arrive at the Palomar Hotel, I'm told by Ernesto, the valet, that Kallistos is out on business. The twentysomething is sporting a pin-striped vest with matching trousers and his ever-present bowler hat. His dark eyes, accentuated by kohl liner, take in everything.

Ernesto isn't just a valet; he's also a vampire. Young and eager to please. In addition to parking cars and carrying luggage, it's his job to keep track of all of the guests' comings and goings, and to report anything unusual up the chain—to Kallistos. My arriving this early in the day is unusual. He's furiously texting someone. My guess? Kallistos. He tries to hide his discomfort as he takes my keys.

"Let me get you a claim ticket," he says, stalling.

He checks his phone. Takes off his hat and wipes his forehead. Checks his phone again. This time whatever he reads brings a smile.

"I'll take you right up," he says. Then he hands my car keys off to one of the other valets and takes my computer bag.

"Do you know when Kallistos is expected back?" I ask as we walk through the great swinging door into the lobby. On the way to the elevators we pass staff preparing the space for the downtown happy-hour crowd. Several nod. Others are too busy lighting candles and laying out drink menus to notice.

"Less than an hour. Shall I send something up? Charlie's behind the bar tonight. She makes a mean pomegranate martini."

We pass underneath the chandelier that hangs over a cluster of sofas and chairs. A collection of lights that resemble jellyfish hang from the ceiling, casting a soft glow, setting just the right mood. I check the time. It's four thirty.

"I think I'll wait for Kallistos."

Ernesto nods. The short ride up to the penthouse is uneventful. He leaves me alone with a promise to have drinks sent up whenever we're ready. I toss my bag on the sofa along with my jacket, then head upstairs.

I'm not sure why I'm here. Since Kallistos isn't, why didn't I go home to work? I could have reveled in privacy and solitude. Had Ernesto page me when Kallistos returned.

And yet, here I am.

I toss my keys on the table beside the door.

Maybe I'm not sure where home is anymore. Maybe I've found it. Kallistos knows I can't allow myself to fall in love or allow anyone to fall in love with me. More important, he knows the cost. He's a realist. He accepts it. While his pragmatic approach may not be particularly romantic, it is a relief. Liz is convinced we're the perfect match—a vampire who makes no demands, except for the most exquisite sexual ones, and the Siren who can fulfill those demands without sacrificing her heart.

When I enter the bedroom, my eyes are drawn to Kallistos' private writing table. My lover may be a vampire King, but he's also a businessman. The eighteenth-century Louis XVI mahogany piece arrived shortly after Kallistos decided to remain in San Diego. I realize that although it appears to be well used, I've never witnessed him sitting behind it. I pull out the chair and run my fingers over the leather-inlaid top. When they brush the keyboard, the desktop computer comes to life. A calendar is displayed. My breath hitches. No password. No security. Why?

Because no one has unsupervised access to this room.

Except for me, now.

Today's appointments are all right here. A click of a button and I'll be able to see the days, weeks, months ahead. My hand hangs, poised, over the mouse.

Instead I go to Finder, hit sleep.

The screen returns to black.

I head over to the closet, kicking off my shoes on the way. The light automatically turns on when I open the door. It's filled with his suits, shirts, and shoes. The scent of Kallistos' aftershave perfumes the air with a delicate and familiar subtlety. I reach for a starched white button-down with traditional cuffs and a spread collar. My blouse and lingerie go into the hamper. The slacks and jacket are hung in the closet. I pad, nude, across the thick caramel carpet into the bathroom, shirt in hand. I hang the shirt on a hook behind the bathroom door, turn on the taps, and add a generous portion of bath salts to the swirling water.

My phone rings. "Bad Moon Rising." Zack.

Rather than race downstairs to get it, I pick up the handset in the bathroom and call him back. "What's up?"

"Heard from Garner. His review of the security footage at the school for the last several days turned up nothing out of the ordinary."

I can hear the disappointment in his voice as he continues.

"So far the school's the only location we can place all three girls. Seems logical that's where whoever is responsible identified his victims. I'm thinking if it wasn't someone on the outside . . ."

"Maybe we should be looking closer at those on the inside."

"Exactly what I'm thinking. I have a list of the faculty and staff. I'm going in to start running background checks tonight."

I turn off the water. "You're going in now? What happened to driving Sarah out to the ranch?"

"She took a cab."

"A cab?"

No reply.

"Zack?"

"You have this idea about what Sarah and I have. It's not what you think." Before I have a chance to respond he asks, "You want to come in and help?"

I hear the door downstairs open, then close.

"Kallistos just came in. I need to talk to him about Lamont. Maybe after."

Seconds tick by.

I hear footsteps on the staircase. "Emma?"

Zack hears Kallistos, too. "I'll let you go. I'll update

Jimmy tonight, put in a couple hours. Meet you in the office tomorrow morning at eight."

"I'll see you then," I tell him. Then I hang up, and slide into the tub. The water is almost scalding. Steam rises up. I close my eyes and try to relax.

"Emma?"

"In here!"

Kallistos appears in the doorway. He's wearing a sleek-cut, single-breasted black suit. In the breast pocket is a neatly folded white handkerchief. It matches the white dress shirt, open at the collar. His dark hair is combed back from his forehead; shoulder-length layers frame his handsome face. I see something in his clear blue eyes that I haven't seen before: worry. "Is everything all right?"

I pluck one of the larger sea sponges from the basket perched on the tub's surrounding rim and hand it to Kallistos.

A smile smooths the worry frown from his brow. He removes his suit coat and hangs it on a hook. His smile broadens when he sees another of his own shirts, the one I brought with me from his closet, hanging nearby. "Need help with those hard-to-reach places, do you?"

He's already removed his onyx cuff links and is rolling up his sleeves.

I lean forward, hugging my knees to my chest. "You came home early. Am I keeping you from something?"

"Nothing as important as you. What is it? Has something happened?"

His voice is low, even, soothing. Water spills down by back, over my shoulder. His strokes are slow and deliberate.

"Nothing. Everything. I'm working a case. Young girls, three of them. It's going nowhere. I'm worried," I confess.

"That you won't find them?"

"That they're already dead. There haven't been any ransom demands, not for any of them." I turn to face him. "But I need to speak to you about something else. Something I heard at lunch today."

"About?"

"You. Well, maybe you. Seamus O'Malley—"

"You had lunch with Seamus O'Malley?" Kallistos drops the sponge back into the tub, then moves to lean against the counter.

The better to watch my face. I swallow a sarcastic retort and, shaking my head, begin, "Not exactly *with* Seamus. Zack and I stopped at Hodad's to grab a late lunch. Asa Wade showed up." Kallistos' vantage point proves to work to my advantage, too. I see no indication that he recognizes the name. "He's Zack's old pack master. They have a history. Bad blood between them. Seamus showed up and diffused the situation."

"Zack involves you in werewolf affairs now?" His tone is sharp and disapproving.

"I'm actually more concerned with what I learned from Seamus about vampire affairs," I reply. "He had a warning. For you."

Kallistos' arms are now crossed in front of his chest. "A warning? What did he say?"

"That Asa came here with Philippe Lamont."

A flash of wariness widens his eyes.

"You didn't know," I add.

He shakes his head. "It's not true. I don't believe Lamont would enter my territory without permission, without going through appropriate channels. Besides, he's being watched. If he'd come here, I'd know. I haven't maintained power for this long by happenstance. I know who my enemies are and I keep close tabs on them."

"Seamus seems pretty certain it was Lamont with Wade. He thinks you may be in danger. He believes that Lamont is here to foment unrest between the factions who oppose the Blood Emporiums and those whom you rule. If it is Lamont, wouldn't the fact that he hasn't made his presence known to you prove Seamus' point?"

He snaps up the handset for the phone and dials. He speaks into the receiver. "When did we last hear from Gideon?" He listens. After a moment, he says, "Find out why he hasn't reported in. I want Lamont's current position." He waits. More seconds tick by. Concern mars his brow.

"What is it?" I ask.

Kallistos holds up his hand. "Call me as soon as you have word." He hangs up, then reaches for a towel, holding it open. "My man didn't answer."

I step out of the bath. His arms, strong and certain, wrap the towel around me. For a moment I lean into him. "What does that mean?" I ask.

"I don't know. But I aim to find out."

He tilts my chin up. My eyes meet his.

"I can take care of myself, you know. Been doing it for a long time. You needn't be concerned." He smiles. "Someone might mistake that concern for caring."

"You know I care."

"Which reminds me . . ."

He takes my hand and leads me back out to the bedroom. On the center of the moss green coverlet is a black velvet box, a little longer and wider than a deck of cards.

"It occurred to me after you left this morning that I haven't been expressing myself very well. This is probably going to come as a surprise to you, but I'm a bit rusty when it comes to negotiating the great relationship gauntlet."

"So you bought me jewelry?"

Kallistos picks up the box. "No. Not jewelry." He appears to measure the weight of the box in his hand. "For months I've been asking you to move in with me. I realized today how that must sound, as if I'm asking you to give up something of yourself—your freedom, your privacy. That isn't my intention. I don't want you to have to give up anything, ever. Not for me. I can be difficult to access, to understand. I've been with thousands of women, but how many have known me? What I've been trying to do, Emma, is invite you in. Not just into the penthouse." He opens the box. "Into my life."

The box holds a hotel card key attached to a short gold chain, one that resembles an old-fashioned watch fob. He holds it out to me.

"Keep your place. Come and go as you please. Commandeer a closet and one side of the medicine cabinet. Or continue to have room service bring you emergency toothbrushes and steal my shirts. I don't care."

"Yes, you do," I say, fingering the key. "This proves it. Thank you."

"Don't thank me yet. My life is often messy. If Lamont's presence in town is any indication, it might be getting messier. He plays dirty, Emma."

"I'm a Siren," I remind him, letting my towel fall to

the ground as I drop to my knees. My hands move to the waistband of his trousers and I unfasten his belt. "We like it dirty."

His long fingers reach down to remove the pins from my hair. It falls loose down my back.

A slow smile forms on his lips. "How dirty?" he asks me, encouraging me to stand. His voice is rough with desire as he kicks off his shoes and steps out of his trousers.

His rock-hard erection brushes the softness of my belly.

I need it. Him. Desperately.

As I work the buttons of his shirt, my heart is racing with anticipation. "What do you have in mind, sire?" The air around us warms, stirring an almost imperceptible perfumed breeze. It's a deliberate crack in the armor, small but effective. His control crumbles.

Suddenly, I'm pinned to the wall. Vampire molded to my body, mouth at my neck.

My breath hitches.

So does his.

It pulses against my skin. "You know what I want," he whispers. "You. I want you."

I thread my fingers through his hair and pull him away. My eyes search his. They reveal more than they should, but then again, mine probably do, as well. I don't have much time to think. His lips cover mine. Hungrily, he drinks me in. Mouth open, tongue probing. A fang pierces my lower lip. I taste my own blood. Surprisingly, this time I don't care.

Kallistos does. He's respected my wishes up until now

and he's prepared to deny himself what he wants yet again.

"I'm sorry." His tongue darts out to lick the drop of ruby liquid from his lower lip.

I shake my head. "Don't be. It's who you are. Don't hold back, not tonight. Not with me."

It's all the permission he needs.

His hands are on my ass. He lifts me, effortlessly. My legs wrap around his waist. I'm wet and wanton. My power rails, begging for release. A wind rises around us. Blinds rattle against the balcony doors. Papers, neatly ordered on the writing table only seconds ago, can be heard beating against nearby walls.

I could stop it, but I don't want to. More important, I don't need to. Not with him.

Lips trail down the length of my jaw. I feel his tongue on my neck.

Then with one sure thrust he's buried inside of me. His hips piston, fucking me with a new ferocity. Something crashes to the floor. Hands grasp, searching for purchase. My light breaks through. The temperature around us climbs, higher and higher until both our bodies are slick with sweat. I'm dizzy. Slipping. All I can hear is my own distant breaths, my own waning heartbeat, my own screams of ecstasy as fang pierces flesh.

I shatter completely, my body wracked by uncontrollable tremors.

I've never been so free.

CHAPTER 10

Day Three: Wednesday, September 4

This time I made sure the alarm was set on my cell phone. I waited until Kallistos was asleep, set it, then secreted the phone in my slipper. Now, as it chirps, I reach down to silence it and feel Kallistos stir beside me.

"So that's where you hid it?" he says, rolling toward me to rest his head on my shoulder. "I wondered why I couldn't find it."

"Exactly why I hid it." But I take his hand and kiss it. "Thank you for last night."

"Want a reason to thank me for this morning?" He's taken my hand and slid it down the flat plain of his abdomen to rest between his thighs. He's hard and ready.

"Can't." It's a reluctant admission. "I have to shower and get to work."

He sighs and lets me remove my hand. "I'm only acquiescing because I know your work is important to you."

"And because you have your own inquiry to launch?"

"You are getting to know me well."

And so we both climb out of bed and head for the shower.

"Time for a soak?" Kallistos asks innocently, eyes on the tub.

"I thought you had things to do?"

His robe is on the floor and his body, long, lean, and oh, so ready, is a hard temptation to resist.

"I'm going to take a shower—a quick shower," I repeat. "Maybe I should take it alone?"

He slips my robe off my shoulders. "I'll be good."

But even as he speaks, his fingers are between my legs, coaxing, teasing. My traitorous body is responding.

"We have to make it quick," I rasp, my body already on the verge of climax.

"Oh, we will."

He brings me to the brink with skillful manipulation, pausing only long enough to turn on the shower. By the time the room is filled with steam, I've come once, twice. We step inside and the warmth envelops us. He wants to keep pleasuring me, but I stop him.

"Your turn."

Then I'm on my knees, gripping his hips. I take him into my mouth, lips first teasing, then sucking, then drawing him deep. He's groaning and moving with me. His hands tangle in my hair. I feel his muscles tense, feel the pressure build. It takes only the subtlest of movements, the pressure of my lips, my tongue sweeping along the ridge of his shaft, to bring him to climax. He shudders, releases, and trembles in the aftershock.

He pulls me up, crushes me to his chest.

"This was supposed to be a quick shower."

"Next time," he whispers. "Promise."

*   *   *

Somehow, I still manage to make it in before seven. When I step off the elevator, the office is already abuzz. Zack looks like he's been up all night. Normally he's all spit and polish. This morning the tie and jacket are off, his shirt is rumpled, and he's sporting a beard thick enough to be attributed to several days of an average man's growth.

"Tell me you haven't been here all night."

"I haven't been here all night." He takes a sip of steaming coffee from his mug, then motions toward the break room. "Fresh pot. And Garner brought in doughnuts."

I sigh. "That man is a heart attack waiting to happen." I look over Zack's shoulder. "Got anything?"

He slides his chair back and stretches his neck. "Besides the great big ball of tension between my shoulder blades? Not really. The night was essentially a bust."

I break off half of the uneaten French cruller on his desk and pop a piece into my mouth. "The school's faculty and staff look clean?"

"Squeaky, as was Julie's computer and the cell phone logs for all of the girls. As anticipated, we found calls between Hannah and Sylvia, but nothing between Julie and the other girls. No texts, no private messages, nothing. Nothing to tie Julie to them and nothing that seemed to shed any light on what each of them was doing to earn that two hundred dollars per week."

He sounds disappointed, and I completely understand why.

"What about Sylvia's computer?"

"Billings is working on it now. But to be honest, I'm not hopeful. We need a break and we need it fast." He lowers his voice. "I think we should have another chat with Rain. More to the point, I think *you* should have a chat with her. It could be she knows something but doesn't understand the significance of it. Or there's something she forgot. Something you could help her remember."

He's right. I just need a few minutes alone with her. My powers extend beyond seduction in mortals. I can also use them to ferret out the truth, though the consequences can be dire for me. "Do we want to try to catch her before school?"

Zack picks up the phone and starts to dial. "I think that would be best. I'll call her house."

"I'll wait for you out front. Tell her we'll see her in an hour. That will give you enough time to shower and change. And to shave. Trust me. You need it."

Rain Johnson's home is quite unlike the other girls'. The cheerful yellow bungalow with the blue planter boxes filled with pansies is surrounded by a small picket fence enclosing a rose garden. Dwarfed on either side by homes four to five times its size, the tiny cottage sits on prime beachfront property at the end of Narragansett Avenue.

The front door opens before we have a chance to ring the bell, revealing a woman who appears to be in her midthirties.

I pull out my badge. "We're here to see Harriet and Rain Johnson. I'm—"

"We're expecting you." She steps aside, inviting us in. "And no one calls me Harriet anymore except Jimmy. I've gone by Harmony since before Rain was born."

"Your paper." Zack hands her the *Union Tribune* he retrieved from the porch.

Harmony tosses it into the mail bin by the door. "I keep telling them I don't want their stupid paper. Establishment propaganda, everything in it. Do they really think a free trial is going to change my mind?" She walks, barefoot, through a small entryway. Her long blond locks, flowing skirt, and peasant blouse are a throwback to the sixties. Whereas Rain is personified by harsh, dark edges, her mother is the picture of softness and light.

"Your roses are quite lovely." I follow her down a hallway lined with family pictures—a recent school portrait of Rain alongside old black-and-white images of bygone years and faded color photos from the sixties and seventies. One of a toddler appears to be a very, very young, very toothless Jimmy Johnson. I point it out to Zack and we share a grin.

"The roses were planted by my great-grandmother," Harmony is saying, drawing our attention back. "The house has been in our family for over a century. I've lived here all my life. So has Rain."

We enter a cozy living room where Rain is waiting, curled up in the corner of a bright green overstuffed sofa along with a ginger tabby. Although the hair, makeup, and clunky boots are the same, the rest of her signature style has been usurped by the traditional school uniform—facial piercings further accentuated by the frame of the stark white Peter Pan collar.

"Rain, you remember Agents Armstrong and . . ."

"Monroe," I add.

The tabby suddenly spies Zack, hisses, then bolts over

the back of the sofa, disappearing behind a wall of royal purple drapes.

"Hmm. That's weird," Harmony says. "Tiger loves everyone."

"Probably smells Zack's dog," I lie. "He's a big ol' wolf hybrid."

That gets a raised eyebrow from Zack, which I ignore as we take seats across from Rain in chairs covered in yellow and pink paisley chintz. Splashes of vibrant color are everywhere—bright throw pillows, braided rugs, and the drapes. It awakens a long-dormant memory of being inside a gypsy caravan. This room has the same feeling—a combination of well-preserved antiques, what looks to be several lifetimes of prize flea-market finds, and a variety of shades and patterns to rival those found in Willy Wonka's closet.

"Are you any closer to finding Julie?" Rain asks.

"We're hoping you can help with that," I tell her. "We have a few more questions."

Rain glances toward her mother, who has yet to sit down. "I can handle this, Harmony. You don't need to stick around."

"You sure?"

Rain nods. "I'm fine, really."

"I volunteer at the co-op on Wednesdays and Fridays," Harmony explains.

Zack rises. "If you're the white Prius, we pulled into the driveway right behind you. I'll walk out with you and move our car." He glances back over his shoulder at me then follows Harmony toward the front door.

Suddenly Rain and I are alone.

I hear the front door close. Zack will stay outside, giving me time to work my mojo with Rain. The ability to extract truth is one of my gifts but it's not an exact science. If I'm not careful, anyone near me when I unleash the power can get caught in the wake. It's happened with Zack before. I need to make sure it doesn't happen again. As Liz keeps reminding me, an encounter like that might awaken feelings in him better left undisturbed. It's the memory of certain events that was altered, not the feelings that led up to them.

I listen to the sound of Zack's voice, drifting in through the open living room window as he makes idle chitchat with Harmony. Assured that we won't be disturbed, I begin the process of lowering my shields and tapping into my power.

The temperature in the room climbs a few degrees. A wind rises up within me, escaping on a subtle, perfumed breeze. A delicate yet complex blend of white florals layered atop citrus begins to permeate the room. The drapes flutter. A strand of hair escapes the coil at the nape of my neck and drifts in front of my eyes. I tuck it back behind my ear.

Rain watches me, eyes wide, lips parted. She leans toward me, attracted by a force she cannot begin to understand. "Something's different . . . your skin."

I fight to contain the glamour, but hints of my true self have obviously begun to leak through.

"I'm trying out a new moisturizer. We don't have much time, and I know you want to help find Julie. Right?"

"Absolutely!"

I move so that I can sit next to her on the sofa. "Rain. I'd like you to think about the conversations you've had with Julie over the past six months."

"Okay."

She's no longer withdrawn, curled up in the corner of the sofa. She's engaged, expectant—sitting up, leaning forward, hanging on my every word and anxious to help.

"Did Julie ever talk about needing money?"

"She used to, but not so much anymore. Not in quite a while."

"We spoke before about the fact that Julie has an account at the bank. That she's been making regular deposits. Do you know where the money comes from?"

There's a long pause.

I wait.

Seconds tick by.

"I'm not sure," she says at last.

"Not sure?"

"I feel like I should know . . . but I can't remember."

I watch as she struggles to answer my question. But it's not her memory that's a problem. Or her willingness, for that matter. She wants to answer—she can't help but do otherwise—and she knows she should be able to. I'm certain of it.

So is she.

Now that I've required her to sift through her store of memories, she's detecting something. A hole. A blank file where something *should* be.

I've encountered this a few times before over the centuries. The possible explanations can be narrowed down to two: a vampire's thrall or magic. Either way, someone wiped a memory, *the* memory. At one point in time, Rain knew something about the money. The realization is unsettling. It means we're up against someone supernatural in nature. And it means finding the girls has become even more urgent.

Rain's level of agitation is rising. "Why can't I remember?"

It would do no good to press her further, so I lie. "It's not important. Don't worry about it. Relax." I wait a moment for my suggestion to take root, to allow her to stop fighting to remember what she can't and focus on the second thing that's stymied Zack and me. "You said before that Julie wasn't friends with Hannah and Sylvia."

"They didn't hang out or anything, if that's what you're asking."

"Maybe not *in* school. But we're trying to look for connections, Rain. Any activities they might have shared outside of school? Anything at all occur to you?"

Her eyes widen.

I hold my breath.

"The college trip," she says.

"College trip?"

"Every year the school takes sophomores on a college trip. A few seniors go along, to share what their college search experience has been like, encourage the younger girls to ask questions, *really* weigh the pros and cons of each college they visit. I just now remembered, Julie was assigned to room with Hannah and Sylvia during the trip."

We're getting close to something. I can feel it. Every case has a turning point, a moment when the pieces, all seemingly unrelated, start to one by one fall into place.

If the trip occurred in the first half of June, that certainly would fit our timeline in terms of the bank deposits. Hannah and Sylvia both opened their accounts in late June. Could Julie have shared whatever was netting her almost a thousand per month with Hannah and Sylvia during this trip? All three girls were scholarship recipients. Money might certainly have been a topic of conversation among them.

I sit back. "Rain, when was the trip?"

"Sometime in June. Right after school got out. I don't remember the exact dates. I didn't go. I already have plans to go to CalTech. They're offering me a full ride. Plus, I'm not so much about the bonding."

"Did Julie mention anything that happened on the trip? Anything out of the ordinary or upsetting? Anything about Hannah or Sylvia?"

Rain shakes her head. "I gave her my condolences when I heard she had to room with the Barbie twins. We didn't really have much of a chance to connect over the summer since, you know, Julie's parents don't approve of me."

"You said the school sponsors the trip. Who does the chaperoning?"

"Teachers, sometimes parents."

Hope sparks. The three girls roomed together for a number of days. Zack didn't come up with anything suspicious about the staff at Point Loma Academy. This new information makes me want to dig deeper. The college trip was an important catalyst. I'm certain of it. We need to follow the money. Rain won't be of any help, but one of these girls must have confided in someone.

Rain is looking at me with big eyes. She senses my

excitement. "Did I help?" Absently, the fingers of her right hand trace the leaf tattoo winding up her left arm. I realize the last time I saw her, she was wearing a jacket. I'd only noticed the lone shoot that trailed from her neckline to her right earlobe. Now I see that the design is much more intricate than that.

It's like a dash of cold water.

A sense of dread washes over me.

I reach out and touch the tattoo gently. "I love this. Is it like the tattoo Julie got?"

Rain shakes her head. "No. She was afraid her parents would freak if she got anything so obvious. She got a tramp stamp. Kind of a butterfly design. No color, at least not yet."

"You took Julie to the same artist that did yours?"

"Yeah. They do great work. Julie was impressed with mine so—"

"Where do you go?"

"Wicked Ink. It's this supercool place in the Gaslamp."

I know exactly where it is. Wicked Ink may be a supercool tattoo parlor, but it's also a front for one of the largest Blood Emporium distribution centers in all of California. Something Kallistos has a huge stake in, both financially and politically.

My stomach clenches. "Did anything unusual happen while the two of you were at Wicked Ink?"

Rain frowns with the effort of trying to fill the gap in her memory. After a long moment she gives in with a shrug. "Whatever it was, I guess it isn't important," she replies.

She echoes the same words I used earlier when she

couldn't answer my questions about the money. At some point Rain was privy to the details about the money. She knew where it came from. Until someone, some vampire, took that memory away.

At least now I know who to ask.

CHAPTER 11

I waste no time pulling in my power, bringing the walls back up. Rain will remember the details of our conversation, including my suggestion that she no longer worry about what she can't remember. The suggestion will continue to bring her solace, a fact for which I'm grateful. I don't want her to think about the void in her memory. Especially since I have a suspicion who might be behind it.

Rain's eyes clear. "Now what?" she asks eagerly.

I stand up. "Now we take you to school."

She frowns. "I was afraid you were going to say that." She glances at her watch. "I missed the bus."

I tell her we will give her a ride and wait for her to gather up her backpack. Then we head out. Zack is alone, sitting on the front porch steps. "We need to take Rain to school," I tell him as I approach. "We made her miss her bus."

He stands, his back to Rain, who's paused to lock up. I can tell he wants to ask how things went. He scans my face, looking for any clue as to the success of my "interrogation."

Rain bounds down the stairs and rushes ahead to the

car. As soon as her back is to us, I give him a stealthy thumbs-up.

"Yes!" Zack starts to pump a fist in the air but catches Rain looking back over her shoulder and stops.

"Very mature," I whisper, keeping my expression studiously neutral. To Rain, "Hop in the back."

"You must have been some spy," I comment quietly to Zack as I pass him on my way to the passenger seat.

Zack keeps Rain engaged in conversation on the short drive to Point Loma Academy, asking her about her classes and her teachers. I'm glad. The gut wrench I experienced when Rain first mentioned Wicked Ink has now turned into a full-blown stomachache. We need to find out whether Hannah or Sylvia was a patron, and I need to arrange for a conversation with Rose, the vampire who runs the establishment. A vampire. Capable of wiping a memory, certainly, but capable of kidnapping? And to what end?

I'm jolted out of my thoughts by Zack's hand on my arm. "Emma? Rain is talking to you."

I blink back to the present. We're in front of the school and Rain is standing by the open passenger side window.

"Will you let me know when you have any news about Julie?" she's asking.

I nod. "Yes. Rain, we'll do everything we can to bring her back. Thank you for meeting with us this morning."

I recognize how perfunctory the reply sounds as soon as the words leave my mouth. Rain recognizes it, too.

She shrugs, frowning. "Yeah. Whatever."

Then she turns on her heel and heads through the school gate.

"Good job, Emma. Way to secure the cooperation of the only person who's provided us with a solid lead." He raises an eyebrow. "What did she tell you?"

I counter with a question of my own. "Remember when I told you about Rose at Wicked Ink?"

"How could I forget. She's a vampire. But what—no, don't tell me. Rain took Julie to Wicked Ink to get her tattoo."

"Yes. And when I asked Rain if anything unusual happened when Julie got her tatt, she couldn't remember. People always remember, Zack, unless there are holes."

"Holes? You mean, her memory's been wiped?"

"I think so. She exhibited all the symptoms. It's like when you get that itchy feeling you're forgetting something but can't bring it into focus. The harder you try, the more the memory eludes you. But Rain did remember that Julie roomed with Hannah and Sylvia during that college trip last June."

"Right before the deposits started for the two of them?"

"She didn't have the exact date, but I think so."

Zack reaches into the backseat for his laptop. Within a few seconds he's logged in and clicking away.

"What are you looking for?"

"Checking to see if Hannah and Sylvia were reported as having any tattoos."

I turn and stare out the window. Should I call Kallistos? Suddenly I'm aware Zack's eyes are on me. I'm wearing a white mock turtleneck under today's black suit jacket. It was a deliberate choice, meant to hide the evidence of Kallistos' mark. Apparently, I didn't choose carefully enough.

Zack reaches out, hooks his finger in the edge of my collar, and gently peels it back, exposing my neck.

I hold my breath. I know what's coming.

"You're letting him feed from you now?" he says. The disdain in his voice is undeniable. It pisses me off. "How old is this bite?"

I pull away. "How is that any of your business?"

"Are you kidding me? You weren't born yesterday, Emma. You know how this works. If he marks you, he'll be able to control you. I'm counting on you. We're partners. I don't trust Kallistos and you shouldn't, either. I don't care how good he is in the sack. Kallistos has one priority. Kallistos."

His words come out in a rush. He's trying to be reasonable and I know what he's saying is true, in part.

"I'm not some naive ingenue. I've been around a long time and I've been with a lot of men. None of them have ever gotten the upper hand, and neither will he. The bite brought me pleasure. It doesn't *mean* anything. You need to trust me."

I can tell he wants to say more. But, to his credit, he lets it go.

"Any luck with the tattoo question?"

He shakes his head and logs out. "Nothing."

"Could be their parents don't realize they have any," Zack points out.

His attitude is once again professional. It's back to business as usual. For now.

"I think we should pay Rose a visit," I say.

Zack glances at the clock on the dash.

"You have somewhere you have to be?"

"Not right away."

"Oh?"

He frowns. "I have a lunch meeting with Sarah. And Seamus."

I wait for more. The set of his jaw tells me I'm not going to get details. "I can cancel if I need to, of course," he finally adds.

"No need. We both have to eat."

"Since we're here at the school, what do you say we nail down the dates of that college trip first?" he asks before dropping his laptop onto the backseat.

I unbuckle and open the door. "We should also ask for a list of the chaperones. Rain indicated some of them could be parents. Anyone associated with the trip deserves a second look, don't you think?"

"Definitely."

He walks around the Suburban and together we proceed up the walkway that leads to the front doors of Point Loma Academy. The grounds are eerily quiet. The students, no doubt, are all safely ensconced in their classrooms.

"The college trip might have somehow connected these girls," he says. "But I'd bet you the recipe for my momma's secret barbecue sauce that the answer to what they were involved in is going to be found at Wicked Ink."

And with Kallistos? Zack doesn't say it, but I know he must be thinking it.

I am.

Zack opens the door for me, then lets out a low whistle. I'd forgotten how opulent the place is. The interior of the building is every bit as impressive as the outside and the grounds. A cathedral ceiling arcs over the foyer and enormous windows spill natural sunlight onto gleaming hardwood floors. In the center, a large, round mahogany table holds an arrangement of fresh flowers. To the right is a door marked OFFICE and, at the far end of the room, a pair of carved wooden doors. I know from a tour during that long-ago fund-raiser that beyond them are the classrooms, the theater, and the gymnasium.

I head toward the office, Zack follows. The door is open. A receptionist greets us, a matronly woman, dressed to the nines in a gray suit that sets off her silver hair.

"May I help you?"

We quickly dispense with the ritual of introductions. Displaying our badges and explaining the reason for our visit gets us through the door and into Principal Robinson's office.

The woman who greets us is not the same principal I remember. The five-foot-seven African-American is slender, incredibly poised, and, if her handshake is any indication, a no-nonsense lady. She motions for us to sit and we settle into the chairs across from her desk.

"This has been a terrible ordeal for us," she says, hands clasped on the top of a neat, orderly desk. "Please, tell me what I can do to help."

Her openness throws me for a moment. I'd been expecting a stonewalling bureaucrat more concerned with maintaining image than doing the right thing.

"We have a few questions concerning the college trip that took place last summer," Zack says.

Her expression clouds. "You think that has something to do with the girls' disappearance? That never occurred to me. Why would you think that?"

Zack reaches into his breast pocket for his notebook. "The three girls roomed together during that trip. What were the dates, exactly?"

Robinson refers to her computer. After a few clicks she answers, "June thirteenth through the sixteenth. Would you like a copy of the itinerary?"

"Yes, and a list of the chaperones," I reply.

She hesitates a moment, and then, "Are you saying one of our teachers might be under suspicion? None of our staff could possibly be involved in anything like this."

I counter with a question. "Were all of the chaperones teachers? I understand parents sometimes go along on these trips."

Another heartbeat of hesitation. "Sometimes we do use parents to chaperone. But on this particular trip, they were all teachers."

"Then we'll need to speak with them. We need to know if any of the girls might have been approached by a stranger or if something out of the ordinary occurred that a chaperone might have made note of."

She sighs. "Then you want to speak with Constance Bertram. She was assigned to four girls—Hannah, Sylvia, Julie, and Roberta Lundquist."

My heart does a little leap. "Roberta Lundquist? Is she—"

"Missing? No. In fact, her parents have taken her out of school temporarily. They're on an extended trip to Europe."

"And you're sure she's with them?"

"Yes. She emails her homework assignments in regularly. We received one yesterday."

Relief that we don't have a fourth girl to worry about washes over me even as Zack says, "Please give us the Lundquists' contact number in case we need to contact Roberta."

Robinson works her keyboard, scrolls a screen, jots a number on a notepad, and hands it to him.

"Thank you. Okay. The interviews shouldn't take more than a few minutes. Do you have a free room we could use to talk to Ms. Bertram?"

"She no longer teaches here."

"Retired?" Zack asks.

Robinson shakes her head. "We had to let her go. I'm afraid we're in the midst of a wrongful termination suit over the matter. Constance and I have had our fair share of disagreements, and I won't deny she has issues, but I just don't believe she would be capable of taking these girls."

Zack opens his notebook to a fresh page. "Tell us, why she was let go?"

For a moment Robinson says nothing. Her lips, which are pressed into a thin line, appear permanently shut.

"We have no interest in pursuing anything that isn't relevant," I assure her. "We could review the court filings. They're a matter of public record. We'd rather save time and hear it from you."

Robinson pulls a file out of her top drawer and flips through it. For a moment I think perhaps she's just refreshing her memory. Then she scribbles something on a plain yellow slip of paper and passes it to me. "The address and phone number of Ms. Bertram. You didn't get it from me. I'm sure with your resources, you could have found it yourself."

"Understood." I tuck the information into my jacket pocket. "Now, what happened?"

"She witnessed something during the college trip that . . . disturbed her," Robinson begins.

Zack and I exchange glances before he says, "What did she witness?"

Robinson pushes her chair away from her desk and leans back in it. I can tell she's choosing her words carefully, as any administrator involved in a lawsuit would. "During her room check she discovered the girls playing with a Ouija board. The hotel had a recreational room with board games. They'd borrowed it, taken it back to their room."

"And that was against the rules?" Zack asks.

"No, it wasn't. When Ms. Bertram saw them she . . . Well, her reaction was disproportionate, totally inappropriate. She began to rant about the devil and witchcraft and . . . she forced the girls to line up on their knees and pray, pray to be saved, pray for forgiveness— to be born again. Apparently it went on for quite some time. All of the girls were upset, but Roberta was especially so. She contacted her parents. They contacted me. I had to fly to Oakland that very night. After interviewing the girls and Ms. Bertram, I had no choice but to place her on immediate suspension and send her home. I personally chaperoned the four girls for the remainder of the trip. As far as I know, nothing else unusual happened."

We waste no time. Once back at the car, Zack starts up the Suburban and I punch in Bertram's number and hit SEND. The call syncs through the car's audio system.

It's answered on the second ring. "Yes?"

I'm a little taken aback at the abruptness. "Constance Bertram?"

Her sharp, abrasive voice projects clearly. "Who is this? I don't accept calls from blocked numbers."

I refrain from mentioning that she just had. She might hang up. "I'm Special Agent Emma Monroe. I'm with the FBI. I would like to make an appointment with you to discuss the college trip you chaperoned—"

"I thought it might be something like that. FBI. CIA. ACLU. I answered to warn you people to leave me alone. Have you even heard of the United States Constitution? A little thing called the First Amendment? I have rights. I've filed suit. Religious persecution."

Her words are fired off in short, staccato bursts.

"I'm not calling about your dismissal. As I said, I need to ask you some questions about the college trip. Three of your charges—Julie Simmons, Hannah Clemons, and Sylvia Roberts—have been missing for four days. I'd like to meet with you to see if you can give us any information that might help in our—"

"It was because of those girls that I was fired." Her voice becomes strained, shaky, as if she's holding her temper in check. "The Academy's administration didn't appreciate how much danger they'd put everyone in. Now maybe they understand."

I raise baffled eyebrows at Zack. "What kind of danger are you referring to, Miss Bertram?"

"Are you recording this?"

"No."

"I'm not giving you permission to record this," she shouts, her voice shrill.

Zack is making finger circles in the air and mouthing, *Obviously her belfry is missing a bat.*

I suppress a chuckle. "I can assure you I'm not—"

Before I have a chance to finish, she interjects, "Most likely, they have been taken by the very evil creature they were trying to conjure up that night."

"Conjure up?" This gets our attention.

"With that board! They were conducting some kind of pagan ritual!"

With a Ouija board? Zack mouths.

Bertram is now on a no-holds-barred rant. "Ouija boards are a conduit into the underworld, plain and simple. I thought I'd saved them in time, saved their immortal souls. But now? Lord knows what's happened to them. Satan is alive. Mark my words—this is the devil's work. A force of evil. I can feel it. That stupid doctor says it's all in my head, but I know better."

"Doctor?"

"At the hospital. Just got out this morning. I was admitted for stress last Thursday."

Well, the phone call accomplished one thing. Once we check hospital records to verify her whereabouts for the last five days, we can eliminate Constance Bertram as a suspect. Before I hang up, I thank her for her time and let her know we'll be in touch if we have any further questions.

"No," she hisses. "You won't. If you have any other questions, you contact my lawyer."

Zack and I exchange looks as the connection is broken. I slip my cell back into my purse.

Zack has gone from finger circling to rolling his eyes. "She's completely unhinged," he says.

I nod in agreement. Zack and I both have experience with things paranormal. But I've lived a long time and as far as I know, a Ouija board has never conjured up anything but teenage nightmares and late-night hysterics.

I sigh. "I think our next stop should be Wicked Ink. If that turns out to be another dead end, we can always circle back and pay Ms. Bertram a visit."

"I wonder if she looks like she sounds?" he asks.

"You mean like an eighteenth-century harridan?" I nod. "Let's hope we never have to meet her in person."

The bell over the door rings as we walk into Wicked Ink. It's Zack's first time in the place. It doesn't look like a typical tattoo parlor, and it isn't. The floors are a dark, polished wood. To our right is a large, round dining room table, surrounded by high-back red velvet chairs. On top of the table, black leather-bound books are piled high. Sterling silver candelabras containing lit black candles blaze from each end. More candles are in the standing candelabras that line the north and south walls. The walls and ceiling are padded, tufted, and covered with an elegant black-on-black brocade. A series of ornate, silver-framed floor-to-ceiling mirrors covers the east wall across from me. It's oddly quiet. No heavy metal blaring from hidden speakers. Only the barely discernable hum of an air conditioner pumping refrigerated air into a room I'd guess was about sixty degrees already.

"Can I help you?"

I turn to see a familiar face emerge from a door cut into the brocade-covered wall so discreetly that it's all but invisible.

"Owen." I hold out my hand. "You look good."

"Better than the last time you saw me," he says, grinning.

Owen Cooper is a vampire. Zack and I know him because we saved him from the finality of the real death just five short months ago. It was my first case with Zack in San Diego. It was also how I met Kallistos.

Owen is dressed much the same as he was the last time I saw him, too. Worn jeans, T-shirt, leather jacket, black boots. His light brown hair looks recently cut. His eyes are clear. His sinewy build is slightly more filled out.

"Emma, great to see you. Hey, Zack, my man, how's it going?"

Zack returns the fist bump offered by the perpetual twentysomething. "Emma's right. You're looking good."

Owen shoves his hands in his pockets. "Back-on the bag. I've been clean since that night."

The night we rescued him from a physician who had been kidnapping and experimenting on vampires.

"You work here now?" I ask.

"Rose hired me. Figured it'd keep me out of trouble. It's good to be working again." Five months ago, the on-again, off-again blood addict was in the throes of detox.

"It obviously agrees with you," Zack says.

"So, how can I help you?"

"We're here on official business," I tell him.

"Cool."

I pull out the photos of Hannah Clemons and Sylvia Roberts. "Can you tell us if either of these girls have been here?"

"They look a little young for tatts. We strictly adhere to the law. They have to be eighteen, no exceptions."

I pull out the photo of Julie. "This one's eighteen. Does she look familiar?"

"No, but that doesn't mean she hasn't been here. You know who you should show these to?"

"Rose," I answer.

"I was thinking Simon."

Simon is the human techie who keeps the Blood Emporiums running smoothly. He's also one of Kallistos' most trusted employees. Recruited straight out of CalTech, the twentysomething operational director of the entire Western Region is smarter than smart. He works in the basement, and as far as I know, he just might live there, too.

"Is he here?" I ask.

Owen shakes his head. "He's up in Orange County today. I can leave a message on his voice mail, have him call you when he gets back."

I nod. "Thanks."

"Do you know when he'll be back?" Zack asks.

"Sorry, I don't."

"Rose?"

He shakes his head again. "Day off. Do you want to call her?"

"I have her number," I reply. "We may do that later."

But for now, another dead end.

Zack and I say our good-byes and walk back toward the car. On the way Zack surprises me by hailing a passing cab. It pulls to the curb.

"I've got to get to my meeting. I'll catch up with you later."

"How much later?"

The set of his shoulders and the tightening of the lines

around his mouth tell me he doesn't want to answer the question. "A few hours, maybe. I'm not sure. It's important. I'll call."

I have no idea what Zack's supersecret meeting with Sarah and Seamus is all about. I can tell it's weighing heavily on his mind, but that isn't enough to curb the irritation welling up in me. Or to stop what to my ears sounded like a completely insincere "Good luck" from springing from my lips.

No reaction. The tone is lost on Zack. "Thanks," he says absently, before climbing into the backseat of the cab.

The taxi pulls away and I'm left standing alone on the curb, battling frustration and annoyance. I find myself hoping this is about Sarah moving onto Seamus' compound. About Zack cutting ties with her once and for all. But then, what would change, really? He'll be free to move on, to find someone with whom he'll be happy. I've noticed the way the women in the office look at him. Now the scuttlebutt is that he has a live-in girlfriend. Once word gets out that his relationship status has changed . . .

I shake my head. Trouble is, he's already met that someone. He just doesn't remember.

I do.

Something's missing. I don't even know what it is, but I know I want it back in the worst possible way.

What is wrong with me?

Something else is missing . . . three girls. And my mind is on Zack's love life.

Focus, Emma.

CHAPTER 12

I head back to the office. Billings is at his desk. He shakes his head as I approach.

"Nothing of interest on Julie's computer," he says. "Just the usual teenage girl stuff between Julie and her friends. Some innocuous boy-girl chatter about homework, teachers. Same on Sylvia's. No word yet on Hannah's computer. I've got the tracking company looking for it."

He pauses and hands me a sheaf of printed pages. "Hard copies of messages from their social networking sites. Mainly posts wondering what happened to the girls and offering words of encouragement to each other."

I thumb through the thirty or so pages, noting that messages for Julie represent concern from every social group on campus—scholars to athletes, band nerds to cheerleaders. Julie may be Rain's only friend, but she's the kind of girl who is friendly to everyone.

Hannah and Sylvia are part of the *popular* crowd and the comments on their pages also reflect worry, alarm, even sympathy for the girls' families.

I take the log back to my desk. Thinking of friendship

makes me think of Liz. And thinking of Liz makes me think of Bertram. I don't place any stock in Bertram's accusation that the girls were dabbling in witchcraft—especially with a Ouija board. To one who is familiar with the *real* evil creatures in the world, the woman's rant had comic undertones. But as an agent investigating the disappearance of three young girls, the undertones, for me, take on a more sinister aspect.

Wouldn't hurt to ask Liz whether she's detected any disturbance in the witching-world force.

I give her a call, and lead with what I know she'll appreciate the most. "Kallistos gave me a key to the penthouse."

I hear her breath hitch. "So, you're moving in?"

"Not exactly. But things have been good, better than good. Listen, I could use your help with something. It's about a case with a possible witchcraft element. Mind if I come over?"

For the last three months Liz has been living with Evan Porter, a thirtysomething attorney vampire. He's hardworking, earnest, loyal, and completely in love with my best friend. The condo that was his home and is now theirs is in the Marina District downtown in the old Soap Factory, one of the largest all-brick buildings on the West Coast . . . and an exclusive address. Units run close to a mil. Liz, per usual, answers the door before I even have the chance to ring the bell.

She's not wearing anything remarkable—jeans, an oversized sweater, and calf-high leather boots. But still, she shines. Liz is five foot seven of stunning. With her long, curly dark hair, almond eyes, and a model's stature, she turns heads wherever she goes.

"So, about this key."

I lift an eyebrow. "Now, you know I'm not here to talk about the key. Besides, it doesn't mean what you think it means."

She leads me through to the living room. The walls that used to be plain white are now a soft yellow. I sink into the overstuffed sofa, now adorned with decorative pillows and a cozy throw. The colorful accents contrast nicely with the funky black-and-white rug under the coffee table.

"Are these new?" I ask.

Her eyes narrow. "Don't try to change the subject. Emma, you know the guy's nuts about you."

"The *guy's* a vampire almost as old as I am. He had a relationship with my sister. A relationship that ended in his death—or undeath? You know what I mean. He knows the score. And he knows the risks. What he feels for me is desire, lust, nothing more. But that's okay. It works both ways."

Liz takes a moment to turn the sound down on the television before claiming her favorite chair. "You expect me to believe that's *all* it is? After *five* months? You forget. I know you. Want to know why you're never with any guy for very long?"

"Because I want to save them from a slow, painful, and inevitable death?"

She dismisses my answer with a casual wave. "Because although you search for safe, you really yearn for something deeper."

I suppress a smile. "I yearn, huh?"

"Shut up. You wouldn't even be thinking of moving in with Kallistos if sex was the only link between the two of you."

"I'm not moving in with him. And I'm not giving up my place. Kallistos said he doesn't want me to give up anything. He just wants me to be a bigger part of his life."

She moves to the sofa and reaches for my hand. "Emma. I know you still have feelings for Zack. But I also see that Kallistos makes you happy. And you deserve to be happy."

I nod. "We understand one another."

"Demeter hasn't raised her ugly head in months now. Relax. As you said, he knows the score. And being with an überpowerful vamp as rich as Kallistos must have its perks, right? I say, enjoy what you have while you have it."

"Easier said than done."

Liz waves off my concern. "I'm dying to see what the penthouse looks like. Think we can run over after lunch?"

"Absolutely!" I stick my hand into the main compartment of my purse and fish around. The old-fashioned fob the key is attached to makes it fairly easy to find. "Ta-da! My shiny new all-access pass." I dangle the card in front of Liz and watch the color drain from her face.

"Son of a bitch." She snatches the key out of the air.

"What is it?"

Liz's expression tells me I don't want to hear the answer.

"Liz?"

"It contains magic," she says, handing it back to me. "A locator spell of some kind is attached to it. And it's a fairly powerful one at that. Think GPS only less conspicuous and more reliable."

"Your magic?"

"No."

My world shifts. In the space of a moment, the solid ground beneath me changes to quicksand. The honesty and trust that I so value in my relationship with Kallistos begins to give way to something else. Something blacker. Darker.

"Shit."

"Don't jump to conclusions."

Even if the key means what he said it means, I know now that it also means something else. I toss it back into my purse. "He wants to keep tabs on me."

"Maybe to protect you," Liz says.

"Like property."

"Like a lover he doesn't want to risk losing. A King always has enemies. Being close to him puts you in danger. Don't stew over this. Talk to him." My cell phone is sitting next to my purse on her coffee table. She tilts her head toward it. "Call him."

I pick it up. After all, even Seamus said I could be used against Kallistos. How did he put it? I'm a vulnerability.

I put it back down. Still, Kallistos should have told me—should have asked me—if I wanted his protection.

Liz watches my face, sees the indecision in my actions. "He could track you dozens of ways. He didn't have to give you a key in order to do it," Liz points out.

She's right, of course. But he could have been honest with me. Should have been honest. Regardless of his motives, I feel betrayed. "I can't deal with this right now."

"Then when?"

Liz's question registers in the back of my mind, but it fades as something else captures my attention. The television. "Hold that thought."

Constance Bertram is speaking to a reporter. Her words scroll across the bottom of the screen . . .

Witchcraft. It has to be. Point Loma Academy is a hotbed of Satan worshippers. The school administrators may be afraid to acknowledge what's going on in the school. But I am not. Three girls missing now. Three! How many more have to be sacrificed before action is taken?

Pictures of Julie, Hannah, and Sylvia flash on the screen. Liz grabs the remote and turns up the volume. "Is this what you wanted to talk to me about?"

I nod.

My phone rings. My shoulders bunch. "Johnson." I connect the call.

"Are you near a television?" he barks, without preamble.

"I'm watching it now, sir."

"What the fuck, Monroe? Did you and Armstrong know about this?"

I feel a headache coming on. "We interviewed her by phone earlier. It was all going to be in our report. She didn't come across as credible and—"

He cuts me off. "The phones are ringing off the hook. Reporters from every television station are calling to ask if we believe three girls have been kidnapped by some damned Satanic cult. News crews are setting up outside the field office. I need an update now. I've scheduled a press conference in two hours. You and Armstrong better get here with a statement I can use. You have one hour. And, Monroe, it had better be something real. Something concrete. Something that will shift attention away from this raving lunatic, Bertram."

He's gone.

"Let me guess," says Liz. "The shit just hit the fan."

"I have to call Zack." Unfortunately, his cell goes straight to voice mail. He's turned it off? Furiously, I leave him a message. *We need to talk. Call me as soon as you get this. We're due at the office in one hour.*

Liz is studying my face. "Zack is AWOL?"

"Had some kind of important meeting to attend. Werewolf business."

She raises her eyebrows. "Now? In the middle of a case?"

I shake my head, too irritated to reply rationally. I take a deep, calming breath. "Liz, I have to come up with a statement for Johnson. Now, more than ever, I need to pick your brain about this." Quickly, I fill her in on the case. Everything, including my "interview" with Rain and our conversation with Constance Bertram just an hour or so ago. "Bertram must have contacted the media right after we spoke with her."

I rub a palm against my forehead. "Do you have any aspirin?"

"Sure." Liz heads into the kitchen. When she returns a few minutes later with two aspirin and a tall glass of ice water, photos of the missing girls are once again flashing on the screen.

"Three victims, young, innocent, blond. For someone who practices black magic, they could be a valuable commodity. But I've heard no rumors of such activity in the area. And I have extensive connections." She sits back down. "Then again, anyone who would do such a thing would be discreet."

I pop the pills into my mouth and rinse them down with a few swallows of water. "Taking three girls at once, though, is hardly being discreet."

Liz agrees with a nod. "I don't think this has anything to do with witchcraft. And certainly not with three teenagers playing with a Ouija board. But—"

"Between Rain's memory being wiped and a tenuous connection to Wicked Ink, I've got a bad feeling a vampire is mixed up in this." I gather up my phone and handbag. "I should talk to Kallistos."

"Yes! That's what I was saying." She releases a sigh, then wraps her arms around me and gives me a fortifying hug. "I love you, you know. Hang in there."

Kallistos' words roll around in my head: *You may be irresistible. But I'm not. At least not where you're concerned . . . I can walk in the light, but I'm not of it. I've done things, had to do things, will continue to do things. Do you understand?*

I wasn't sure I did then.

Now I'm beginning to.

"Come on, Liz. I meant I need to connect with him about the *case*. Three missing girls trumps the disaster that is my love life."

Her eyes narrow. "I know. But at some point you're going to have to stop avoiding it."

"I'm not avoiding. I have a plan."

"Which is?"

"Ignore it for now. Deal with it later. I've got to start working on this statement. I'm going to head over to the

Palomar. With luck Zack can meet me. Keep your ear to the ground?"

She nods. "If I hear anything, I'll call you. Go."

I do, my head spinning with thoughts about Kallistos and the case. By the time I get to my car, I'm weighed down by questions for which there are no answers.

My cell chimes.

The incoming text is from Zack. He received my voice mail along with one from Johnson. He's wrapping up his lunch appointment and is ready to meet.

I type, *Come to the Palomar.*

First and foremost, we have to deal with Johnson's request. What can we say? That no, it's probably not a coven of witches or a satanic cult that's responsible for the disappearance of three girls.

It may be vampires.

And, by the way, my lover is their King.

CHAPTER 13

I slide the key into the lock, turn the door handle, and slip inside the penthouse.

The only sound I hear is the low hum of the air conditioner.

I'm alone.

The two-story penthouse is enormous, but I feel claustrophobic. I drop my purse and the bag containing my laptop on the sofa, then walk over to the floor-to-ceiling panels of glass that separate the indoors from the balcony and push them aside. Despite the warmth of the day, I can feel a breeze coming off the ocean. The streets below are filled with cars. San Diego has a population of 1.3 million people. One of them had to have seen something, heard something, has to *know* something.

I head back inside and wander over to the kitchen. I grab a pitcher of iced tea from the refrigerator and pour myself a glass. Johnson will be able to discredit Bertram fairly easily. With a little finesse we can craft a statement that will allow the press to read between the lines and encourage a few follow-up questions.

I send a text to Kallistos.

Can you reach Simon?

I pull my laptop out and set it up on the dining room table. Before I have a chance to sit down, my cell chimes.

He's with me. What's up?

I hesitate. Consider calling. Decide against it.

Need to show him something.

I wait for a response. A full minute passes. Halfway through the second, a response comes through.

On our way back from OC. Meet you at the Palomar in ten minutes?

It's not really a question, of course. He knows I'm here.

I resist the urge to take the key card out onto the balcony and use it for target practice. Instead I spread the photos out on the table and stare into the faces of the missing girls. I start to organize my thoughts in preparation for writing Johnson's press statement. At first I just let them flow, reordering as I go. Within a few minutes, the blank page on my laptop is full of notes. And I've managed to boil it down to five concise talking points.

1. We've found no evidence that any of the victims were involved in the occult.
2. Yes, as was reported by several local news stations, the girls used a Ouija board while on a college trip. They've all seen an episode of *Charmed* and read the *Harry Potter* series. Those things don't make them witches or Satanists.
3. They are victims.
4. What *we* need to focus on are solid leads from credible, reliable sources.
5. The Bureau has dedicated significant resources to

this investigation and we are following up on several key leads at this time.

Then I dial Garner at the office.

"How quickly can you get a hotline in place for tips?"

"How soon do you need it?"

I smile. "In time for the press conference."

"Done."

I email a draft of the talking points to Zack and tell him to get here ASAP. I'm about to begin writing the statement in earnest.

My progress is interrupted by the whir of the door's electronic lock. I look over my shoulder in time to see Kallistos cross the threshold, Simon right behind him. The two men couldn't be more different. The vampire King is tall and imposing. Today's suit is a black-on-black pinstripe, his shirt a deep aubergine. His normally piercing blue eyes have an almost violet cast.

Simon is a good foot shorter than Kallistos. Dressed in a pair of baggy khaki cargo pants and a rumpled T-shirt displaying a map of Middle Earth, he looks more like a scruffy college student than someone worthy of the title of operational director.

Kallistos is ahead of him by several steps. His tie is off before he reaches me, the top two buttons of his shirt undone. For a moment I forget I'm angry. But then he bends down to kiss me and I remember. His hair brushes the side of my cheek. His mouth covers mine. I try not to stiffen, not to pull away.

"What's wrong?" he asks. Then he glances at the photos on the table and draws his own conclusion. "Still no progress on the case?"

I close the lid of my laptop.

"Actually, that's why I want to speak with Simon."

"You want me to solve a case the FBI can't? Bring it on!" The high-strung genius pulls a Red Bull out of the worn, leather messenger bag that's slung over his shoulder, pops the top, and takes a sip.

I tilt my head toward the photos on the table. "These girls are missing. We believe we've found a connection between them and Wicked Ink."

No comments. No questions. No arguments. His messenger bag slides to the floor. He pulls out his laptop, some other hardware, and a handful of cords. "May I?" he asks, holding his phone above the photos. "We use facial recognition. I can upload their images and do a comparison against our database."

I give my consent.

Kallistos sits down alongside me. "Tell me about this connection."

"It could be nothing," I tell him. "But it's the only real lead we have—"

We watch, silent, as Simon scans, clicks, works the keyboard. In a few minutes, the computer sounds.

"We've got a hit. Julie Simmons." Simon turns his laptop so we can see the display. Her name is flashing underneath the image Simon scanned and uploaded. The images of Hannah Clemons and Sylvia Roberts appear, too. Alongside them a blur of faces pass by as the facial recognition software searches the database for their images, as well.

Kallistos leans forward and for the first time takes a long, hard look at the faces of the victims. "How long could this take?"

"I entered some parameters to narrow it down. Female, blond, eighteen to twenty-five."

I shake my head. "The other two victims are under eighteen. Of course, they might have lied or had fake IDs. We know Julie has a tattoo and that she got it at Wicked Ink." I turn to Kallistos. "I interviewed someone who went with her. She'd been put into thrall. I believe a significant portion of her memory was wiped."

"You couldn't recover it?" Kallistos asks.

"Unfortunately, no."

Simon pauses the search. "Let me try something. These girls fit the profile for the YBV program. Some of those participants are as young as fifteen." His fingers fly across the keyboard.

The search restarts.

Simon takes another hit of his Red Bull.

Kallistos leaves the table and heads for the bar.

"YBV." I search my memory. Then I remember. The first time I interviewed Simon, it was in his office in the basement of Wicked Ink. Rose took me down. We passed the big refrigerated units used to store blood. One of them was marked YBV. When I asked Rose about it she replied—

"Young. Blond. Virgin." This time it's Simon answering. "It's a signature blend. Very popular."

I turn around and glare at Kallistos' back. "You've got to be fucking kidding me. You're tapping kids to boost your blood supply?"

The computer sounds.

Hannah's name now appears under her photograph.

Kallistos returns with a generous pour of scotch. "You make it sound so nefarious. Since the Blood Emporiums have been put into place, vampire-on-human assaults have decreased considerably. But you know that. These girls are willing. We place careful limits on how much and how frequently we allow them to donate. And they are compensated. They are giving up something they don't require, something that without effort they can make more of. How much are we paying?"

Simon and I answer in unison. "Two hundred per week."

"You can hardly accuse us of exploitation," Kallistos reasons.

"It's more than double the going rate," Simon chimes in. "We explain everything to them up front, the risks, the benefits, the compensation package, grounds for termination, the necessary security measures—"

I feel another headache forming behind my eyes. "By 'necessary security measures,' do you mean wiping their memory?"

Simon nods. "Yes. Yes, but only after they sign and agree."

"Sign and agree? Some of these girls are minors. They couldn't legally agree to anything."

"Well, yes," Simon concurs. "But it's the formality that lends credibility."

The pressure behind my eyes increases. "So, you tell them they are contributing to some boutique blood blend for vampires and get them to sign a consent?" I ask.

"Not exactly."

"Why do they think they are donating blood, exactly?"

"We hint that it might be used for top-secret medical research."

"You *hint*?"

"We require them to fill out a questionnaire for government clearance and to sign some major confidentiality statement."

"Then you mess with their free will. Take away their memory. Eliminate any chance that they'll change their mind."

"No. Their memory is only wiped regarding our procedures. They can quit anytime they want. They believe they are contributing to an experimental medical program that may benefit all mankind." He pauses. "And in effect, they are."

I shoot him a black look. "And by *benefiting mankind*, you mean keeping mankind safe from rogue vampires."

"It's working, isn't it? And by the way, have you any idea how hard it is to find young blond virgins in Southern California? I'm telling you, this is a win, win, win," he insists.

Kallistos has been listening quietly. I reach for his scotch, take a sip, savor the bite, then place the glass down on the table. "You approved this business plan?"

"How do you think we keep attacks down and blood in stock? We can't simply let donors go without taking precautions. We're vampires, Emma. We need blood to survive. We need *human* blood to survive. This may not be ideal. It may offend your sensibilities. But it's a system that's working."

"For who? Not for these three girls!"

Kallistos rises from his seat and circles around the table to where Simon is sitting. "Check for other missing girls. Others who have missed appointments."

I open my laptop and fire up my computer. "Give me

the names of anyone who's missed an appointment. I'll have to cross-reference."

Simon frowns. "Please. Child's play." He makes a grand show of cracking his knuckles. Then he pulls out a set of headphones from his messenger bag, plugs them into his laptop, and goes to work. Seconds tick by. The silence in the room is broken only by the clacking of keys and Simon's superspecial rendition of Prince's "Kiss."

The house phone rings. Kallistos answers, listens, then mutters, "Oh. My day is complete. Send him up." To me, "Armstrong is here."

"Things blew up this afternoon," I tell Kallistos, wondering why I should explain. But I continue. "A former teacher of the Academy went on record with the press, saying there were connections to the occult. Johnson has scheduled a press conference. Zack and I have to put together a briefing in the next twenty minutes."

"The Emporiums can't be implicated," Kallistos says. "There's too much at stake."

"Too much money to be made, you mean?"

Kallistos seems to finally register that the bite to my tone can't be attributed solely to concern over a case. He tilts his head to study me. But before he can ask the question, a knock sounds at the door.

"That would be Zack." I make a beeline for the door. "Let me fill him in."

"This is vampire business."

I stop dead in my tracks and turn to face him. "With all due respect, Your Majesty, I've been charged with finding these girls. This is *my* business. And it's Zack's business." I don't wait for his permission. I resume my course. Although I'm only a few feet from the door, he beats me to it, placing one hand on the handle, the other on my elbow.

"I want to find these girls, too," he says, his blue eyes searching out mine. "I may be a monster, but I do have some morals, you know." His teasing tone then becomes quite serious. "I value human life."

"You need blood to survive. You need *human* blood to survive. And you profit from it."

His eyes become cold, his face rigid. "Something you've known from the beginning, Emma."

Then he backs away so I can open the door.

Zack's leaning, shoulder to the doorjamb, arms crossed, expression stern. "I think the two of you had damn well better catch me up."

CHAPTER 14

"Thought your talking points were solid, Emma." Zack bows his head slightly as he passes Kallistos. "Your Highness."

No sarcasm there.

Kallistos bristles. "Armstrong."

It's like watching two porcupines dance.

Simon has moved on to "Little Red Corvette." I wave toward him. "That would be Kallistos' operational director."

Zack stares. "Seriously?"

I nod. "He's quite brilliant."

"I hope so. He sure as shit can't sing."

"We've uncovered another connection," I tell him. "And the source of the money."

Zack's shoulders tense. "We?"

"Simon confirmed the three missing girls were all enrolled in a program run by the Blood Emporium."

Zack heads for the dining table where Simon, oblivious to Zack's presence, is working. "What kind of a program?"

The data on Simon's screen looks like gibberish. He watches intently as it scrolls past.

I look over my shoulder toward Kallistos. He's leaning against the back of the sofa, arms folded in front of his chest. Whether it's a defensive or contemplative pose, I can't tell. His eyes are on Zack.

I take a deep breath, then dive in. "The Emporium has been marketing some unique boutique blends in addition to the run-of-the-mill A, B, AB, O."

"Blends of the four blood types?" he asks Kallistos.

"Our master blender also develops samples that are pure with respect to certain characteristics. The missing girls were all voluntary contributors to our YBV blend." Kallistos walks over to the bar, opens the mini-fridge concealed in the cabinet underneath, and pulls out a blood bag. "Very exclusive. Basically, we add a small amount of their whole blood into a bag of AB negative." He tosses the pack to Zack.

"Young Blond Virgin?" he asks, after glancing at the label.

"Highly valued and hard to find."

"I can imagine, what with the shortage of nunneries." Zack turns to me. "Tell me these girls haven't been bled dry and disposed of."

I shake my head. "If they have, these two didn't have anything to do with it. To them, these teens are like prize cows."

Kallistos frowns. "We don't think of them as cows."

"Actually, that's not a bad analogy," interjects Simon, headphones now off. "You know, cows produce milk. Our YBVs produce highly coveted blood of the innocent." He extends his hand toward Zack. "I'm Simon."

I sit back down in front of my laptop. "My partner, Zack."

The two men shake hands.

Simon's attention is caught by something on the computer screen. "I'm afraid you might have more missing girls." He turns the laptop so that I can see. Kallistos and Zack crowd behind him. "Four girls in the Los Angeles area didn't show for their appointments today." With the click of a mouse, one by one their images appear on the screen. "Three different girls in the Orange County program were no-shows, too. Searches have been initiated for two of these seven girls, one in Los Angeles, the other in Newport Beach. It's possible the other five haven't been missed yet. School just got out a couple hours ago. Two of the five were absent from school today—unexcused absences—the other three attended all classes."

Zack bends closer to the screen. "Where the hell are you getting this information?"

Simon cracks his knuckles over the keyboard. "Do you really want to know?"

Zack grimaces. "Christ. On second thought, no. Just . . . stop. I'd hate to have to arrest you for hacking." He looks at me. "All seven girls fit the profile—young, blond, and presumably virgin. Six of the seven are under eighteen."

I release a breath. "Shit, Kallistos. They're just kids."

"We'll need those names," says Zack grimly.

Simon looks to his boss for direction.

Zack presses forward. This time he addresses Kallistos, his tone far more tolerant and understanding than I anticipated. "You know this can't be a coincidence. Philippe Lamont is in town. Asa Wade accompanied him. Word is neither were invited."

"I've heard the rumor. Lamont's presence hasn't yet

been confirmed," Kallistos says. "But we do have confirmation from Seamus' camp that Bill Ford was sighted. He's checked into the US Grant Hotel. We're having him watched."

Bill Ford? The two men are exchanging knowing glances. It's a name they're obviously familiar with.

"Someone want to clue me in?" I ask, not bothering to mask my irritation. "Who the hell is Bill Ford?"

Zack reaches for my computer, places it beside Simon's, and does a quick search. A fan site comes up. A series of images is displayed. "He's a former football player for the Saints. Retired a few years ago. Dropped out of the public eye when he became Blood of the King. If he's in town, so is Lamont."

Blood of the King. It's an obsolete title I didn't realize was bestowed any longer. It means that Ford and Lamont are bonded. It's not uncommon for the vampire sovereigns to take on human blood slaves and paramours. Some have harems full of them. But to bond with one, to name one Blood of the King, is unheard of these days. Ford is more than Lamont's mate. As long as he's alive, he's his main source of sustenance.

"You think Lamont is behind this?" I ask Zack.

"Either of you have a better idea?" He looks from Kallistos to me. "These girls are being deliberately selected. Quite possibly eliminated. Whatever else they may have in common, *we* in this room know every one of these girls can be linked to the Emporiums and, by virtue of that, to you." He fixes his gaze on Kallistos. "You represent everything Lamont hates. Everything he's been fighting to eliminate. Vampires mainstreaming into society. Making them less dependent on a sovereign. Usurping Lamont's power to control them."

"It's just a matter of time before those other girls are reported missing," I add. "The local police will start to search for patterns. It might take them a while, but just like we did, they *will* find the connection. Your Emporiums will be discovered."

Kallistos' tone is somber. "How long is a while?"

Zack answers, "Federal law requires law enforcement to enter information about a missing child into NCIC, the National Crime Information Center Missing Persons database, no more than two hours after the receipt of the report. The reality is, it almost always takes longer. The California DOJ maintains records, as well. Parents can even go to their Web site and search parameters like age, eye color, hair color. How long could it take to connect these cases? Days, weeks, months. Maybe hours."

"How many of these searchable databases do you know of?" Kallistos asks.

"In addition to NCIC and the state clearinghouses?" Zack asks.

"NCMEC is a private nonprofit. They're likely to get involved with some of these. Then there's NamUs," I add, "The National Missing and Unidentified Persons System."

"My point is," interjects Zack, "once an investigator finds a pattern among the missing, they will start to look for other connections and similarities. It's just a matter of time before the network of businesses that front the Emporiums, businesses you own, are implicated. In fact,

I have a sneaking suspicion Lamont, stand-up guy that he is, has a plan up his sleeve to help connect those dots. Nothing would make him happier than complete disintegration of the status quo."

"We need to stay ahead of this," says Kallistos. He skewers Simon with a frown. "How did they access our secure server? How was security breached without you knowing?"

Simon holds up his hands. "They didn't. I don't know yet how they identified the donors but I will find out."

I shake my head, drawing Kallistos' attention back to me. "The best way to stop this is for us to find these girls, and fast," I tell him. "Unfortunately, I haven't a clue where to start."

Kallistos nods. "I do. I'll make some calls."

Zack closes my laptop and scoops it up. "And you and I have got to get that press release to Johnson. You drive. I'll type."

I feel Kallistos' eyes on me as I pack up my computer and files. I don't turn as Zack places his hand at the small of my back and steers me toward the door. The echo of Kallistos' words rattles around in my head. I have known from the beginning that he needs human blood to survive. I've known about the Blood Emporiums. Known about human donors. Known, while it isn't the only source of his income, he's gotten richer off those human donors. Off the missing girls.

I've known all about it. Enjoyed the lavish lifestyle right along with him. A lifestyle paid for with blood money.

Real blood money.

*   *   *

Johnson is waiting for us, pacing in front of the elevator, when we get to the office. Zack goes directly to a printer, inserts a flash drive, and in less than thirty seconds hands Johnson a hard copy of the press release.

Johnson's eyes scan the page, his brow furrowing. "Better than what I am tempted to say—that Bertram is a fucking wack job." He looks up. "We found out she spent the last several days under psychiatric observation. She's been released but let's hope our erstwhile reporter friends have done their due diligence, too."

He motions to Zack and me to follow him. "I want you two behind me at the podium. I don't expect you to field questions but it won't hurt to show the public we have our best team working the case."

Zack follows Johnson to the elevator. I reluctantly trail behind. No matter how many times I'm involved in these things, I still get a nervous stomach when in front of a camera and microphone.

Ridiculous, I know, but behind the queasiness is the fear that someone will see me and think, *She looks just like the girl who lived next door to us fifty years ago in Malibu. Groovy chick. No. It can't be.*

But it can.

I fidget in apprehension. My handbag slips off my shoulders and crashes to the floor. Shit. You'd think after centuries of close calls, I'd be used to this.

"Relax." Zack's voice is at my ear as he crouches to help me gather it up.

Johnson half turns toward us. "Yeah, Monroe. Relax. It's not like this is your first news conference."

I straighten and tug at the hem of my jacket. "I hate them."

"Just stand beside me and look professional. And concerned," Johnson says, holding the elevator door open.

I step around him, wanting to snap back, *I am professional and concerned.* Zack's hand on my arm, however, encourages me to swallow hard and stay quiet. The sooner we get this done, the sooner we can get back to Kallistos' and see whether Simon has anything new to report. The thought that we may be looking at girls missing all over Southern California, and that in a matter of hours, all those cases may be connected to ours, makes it imperative to find out what the hell is going on.

We step through the front door of the FBI building. A crowd of about twenty reporters has gathered around a podium set up on the top step of the entryway, some with cameramen, all with microphones. Behind them, at the bottom of the stairs, held away by uniformed policemen, are thirty or so protestors bearing signs that herald the slogan: PROTECT OUR CHILDREN FROM SATAN'S INFLUENCE. BAN WITCHCRAFT.

"Jesus," Johnson whispers to us. "Now we're in for it."

When they spy us, the protestors start chanting, something unintelligible that sounds like a combination of song and prayer. I search the faces for Bertram, but she either had the good grace or was cautioned by her attorney not to appear. I have no doubt it was at her encouragement, though, that these people assembled.

Johnson raises his hand for silence and they drop the decibel level but don't stop altogether. He shakes his head and turns on the microphone.

Johnson clears his throat. "Good afternoon. We are here to address the disappearance of three young girls, each taken on a different day, but all within the past four days and all from the same school. Our office lines have been flooded in the past couple hours with phone calls related to this case, demanding response to an ill-informed and quite possibly harmful allegation that these disappearances were connected with the occult. I'm confident you can all appreciate how vital it is that at this juncture the investigators stay focused and on track. So, we're here to address that question. Then we plan to move on."

The chanting increases in volume for a moment, but a policeman moves through the crowd, and whether he is threatening to arrest them or move them farther from the steps, the ploy works. The voices drop.

Johnson reads my statement practically verbatim. No evidence of any connection to the occult has been found.

A young reporter in the back shouts out, "According to Constance Bertram—"

Johnson raises his hand and speaks once again into the microphone. "We need solid information from credible and *reliable* sources." He stares at the crowd. "Let me repeat. No witches. No Satanists. The Bureau is dedicating significant resources to investigate a real crime. Not an imaginary one."

The crowd in the back begins to stir. Someone is trying to rile them up, but Johnson cuts it short by continuing. "We have agency personnel combing through the girls' computers, cell phones, social media contacts, and school records. Agents Monroe and Armstrong are heading up our team." He half turns to acknowledge us, then faces the microphone once again. "They are following up on several promising leads at this time. We are passing out photos of the girls and information sheets with a tip number we hope you will run. Now I will take a few questions. But remember, as in all such cases, we are limited as to what we can release to the public."

A general shout-out of questions erupts from the reporters. The first reporter Johnson chooses asks one of the questions I expected would be thrown out first.

"Why was no Amber Alert issued when the girls were first reported missing?"

Johnson bobs his head in acknowledgment. "The circumstances didn't meet the criteria. The third girl to have gone missing, Julie Simmons, is eighteen. The first two girls, Hannah Clemons and Sylvia Roberts, went missing one after the other. Since they were friends, an explanation other than abduction had to be considered. Especially since no one witnessed any of these girls being taken. It was when the third girl was reported missing that the local police called us in. We are here to ask for the public's help." He glances down at his notes before continuing. "In a city of 1.3 million people, someone must have seen something. Please, encourage anyone with information related to these cases to come forward. Our hotline is up and running. We have agents standing by." He recites a number. Pauses, then repeats it.

Another reporter calls out, "What about Constance Bertram's allegation?" He consults a notebook in his hand, then glances up. "That Point Loma Academy is, and I quote, 'a hotbed of Satan worshippers' and that the administration refuses to acknowledge it."

Johnson sighs. "I think I've answered that but let me make it clear one more time. We have found no evidence to suggest these girls—or any students at the Academy—

are anything but normal teenage girls. I can't begin to explain what might be motivating Ms. Bertram's allegations. Or should I say accusations." He smiles, as if begging the reporters' indulgence. "In fact, if any of you figure it out, let me know. All I can tell you is that *we* haven't found any basis for them."

My cell phone vibrates with an incoming text. When I check it, I see it's a message from Simon. *Monitoring additions to the relevant databases and searches. Taking necessary steps. Kallistos asked that I keep you apprised.*

Necessary steps?

I tilt the phone so Zack can see the message, too. He whispers something to the agent standing next to us on the podium, then motions for me to follow him back inside.

Johnson doesn't see us leave. He's too busy with the reporters.

"What the fuck?" Zack hisses as soon as we step into the foyer.

I'm already dialing Simon. "What are you doing?" I snap as soon as he picks up.

"Helping," he replies, no trace of surprise or irritation in his voice at my abrupt greeting. In fact, he continues as if I'd begun with a sunny "Good morning."

"Listen," Simon continues. "You heard me tell Kallistos our system was not breached and that the victims must have been identified another way. I'm betting good old-fashioned surveillance was used to find them. Ninety-six girls are in the YBV programs in San Diego, Los Angeles, and Orange Counties. They are now all under guard. Round-the-clock protection. Discreet, of course."

"Of course." Sarcasm drips from Zack's voice. His cheek is pressed against mine, the cell phone sandwiched between us. "Simon, I wasn't kidding before. You realize what you're doing could get you arrested," he whispers.

"Only if you can prove it. And you can't. Besides, you have bigger fish to fry."

"Unlawful surveillance is a Class D felony," Zack persists.

Zack's admonishment doesn't faze Simon in the least.

"Don't think of me as an evildoer. Think of me as a difference maker. Like Tony Stark, only without the awesome iron suit."

"Is Kallistos with you?" I ask.

"No. I'm back in the office. But, hey, remember he mentioned we were going to place Ford under surveillance?"

A sense of foreboding washes over me. "Yeah."

"Well, the good news is that some photos our guy took just came in. You'll never guess who he was meeting with just a few hours ago."

Zack's holding his breath, waiting for Simon's answer. I'm pretty sure I know what's coming.

"Asa Wade," he says.

"When it rains, it pours," I grumble.

"Shit," Zack says. "He's back? Wait. That was the good news? What's the bad news?"

My heart sinks. My stomach roils. "What happened?"

"Ford left the hotel on foot. Paul lost him."

"What the hell do you mean he *lost* him? How does a vampire lose a human in broad daylight?"

Simon doesn't sound the least bit worried. "Never fear, fellow crime fighters. I have a plan to draw him out."

CHAPTER 15

After Simon gives Zack and me the details of his plan, we head for the Wellington in Mission Hills to await Seamus and Sarah—and put the first part of Simon's "foolproof" plan into action.

It takes a minute for my eyes to adjust after we step through the large wooden door that leads into the steakhouse. Zack, of course, doesn't have the same problem.

"Looks like we have our pick of tables," he says.

"Emma? It's been a while."

I recognize Vasilis' voice. As a fixture at the Wellington, it's his expertise behind the bar that has earned the restaurant its reputation for serving the *perfect* martini.

"Vasilis, this is my partner, Zack."

As he gets closer, I see he's wearing his standard "uniform," black shirt and trousers. His dark hair is neatly trimmed. The black horn-rim glasses he wears were fashionable when he was turned in the late forties. Now they're all the rage again. At five-ten, he's shorter than Zack, but I wouldn't necessarily assume he's weaker. Zack doesn't make that mistake, either.

Vampire and werewolf shake hands warily, each cautious of the other.

"We're meeting someone," I say. "Mind if we take the corner table by the bar?"

"Help yourself. I think it's going to be a slow night. Drinks?"

Zack and I slide into opposite sides of the L-shaped black leather booth.

"Club soda," Zack says.

"Make that two," I add.

As soon as Vasilis leaves, Zack leans across the table. "You come here often?"

I shrug. "Often enough. My place is close. They have good food. It's quiet."

Quiet is right. The dimly lit steakhouse holds less than a dozen tables. Even on a busy night, the setting lends itself to intimacy.

Zack eyes Vasilis, who is busy scooping ice into a cocktail shaker. "He the owner?"

"No, he manages the place. We go back."

I've piqued his interest. "How far back?"

"We met in New York City shortly after he was turned. I was tracking a suspect who was connected to a missing persons case. Vasilis was bartending at the Waldorf where the guy was staying. He slipped him a Mickey during last call. Helped me catch the bastard. We lost touch for a while."

"Here you go." Vasilis is suddenly at our table. "Traditional martini with olives for the lady. An old-fashioned for the gentleman."

Glasses are set before us.

Zack frowns. "We ordered club soda."

Vasilis nods. "Trust me. You'll like this better."

I learned years ago not to bother arguing. "This is what The Wellington is known for," I say, lifting my glass. "A toast. To thwarting Wade's plans—whatever they may be."

The rim of Zack's glass touches the side of mine. "And hopefully catching the bastard." He checks the time on his cell. "It's five thirty. Sarah and Seamus should be here by now. Should we call Liz and tell her we're going to be late?"

The plan Simon concocted is simple. Seamus is to bring Sarah here to meet us, and when we've established that they haven't been followed, the plan is to take Sarah to Liz for a magical makeover. Then I act as a decoy Sarah while one of Seamus' men escorts the real Sarah to the six-bedroom, six-bath, eleven-thousand-square-foot mansion on Billionaire's Row in San Francisco that Kallistos occupied before moving here. I'll return with Seamus to the ranch. By the time darkness has settled over the compound, Kallistos' security team will have moved in to back up the resident Weres. With luck, Wade will come after Sarah, get captured, then become the perfect bait to draw out Ford and Lamont.

I pull out my phone and dial. As Liz answers, Seamus walks through the door.

Alone.

"Let me call you back," I tell her.

Zack's shoulders sag. "She's not coming," he says once Seamus reaches the table.

The pack master pulls out the empty chair and sits. "No. I'm afraid not. Sarah doesn't want to see you, Zack. And she doesn't want to leave the ranch. She feels safe with us. This feeling of obligation, or whatever you want to call it, you have to let it go. Sarah isn't yours to care for. You're not responsible for what happens to her."

Zack isn't so easily dissuaded. "She wouldn't be in this predicament if I hadn't left."

"Even if that's true, it doesn't matter. Look, you told her to move on. She's moving on. Let her go."

Vasilis approaches the table, presumably to take a drink order, but Zack waves him off.

"I can smell her on you," Zack says, his voice low, rumbling.

Seamus leans back in his chair. "It that a problem?"

Zack swallows, then, after a moment's hesitation, "No. No problem." He knocks back his drink, catches Vasilis' eye, and orders another. "He'll come for her, you know."

Seamus rises. "If he does, we'll be ready."

"The King's offer stands. You could use the help."

"Kallistos Kouros has his own problems. Word has it heads of state from the other territories are hedging their bets and won't choose sides. By choosing none, they may become enemies of both." Seamus turns to me. "I spoke to him a few minutes ago. Told him we can handle Wade ourselves. If Wade's sorry ass breaches my compound, I'll have no problem wrapping him in silver chains and delivering him personally. Then Kallistos can do whatever the hell he wants with him."

With that, he's gone.

"Now what?" I ask Zack.

Vasilis arrives with Zack's drink.

He accepts it and says, "So much for Simon's plan. I may get drunk." He motions to me. "The lady will have another. And menus, please."

I suppress a smile. "How much does it take to get you drunk?"

Zack fishes the cherry out, pops it into his mouth, and crunches down on it. "A lot."

I raise my glass. "Well, I don't have your metabolism. So don't expect me to match you drink for drink, big guy." I study him for a moment. The line of his jaw seems softer, the shoulders more relaxed. "I can't tell if you're celebrating or trying to drown your sorrows."

I get the shrug. "Maybe a bit of both."

"So Sarah and Seamus?"

He nods. "It's a good thing. Seamus was right. I asked her to move in with me out of a sense of obligation, of duty. She always wanted it to be more." He pauses to take a sip of his drink. "I didn't."

Vasilis arrives with menus and my second martini. I've barely touched my first and my head is already spinning. What is Zack saying? I put my menu aside and in a hushed voice I ask, "Are you telling me that you and Sarah weren't really . . . together?"

"By together you mean—"

"Having sex," I whisper.

His eyebrows shoot up.

"Never mind," I tell him.

Only he doesn't want to let it go. "We broke it off before I left South Carolina. I told you that."

"But then you asked her to move in with you. This entire time I thought . . ." This is dangerous ground. The last thing I should be doing right now is dredging up the past. I shake my head. "It's none of my business."

I feel his fingertips brush mine. The touch is hesitant, barely there, then gone. "Do you ever wonder?" he asks, softly. "Do you ever think about how things might have turned out?"

My heart is hammering in my chest. I'm certain he can hear it. "Turned out?"

"That night at the Hotel Del. We were in the court-yard. I've replayed that moment over and over in my head. I have a thousand different endings." He smiles down into his drink before finishing it off. "None of them end with you just walking back inside, leaving me alone." The hand that was so close to mine slides back.

Of course, I know what really happened. That was the moment of our first kiss, the night we made love. It seems a lifetime ago. "I think about it," I admit, surprising even myself.

"But not with regret." He lifts his empty glass into the air so that Vasilis can see it.

"My situation, *our* situation, is complicated." I resist the temptation to reach for his hand. "There's so much I've regretted doing. And so much I regret not doing. But my life is what it is."

He fixes his gaze on me. "I told you once I could pretend, keep my distance, not push. I've kept my word." He leans forward, lowers his voice a notch. "I know there are a million reasons why you wouldn't want to be with me. I get that. What I don't understand is why you're with him."

"Are we ready to order?" Vasilis places the old-fashioned on the table and collects the empty glass.

"I'll have the usual," I answer.

Zack glances at his menu for the first time. "The house wedge. Rib eye, rare, with the seasonal vegetables and the mac-n-cheese."

"Excellent choice," Vasilis tells him before taking his leave.

Zack is waiting for an answer.

I stall.

I finish my first drink. Then lift the second one to my lips—seeking inspiration more than liquid courage. I'd been trying to avoid eye contact, but I can't help stealing a glance over the rim of my glass.

He's smiling. "You don't have an answer."

The hope in his eyes is almost too painful to bear. The truth is, I don't have a *good* answer. I've yet to clear the air with Kallistos about the key card. On top of that, he's taking circumspect and completely unsanctioned actions. He's acting the part of a King, protector of the realm. While I understand his need to do so, I fear it may compromise our investigation. Our goals are not the same. In fact, they may be at cross purposes.

"I—"

He holds up his hand. "Let me savor the moment."

We sit in silence.

Our salads arrive.

Zack eats his with gusto while I pick. About half of the tables in the restaurant are now occupied, some with faces I recognize from the neighborhood. My mind wanders back to safer territory. I retreat into the case, letting the details roll around in my head like stones in a polisher. I sift through the evidence, replay interviews.

"Why'd you order the Caesar if you don't like it?" Zack asks.

"I like it. I guess I'm not all that hungry."

He reaches across the table with his fork and spears a

leaf of romaine. "I have an idea. Something that might lead us directly to Ford or the missing girls."

I'm surprised how relieved I feel to be getting back to business. "I'm all ears."

"Remember that thing Liz tried to do when her boyfriend, Evan, went missing last spring?" he asks.

"Scrying?"

"It didn't work because he was in a coma."

"Divination isn't her strong suit. Otherwise I would have asked days ago."

"So, it's a long shot. What do we have to lose?"

"We'll need something personal."

"We have laptops belonging to two of the girls."

I shake my head. "No. Tech doesn't work. We'd have to call their parents. We could tell them we want DNA samples on file. Hair from a comb or brush would easily work." I pause, wondering whether it would be possible to tie Ford to the girls. "You know, being able to place Ford and the girls in the same place at the same time would all but cinch Lamont's involvement in all of this. But that means we'd need something from him, too. That won't be as easy to get."

Zack's busy scrolling through something on his phone. He holds it up so I can see. It's one of Ford's football jerseys on eBay—game used and signed. The current bid is twelve hundred. The auction closes at midnight. "Would this work?"

"Can you tell where the seller is?"

He scrolls again. "Ships from Denver. We could have it in hand by early afternoon. I need to set up an account."

"It's not too late. If Ford doesn't lead us to the girls

tonight, we can call their parents and make arrange-
ments to have their items picked up in the morning. It's
worth a shot." I wave to get Vasilis' attention. "Let's box
up dinner. I'm just a few blocks away. It'll be easier to
monitor the auction on a laptop. Go get the car. I'll get
the check."

I pull my wallet out of my bag. When I do, the key to
the penthouse falls out, onto the floor.

I don't pick it up.

Zack's picked me up and dropped me off on occasion,
but he's never been inside my place. I live in a converted
carriage house in one of the oldest sections of town. I use
the term *house* loosely. At less than four hundred and
fifty square feet, the entire place is about the size of
Zack's master bedroom. I unlock the door, flip on a light,
and head straight back to the dining room.

I don't have a designated workspace. I work anywhere
and everywhere. The tiny dining room is but a few steps
away from the kitchen, making it the perfect place to
work tonight. We can eat and obsessively monitor eBay.
I unpack my laptop and plug it in.

"Plates are in the cabinet to the left of the sink. Silverware in the top drawer to the right," I call out. I remove
my jacket and drape it over the back of one of the chairs.
Within seconds my laptop is fired up and my fingers are
flying, trying to find the jersey that Zack showed me in
the restaurant. "Bourbon's above the fridge."

"Want me to open this?" He's standing in the doorway, holding a bottle of cabernet sauvignon in his hand.

Aside from the modest table and chairs, the only
other piece of furniture in the dining room is an antique

sideboard. It holds my *good* crystal and china and sometimes doubles as a bar. I tilt my head in its direction. "You'll find glasses on the shelf and a corkscrew in the middle drawer." Then, "How did you find the jersey? I'm not seeing it."

Zack circles around the table and looks over my shoulder. "Search *Ford football jersey signed*."

The listing comes right up.

"It's still twelve hundred."

He's moved back into the kitchen. I hear the cork pop, the wine being poured. When he returns, I'm watching him, my arms crossed, my hands attempting to rub away a sudden chill.

"Are you cold? Do you want to turn on the heat?"

I accept the wine he's holding out. "How about a fire? There's a stack of wood on the back deck."

Zack opens the French doors and heads outside. My heart starts to pound. Is it the chill of the evening or something else making my skin go cold? Is Demeter subtly reminding me that she's ever present, ever watching?

"Matches?"

Zack's voice brings me back. His back is to me as he assembles wood for the fire. His suit coat is off, tie loosened, shirtsleeves rolled up. His rugged handsomeness momentarily takes my breath away.

"In the urn on the mantel." My voice sounds strained.

He turns. "You feel all right?" His eyes search my face. "A second ago you were complaining of the cold. Now you look flushed."

"Just hungry." I reach into the sack from The Wellington and pull out the containers of food. "Be right back. I'm just going to go grab plates."

I exit the dining room, but don't make it to the kitchen. Instead, my eyes are drawn to my bed. I move toward it. How many nights have I lain here alone, unable to sleep, thinking about Zack. Missing him. I unfasten the ties to the drapes that curtain off the bed area from the living space and yank them closed before moving to the kitchen.

Demeter took care of such fantasies. And that was before Kallistos, before I gave in to his relentless efforts, his persistent charm. Before I fell into his bed and found distraction and comfort in his arms.

Why am I with Kallistos?

Because I enjoy how free I can be with him.

Although that's only part of the answer, isn't it? If I'm to be honest, the rest is far less complicated. And it's a truth that's easier for Kallistos to admit.

Because, Zack, I can't be with you.

CHAPTER 16

Day Four: Thursday, September 5

I wake to glaring light and the persistent thrum of rhythmic pounding in my head. I sit up. My eyes land on the coffee table. My laptop. Next to it, my Glock and an empty bottle of wine. I recall it was the second we opened last night, likely the one responsible for the one-man band playing inside my head.

Big mistake.

The last thing I remember, Zack and I were both in the dining room, trading stories about old cases and watching the auction. It was getting close to midnight, and I was going to lay my head down for just a few minutes. I must have fallen asleep, and he must have carried me to bed. I peek under the blanket. Save the shoes, I'm still fully dressed.

I pull back the throw covering me and slide out of bed. The first thing I do is close the drapes to the outside windows. The darkness takes the edge off the headache. A hot bath, a couple aspirin, and a cup of strong coffee should knock out what remains. And water. Lots and lots of water. I remove my blouse, slip out of my trousers. Drop them in the dry-cleaning bag. Bra and panties are deposited in the hamper. Then I pad over to the kitchen. Our dishes from last night are already washed and in the drying rack. A note is stuck to the coffeepot.

We won the auction. The shirt should be here sometime in the afternoon. Took the car. Will be back for you with breakfast around eight thirty.

I glance over at the clock hanging in the kitchen. It's already eight.

Hydrate and bathe now. The caffeine fix will have to wait. I quickly fill a glass with cold, filtered water from the fridge, then head into the bathroom and run a tub, dumping in a generous amount of bath salts to soothe body and soul. I swallow two aspirin with the water, then quickly wash my face, brush my teeth. When I close the medicine cabinet, I catch a glimpse of myself in the mirror. My hair is a disaster. The few remaining pins come out. The long, dark waves tumble down around my shoulders. I brush it out, then quickly wind it back into a tight bun and secure it once again at the base of my neck.

I shut off the taps, slide into the tub, and lean back. Like always, the hot water does wonders. The din behind my eyes begins to subside. My shoulders start to relax. I inhale deeply, breathing in the familiar scent of lavender and vanilla that I've long used in my baths. My stomach growls. Now that my head is feeling better, hunger pangs set in. Just as I begin to wonder how much longer it will be before Zack shows up with breakfast, I hear the front door open, then close.

"Thank goodness! I'm starving," I call out. "Think I can get you to make a pot of coffee?"

My only answer is the sound of footsteps crossing the wooden floor.

"Zack?"

The doorknob to the bathroom turns.

Instinctively, I reach for a towel. It slides off the nearby rack, onto the floor and out of reach.

Liz's statement from yesterday flits through my mind. *A King always has enemies. Being close to him puts you in danger.* My eyes flash to the Glock, sitting on the coffee table. Nothing nearby can be effectively used as a weapon. All I have is myself, my innate power to influence, to seduce. I begin to lower my shields.

The door opens.

It's Kallistos.

I breathe a sigh of relief and quickly pull my powers back in. The extreme energy required leaves me feeling drained.

Kallistos doesn't look like he feels any better. Perhaps it's due to the power shift he was unexpectedly exposed to. Perhaps it's the combination of head-to-toe black clothing—cashmere mock turtleneck, light wool slacks, polished boots—and the unforgiving fluorescent lighting in the bathroom. For the first time since we met, he looks a little worse for the wear—paler than usual, with a light blue cast under his eyes.

"Everything okay?" I ask, suddenly concerned.

He crouches down next to the tub. "It is now." His hand slides around the back of my neck. He lowers his forehead to mine. "I spent the night monitoring the situation at the ranch. Wade never showed."

"No sign of Lamont?"

"None whatsoever. I came home right after sunrise.

You weren't in my bed. You didn't answer my calls. I was worried."

"I'm sorry. I worked late last night, overslept this morning. I didn't check my messages."

After releasing me, he slides to the floor, back against the bathroom door, legs stretched out. He rubs his eyes. Then sighs. "I was worried."

I fold my arms on the rim of the old-fashioned cast-iron claw-foot tub. "You said that."

"And then . . . jealous. Did I mention jealous?"

"You were jealous?"

He fixes his gaze on me. I see how serious he is. "Did you sleep with him, Emma?"

"Who?"

"Armstrong." He reaches into his pocket and pulls out the key to the penthouse. "You left the key at The Wellington. I know you were there with him last night. And I know you left with him. You brought him here. I can smell him. You're expecting him to return." He looks down at the key. "I'm not used to feeling these things," he confesses. "They soften me. Weaken me. The well-being of my charges, the safety and security of my realm, need to be my primary concern. It's the duty of a King. Above all else, that's what I am, Emma. What I must be. This . . . concern . . . is a distraction."

He means I'm a distraction. I don't know whether to be flattered or insulted. "We were working," I tell him. "We met Seamus at the Wellington to fill him in on Simon's plan. Sarah's not going to cooperate. It didn't pan out."

"I'm sorry." It sounds as if he means it.

I continue. "Fortunately after a couple of old-fashioneds,

Zack landed on an idea that might just work. Liz is going to take a shot at scrying. We came back here with takeout and spent a few hours lining up personal belongings. I went to bed just before midnight—alone. Zack's supposed to pick me up around eight thirty and bring breakfast. I haven't been staying here much during the last few months, you know. I don't have any food."

At that, a smile touches his lips. "You haven't asked me how I traced you to The Wellington."

"I *know* how you traced me to The Wellington. It's why I left the key. I was angry. It took Liz all of two seconds to notice it was charged with enough mojo to power a small city. Why the deception? The pretense?"

He looks away, leans his head back against the door.

I wait patiently for an answer. Finally it comes.

"It wasn't pretense, not exactly."

"Then what?" I push myself out of the bath, reaching for the towel on the floor.

He grabs it first, rises, and holds it out for me. "I told you I've done things, had to do things, will continue to do things."

I step out of the tub and allow him to wrap the towel around me, like he's done so many times before. Then I turn to face him. "Are you saying you did it to purposely piss me off? To push me away?"

He lifts my chin. "Be careful. It would be dangerous to believe my intentions are noble. I'm anything but."

"Really?" My taunting tone gets an unexpected rise.

I find myself pinned to the door. Hard, aroused vampire hovering over me. His mouth poised just above my neck. "Don't push. I haven't slept. Or fed."

I feel his breath and hold my own. I respect he's used

to taking what he wants and the fact that he's showing restraint. Despite my ire and doubt, I find my arousal begin to build, feel an impulse to invite him to feed, to sate what I recognize as incredible desire. I push it away.

"I have to get dressed," I tell him.

"Armstrong can wait." He snakes his arm around my waist, pulling me closer. Pressing his cock into the softness of my belly. His fingers slip between my thighs.

"Don't," I whisper.

He pauses, lifts his head, searches my eyes. His fangs have descended; his normally vibrant, blue eyes are like lightning cutting through a cloud-filled sky—dark, swirling rays of silver slice through irises that are now black.

"I have to feed."

"Is that the only reason you're here?" I ask, although I already know the answer.

"Yes . . . No."

Uncertainty is not an emotion Kallistos is comfortable with. The admission, even to himself, costs him. "Because I wanted it to be you. I *need* it to be you. Will you deny me?"

"Your priority right now is your Kingdom. Please understand, mine is finding these missing girls."

I hear a knock. "Emma?"

It's Zack.

He's let himself in.

I place my hand on the side of Kallistos' face. "You need to go. We need to start gathering the girls' personal items. An old shirt belonging to Ford is being flown in. Everything we need to give scrying a shot will be here by this afternoon."

He nods, his emotions now reined in. His fangs

sheathed. Eyes back to that intensely captivating and deceptively pure blue. "Maybe I'll take a sip or two from Armstrong before I leave to tide me over."

I can't help but smile. "You'd resort to that? Now you're just trying to be purposely pitiful so I feel sorry for you."

"I'd like to see you try, Kallistos!" Zack calls out.

Kallistos rolls his eyes. "Please. I could go months without feeding and still kick his furry ass."

I push him away, drop the towel, then grab the robe hanging on the back of the bathroom door. "I'll let you know how things go with Liz."

As I cinch the sash around my waist, Kallistos reaches out and drops the key into the pocket of my robe.

"Keep the key," he says, then rephrases. "I'd be grateful if you kept the key." It took pains, I'm sure, to make it a request instead of a command.

Before I can acknowledge the effort, he's out the bathroom door. I hear Zack mumble something under his breath as Kallistos passes him, but whatever it was gets only a grunt from the vampire. The sound of the front door closing is like an effective dismissal, followed a moment later with Zack calling, "Coffee?"

I quickly slather sunscreen on my face. "Be your best friend."

"Seriously? What would a bagel and cream cheese get me?"

My stomach growls unceremoniously, reminding me once again how hungry I am. I open the door to the bathroom. "You brought me a bagel?"

Zack is sitting on the sofa. He's dressed in a fresh dark gray suit, starched white shirt, and black tie. A brown paper bag sits in front of him on the coffee table along with a cardboard coffee holder containing a single cup. He's holding the second one in his hand. "Ate my bagel on the way over. Dig in. Mr. and Mrs. Roberts expect us by nine fifteen."

I pop the lid off the coffee cup, lift it to my lips, and breathe in the aroma before taking a sip.

"How you feeling?" he asks as I sink down onto the sofa.

I lean my head back and close my eyes. "Like I drank too much wine, passed out, and slept in my clothes."

A whiff of cinnamon forces them open again. Zack's holding a bagel in front of my face. I reach for it and take a grateful bite. "How are you feeling?"

"Answering that will only annoy you," he says.

Damned werewolf metabolism.

Then, a moment of hesitation before he asks, "Is he still feeding from you?"

As if that question won't annoy me at all. I leave the bagel and coffee on the table in front of the sofa and head for my closet. "I thought we agreed that was none of your business?"

When he doesn't answer, I turn around.

Instead of being across the room, where I'd left him, he's right behind me.

"*You* agreed," he answers. "You know the more you allow it, the more you'll want it, crave it, crave *him*. I worry about you, Emma."

I gaze into his eyes and I see the ache in them, the longing.

"Why?" I ask.

I get a sad smile. "You know why."

His thumb glides across my cheek. I should have pulled away, but instead I lean into the caress.

His other hand moves toward my shoulder, ghosts across my collarbone. He pinches the fabric of my robe between his fingers and peels it back a few inches. I hold my breath.

"Zack."

Fingers over my mouth force me to silence. Then they slide the other side of my robe from my shoulder. He circles round me. Warm hands slide down the length of my neck, over my shoulders. They pause.

"He didn't just bite you. He marked you." His fingers trace the scar. "This should have disappeared by now. He'll mark you again. And then again and again. He's not just feeding from you. He's building a connection, one he'll use to control you, manipulate you."

Zack's normally warm, brown eyes are now sky blue.

"Your eyes—"

He closes them. "Sorry. The beast isn't as good as I am at pretending."

"I should get dressed. We need to go." I reach for the last clean black pantsuit that's hanging in my closet and head for the bathroom.

Again, he follows. "My wolf, he wants to take away Kallistos' mark." Zack stops, filling the doorway. "Just say the word. I can break the cycle."

"How? By trading one mark for another?" I hang my suit up on the shower rod.

"I'm not offering to mark you for myself. I'm offering to free you from him. Unlike a vampire's, a wolf's mark means something. It's a mutual commitment. One made for life. That's not what we're talking about here."

"What are we talking about?"

Zack appears to be weighing his words carefully. "We're talking about doing what's smart, what's necessary. You said Kallistos would never get the upper hand. But it seems he has."

Suddenly I feel trapped. I need to put distance between myself and Kallistos. I step back and stuff my hands into the pockets of my robe. My fingers wrap instinctively around the key card. It's a tangible reminder of the truth of Zack's words.

"Yes." It comes out in a rush.

"You want me to remove the mark? Are you sure?"

"Yes. Do it." I'm trying to focus on what Zack said about this being smart and necessary, nothing else. A wolf's mark means something. But this will mean nothing. "Hurry. Let's get it over with."

But Zack doesn't hurry. He takes his time, pulling me back, gently curving his body over mine. His is warm, impossibly warm, and I can feel it through my robe. Just as I feel his breath on my neck, feel the echo of his heartbeat in my own.

"Trust me?" he asks, his voice a low, intoxicating rumble.

I do trust him. "Completely."

His fangs graze my skin. His cock, long and hard, presses against my back.

My breasts ache. My knees feel weak.

The familiar feel of him. It's too much.

It's not enough.

I brace my hand against the frame of the bathroom door and push back, offering him the friction I so desperately want for myself.

For a fleeting moment, his hand finds my breast. Then it slides down to my hip, stilling my movement. "Christ, Emma. I want you. You know I do. But not like this, with him between us. Just . . . let me do this. Hold steady. It will be over in a minute. Once it is, we'll never speak of it again," he says. Then he covers the mark with his mouth.

The feel of his lips at my neck makes my breath catch. His hands never stray from their steadying grip. He doesn't press his body against me. He doesn't allow me to press my body back against him. And yet when his fangs pierce my flesh, I start to tremble. Desire, violent, white-hot, threatens my control. I want him, over me, in me, loving me.

I can't have what I want.

I clench my teeth to keep from crying out. It takes every bit of strength I have to remain still, to keep my traitorous body from responding to this touch.

In a minute, it's over. Zack steps back. His hands fall away. He leaves me without a word, softly closing the bathroom door behind him.

I sink to the floor, breathless, heart pounding.

We came so close.

I rest my head against the cool porcelain of the bathtub, remaining still until I can breathe normally, until my heartbeat slows. Zack, intending to heal one wound, opened up so many others.

CHAPTER 17

The ride to Liz's is quiet. Zack is driving. The package from Denver sits on the car seat between us. Evidence bags containing personal items from the three missing girls are in the backseat. We've barely spoken a dozen words to each other since leaving my apartment. I pop down the visor, pull back the collar of my black silk blouse as I check the mirror. My skin is pristine. No sign of Kallistos' mark. More miraculously, no sign of Zack's.

From the corner of my eye, I catch Zack watching me. Finally, he says, "This silence is unnerving."

I flip the visor back up. "You're the one who said we couldn't talk about it."

"We could talk about a million other things," Zack says.

"Yeah. Name one."

I drum my fingers on the FedEx box and wait. But his silence speaks volumes. I'm sure he's thinking the same thing I am.

"You know how when someone tells you not to think about an elephant and the *only* thing you can think about is the damned elephant?" I ask him.

He nods.

"Well, this is one huge mammoth of an elephant, and what happened in my bathroom—what *could* have happened in my bathroom—has my stomach in knots."

Zack doesn't answer. His eyes remain studiously on the road but his hands clench and unclench on the steering wheel as if expecting a reply to be telegraphed to him through the leather. Finally he whispers, "Did you want something to happen?"

Yes. No. "We're partners. We agreed that's all it could be."

Something as cold as an arctic breeze brushes the back of my neck. Demeter. Reminding me we're navigating into dangerous waters, Zack and I, and of the consequences I risk. I straighten in my seat, pinch my shoulders back, put steel in my voice. "Partners, Zack, that's all."

His turns his face from the road. His eyes, when they meet mine, are as hard as my tone. "I remember. I thought for a minute *you* might have forgotten."

I feel color burn my face. He's right. I let him touch me under the pretense of removing Kallistos' mark, but I wanted more. He felt it. How could he not?

"I'm sorry. It won't happen again."

"What won't happen again?" The words are sharp as a rapier. "Your letting Kallistos feed from you? Or taking pleasure from allowing me to remove evidence of it?"

How can I answer that? Before he pushes it, we've arrived at Liz's condo. I've never been so happy to drop a subject. "Pull into that visitor's space," I say, nodding toward a vacant spot.

"I've been here before."

Zack's tone hasn't softened. Liz is going to pick up on the tension between us the moment she opens her door.

"Look, Zack. Let's not drag Liz into our drama. We're here because Liz has offered to help us find the girls. That's all we should be thinking about right now."

Zack has already pushed open his door. He doesn't so much as glance at me, but reaches into the back to pull out the evidence bags. I grab the FedEx box and meet him at the driver's side of the Suburban. "Are we okay?"

He won't meet my eyes. But he does release a breath and tension seems to drain from his shoulders. "I know we have a job to do. Let's hope Liz can help."

Liz has an uncanny ability to sense my presence. We approach and she's swung open the door before my hand touches the bell. Her eyes dart from my face to Zack's and narrow when her gaze meets mine. "What's going on?"

"Nothing."

She grabs my hand and pulls me inside, motioning for Zack to come in with a flutter of her free hand. "Zack, excuse us for a minute, will you? I have to speak with Emma. Go on into the dining room. We'll be right back."

I don't bother to argue. Zack looks surprised but takes the FedEx box from my hand and moves toward the dining room. Liz pulls me into the kitchen and closes the door behind us.

"What on earth—"

She turns her back to me. Her arms are outstretched. The kitchen hums with power. I know what she's doing. I wait, patiently, while she erects a shield to prevent Zack from hearing our conversation.

"Something happened between you and Zack," she

says as soon as she's finished. It sounds like an accusation. It is an accusation. "You slept together again, didn't you? You know how much danger that puts him in. You don't want to awaken—"

I rub the back of my neck where I still feel the chill of Demeter's cold breath. "No, Liz. We didn't sleep together."

My words come out much harsher than I intend.

"But you came close." It's not a question.

I close my eyes, nod. "We came close."

"Damn it, Emma." Liz grabs my shoulders. "You know what will happen to Zack if you give in. I thought you were smarter than this. I can only do so much to help."

"I know, Liz. I know." Tears burn my eyes. I brush them away. "It would be so much easier if I could tell Zack about Demeter, make him understand."

"But you know he won't understand. That's why you didn't tell him about Demeter in the first place. You know what his reaction will be. You said it yourself. He's a fighter and he loves you. He won't walk away. Give him a target and he'll go after it. Demeter will crush him. You know that, Emma. You've seen it happen before. If you care about him, you won't risk this."

"I know." I draw a ragged breath. "Nothing can happen. I'll be more careful."

Liz lays a gentle hand against my cheek. "You have an answer, you know. Kallistos. Concentrate on your relationship with him." She grins. "And I know how good vampire sex is. Like nothing else."

I return her smile. She does know. But the sad truth is one element is missing in my relationship that is present in hers. She and Evan are in love.

*   *   *

Liz has pushed the dining room table and chairs against a wall to clear a space in the middle of the floor. On the hardwood she's drawn a chalk circle, and in the circle, a pentagram. On the pentagram she's placed a map of San Diego County. When Liz and I join Zack, he's examining the map.

"You think the girls are close?" he asks.

"It seems logical to look close to home first," Liz says. "If nothing shows up, I can extend the range."

She's taken the objects we obtained from the girls' parents and is placing them on the points of the pentagram: at the top, Julie's hairbrush; to the right, a toothbrush of Hannah's; to the left, nail clippings retrieved from Sylvia's bathroom trash. At the bottom of the pentagram, Ford's football jersey. When Liz is satisfied that the objects are laid out the way she wants them, she lights five candles, also at the points of the pentagram. She's already pulled the dining room curtains closed against the bright afternoon sun, and when the candles blaze to life, the room is bathed in a soft, golden glow. The beeswax candles give off a faint odor, church-like and comforting. When I glance at Zack, he's watching Liz with rapt attention.

Liz is ready to begin. She's taken a chain from a small velvet bag. At the end of the chain, a crystal sends slivers of reflected light dancing around the room.

"Will you be working a spell?" Zack asks, his tone hushed and reverent.

She smiles. "No spell. No invocations. This is elemental magic. Tied into the physical rather than metaphysical. You and Emma just stand back and let the crystal do its thing."

Zack and I take a step back. Liz holds the crystal over the pentagram and lets the chain swing free.

It rotates a couple of times, then stops.

Zack and I lean forward expectantly.

"That was fast," Zack says. He's following the point of the crystal to the spot it's hovering above on the map. "Wait. That looks like the middle of the bay. Are they on a boat?"

Liz frowns. "No. Something's wrong. Let me try again."

Zack and I retreat to the edges of the circle while Liz draws the crystal into her palm. She releases it again. The crystal spins from the energy of being released, circles twice, then stops again. Dead stop.

Liz looks over at us.

"What? Ford's in the middle of the harbor?" Zack asks.

Liz frowns. "No. There was no *pull* on the crystal the way there would have been if Ford or the girls were in the area. I hate to say it, but this is exactly what I experienced when I tried to find Evan while he was being held in Barbara Pierce's lab. I think the girls are being shielded somehow."

I give voice to what I know we're all thinking. "Or they're dead."

Liz takes my hand. "Not necessarily. Remember Evan was unconscious, drugged. Maybe the girls are, too. Let's not jump to conclusions."

"Call Kallistos," Zack adds. "Maybe he found Ford."

I dial the phone. It's answered on the first ring.

"Hey, Emma."

The voice isn't the one I expected.

"Simon?"

He sighs. "Before you ask, I have no idea where Kallistos is. I was hoping maybe he was with you. He left this damn thing in my office and it's been ringing off the hook. I'm afraid to answer it and afraid not to."

"Find Kallistos and have him call me." I hang up.

I instantly feel the heat from Zack's glare.

This isn't my fault, but somehow I feel responsible.

Liz saves me before I have a chance to reply. "I might have an explanation for why the scrying isn't working."

"Please, tell us. We could use some good news right about now," Zack says.

"They may be in a place that naturally interferes with magic. A place with its own spiritual energy. A holy place."

"You mean like a church?"

"A church. A synagogue. A mosque. Even a cemetery. Any hallowed ground."

"Great." Zack releases a breath. "I'd guess San Diego County has a couple thousand churches and cemeteries."

Liz places the crystal on the dining room table. "Let me make some calls. I know others who are better at scrying than I am. Maybe we can narrow down the options a little." She shrugs. "Or maybe I'm completely off base. At least we'd know. Do you mind if I keep these things?" She motions to the items on the pentagram. "If I can get some help, we'll need them."

Before I agree, Liz's cell phone chimes. She glances at it. "It's Evan. Just a sec." She connects the call. "Hey, you.

Emma? Yes, she's still here." Liz listens, her eyes widening. "I'll tell her."

She disconnects. "Well. You may not need the scrying, after all. Evan is sending Owen Cooper over. He's got some information that might shed some light on your case."

CHAPTER 18

"What did he say, exactly?" I ask Liz.

The question elicits a sigh of frustration. "Just that he was on his way to a meeting and that he was sending Owen here."

Zack stops pacing long enough to add, "With some information."

"Yes." Liz nods. "With some information that might shed light on your case. We've been over this."

"The elevator." Zack stills. Listens. Then frowns. "Never mind. Sounds like two people. A man and a woman."

Liz heads for the door anyway, probably just to get away from the two of us. Before she's reached it, there's a knock. Liz swings the door open.

"I believe you're expecting us?"

I recognize the delicate voice at once. "Rose from the Emporium," I whisper to Zack.

Rose was turned when she was sixteen, but that was more than a hundred and twenty years ago. Her youthful face and form are showcased today in a long gown of dark purple taffeta. I hear the brush of crinoline as she sweeps past.

"Owen needed a lift and I've been dying to meet Agent Armstrong." She approaches him, and then bows ever so slightly. "I've heard so much about you. I'm pleased to finally make your acquaintance."

"The pleasure is mine," he replies, turning on the Southern-boy charm and doing his best not to stare.

Although Rose's attire appears to be straight out of the Victorian era that she came from, her hair and makeup are contemporary Goth. Smudged kohl eyeliner, red-black lipstick, dark hair swept into her signature style of carefully crafted messiness dotted with violets. A spill of escaping tendrils frames her flawless face and cascades down her back. The décolleté of the gown shows off her dramatic tattoo—a tangle of black thorns and bloodred roses emerges from underneath her dress, covering her chest, creeping up her neck. Not for the first time, I wonder if she's always dressed in the manner she was accustomed to when she was alive.

"Wicked Ink?" Zack asks, reaching for her hand and examining the thorns and roses.

"Of course." A flash of coquettishness flares in the look she gives him. "You should stop by. I could fix you up."

"Why on earth would a werewolf get a tatt?" Owen, who followed Rose inside, speaks for the first time. "First full moon it'd be ripped to shreds." He grins. "You just want to see his chest." He pulls a sheet of parchment from his back pocket and holds it out for Zack. "This is what *you* want to see."

So much for preserving the chain of evidence. Whatever it is, or whomever it was from, it now has Owen's fingerprints all over it, too.

Regardless, Zack pulls a pair of gloves from his jacket pocket. While he slips them on, I fish through my purse for an evidence bag.

"What is it?" I ask, laying the bag on the coffee table.

Zack places the parchment on top. It's folded in thirds, a broken wax seal on one side. *You are cordially invited* is written in an old-fashioned script on the other. Zack carefully begins to open it.

"Craig, this vamp in my support group, found it under his door," Owen says. "Just the promise of it sent him off the rails. He relapsed. Big-time. Practically drained some co-ed in the college area last night. He came to me for help this morning. We're about the same age and, like me, he was an addict before he was turned. Only his drug of choice was a little more highbrow—cocaine. I called Evan. He needs a seasoned sponsor and I'm not ready for that. Thirty days of sobriety and he threw it all away." He smiles sheepishly. "Of course, I've thrown it away hundreds of times."

"But not this time," adds Rose, reaching for his hand.

He kisses hers and leads her to the sofa. It's the first time I've seen them together. I'd been under the impression, from references made, that Rose was more than Owen's boss. She was also his sire. What I hadn't realized is that they're obviously also lovers.

Zack and I lean in to examine the invitation. The message reads:

One-time Opportunity Only
Auction of 100% PURE YBV—Ten Units
Drink from the Source
Email: sales@drinkfromthesource.com for details

The bottom of the message is date-stamped—noon yesterday—and an added note reads: *You have twenty-four hours to respond.*

My heart sinks. Ten units. "The ten missing girls." I check my watch. It's coming up on noon. We don't have much time. "Does Kallistos know about this?"

"Simon's tracking him down. He left earlier in a mood and hasn't returned."

Zack and I exchange a glance. My refusal to let Kallistos feed probably didn't improve his disposition.

Zack points to the email address. "We should try to trace this."

"We can't put one of our guys on this. How would we explain what the message means or how it's connected to the missing girls?" I ask.

Zack's already typing away. "The registrant information is marked private."

I dial Simon back.

"He came. I gave him your message."

"I may need you to trace who owns a privately registered domain," I say without preamble.

"Why, aren't you a little minx," he teases. "My mother warned me about girls like you."

"We're hoping it can be traced to Lamont," I continue. "If we can figure out where their email communications are coming from, all the better—drinkfromthesource .com."

Simon's tone turns serious. "Do you have any emails from them?"

Zack hears the question and chimes in, "We need to get Craig to respond to this written invitation. Say he's interested. It will buy us some time. And when they respond to his email we'll have more information to run a trace."

"Are you kidding?" Owen says. "Craig responded the instant he received the damned message. Evan's with him, trying to talk him down. I'll call and see if he's received a response." Owen dials, then hangs up. "Straight to voice mail."

"Meanwhile, I'll see what I can do. I'll call you back when I have something," Simon says before hanging up.

"Try Evan," I suggest. "We're going to need Craig's cooperation. If we can't pinpoint where they're currently holding the girls, then the next best thing would be to find out the time and place of the auction. They're bound to be present, don't you think?"

Owen nods. "No one's going to fork over the kind of money they're sure to be demanding without testing out the merchandise." His phone chimes. Owen scans the screen, then starts to type. After a moment, he sends the message and looks up. "That was Evan. Whatever your plan is, it can't include Craig. Evan says Craig's sire just showed up. Pissed. He's placing Craig in restoration. Hopefully he hasn't taken him yet."

Everyone in the room falls silent. Restoration is an arcane form of discipline—or torture, depending on one's perspective. Ironically, the end result is usually far from restorative. Vampires who survive the period of isolation and encasement in silver usually end up irreparably broken.

"Maybe Kallistos can intervene? Surely he can't condone such measures." I dial his number.

Rose clears her throat and then ever so slightly shakes her head.

"What?" I ask her.

I get a disapproving look. "You should not ask it of him."

"Because?"

Her lips press into a thin line. "It pains him to say no to you, but he will have to."

I dial anyway. The phone rings once. Twice.

This time he answers. "I'm on my way up. Getting into the elevator now." It's all he says before disconnecting.

Liz sidles up next to me. "You know. We don't necessarily need Craig. Any vampire around his same age would do. Owen would work and, hello, he's right here. A little DNA, a lot of mojo, no one would be the wiser."

Her suggestion alarms Rose. "No. You're not sending Owen to that auction."

Owen looks confused. "How could I go to the auction?" he asks.

But instead of answering, Liz holds her up hands. "I'm just saying it could be an option."

"We'll let Kallistos decide." Rose folds her arms across her chest, her tone conveying confidence he'll rule in her favor.

Owen looks back and forth from Rose to Liz. "How could I go the auction?" he asks again.

But the doorbell chimes and this time it's me who heads for the door. Not only do I want to fill Kallistos in, I want to make sure things are okay between the two of us.

The vampire who stands in the doorway looks nothing like the one I saw a couple hours ago. This Kallistos looks like he's just stepped off the page of the newest *GQ*. His charcoal gray suit is freshly pressed and paired with a cobalt blue shirt and silver-gray tie. The pale cast to his skin is gone, as is the weariness in his step. He looks strong, steady, powerful. His eyes are once again bright and piercing. His skin is radiant. He's fed, but not from me. Maybe from a bag. More likely from a willing human donor.

I feel a strange pang of . . . something. Guilt? Sadness? Jealousy?

I close the door behind me. "Are we okay?" I ask.

He reaches for the edge of my blouse, pulls it away enough to expose the place where his mark had been. "You tell me."

I step back. "How—"

"You thought I wouldn't feel such a thing? The removal of my mark? I feel all I'm connected to. It's one of the privileges. Sometimes one of the pains."

He cups my face in the palms of his hands and sweeps me into a long, slow kiss. I let him not only because Liz's words—about the wisdom of maintaining a relationship with Kallistos and the benefits of vampire sex—are ringing in my head, but because I can tell he wants it, needs it. So do I.

When he releases me, he steps back. "We have a lot to talk about," he says. "But not now, later. Now we must attend to other things. Rose is not . . . in favor of your plan. She feels it might endanger Owen. That he might once again become out of control."

The heat of my desire quickly becomes a flame of resentment. "She's already communicated with you? So I'm wasting my breath. Is that it? She's already pleaded her case." I hold up my cell phone. "It's really annoying that I have to rely on this and she has a direct line to you anytime she wants."

A vampire can't execute thrall outside of someone's presence. But some of the more powerful are able to communicate with or call out to their progeny. I've seen Kallistos do it before with Rose. They've had a lot of time to practice. They've been together for more than a hundred years.

Kallistos came across her at the Seabrook Sanitarium in Brighton in the late eighteen hundreds. He was meeting with a young doctor who claimed to have isolated the contagion responsible for vampirism. Rose had been a long-term resident and was about to lose a battle with consumption. It wasn't only her heart-shaped face and hollow green eyes that called to him. It was her refusal to accept death and her unflinching and unapologetic desire for eternal life. As it turned out, the doctor was an idiot who had been experimenting on some of the children—infusing them with the blood of half-starved, half-mad fledgling vampires. Kallistos killed the doctor, released the vampires, then turned Rose. She's been his most trusted and favored child since.

"You get other special privileges." His hands fall to my waist. He takes a step closer, lowers his voice. "Besides, I haven't made up my mind. I intend to hear you out and that has Rose worried. She knows you can be . . . persuasive." Kallistos reaches for the doorknob behind me. "And we need to see how Owen feels."

I stay his hand. "Do you think he can do it?"

The door opens. It's Rose. "Wouldn't it make more sense to continue this conversation inside? It's getting a bit tiresome, having to repeat everything the two of you say to Liz."

Zack's right behind her. "Evan just sent Craig's email

log-in, password, and IP address." He holds up his keys. "I'm going to get my laptop from the car."

Rose moves to let him pass.

Suddenly I'm stuck in the middle. Zack in front of me, Kallistos at my back. Under other circumstances, perfect fodder for a sexual fantasy—the vampire, the Siren, and the werewolf.

I swipe the keys from Zack's hand. "I'll get it." I don't have the time to indulge in foolishness. A happily-ever-after isn't in my future. And more important, if we don't pinpoint the location of these girls soon, they'll have no future at all.

I close the door to the Suburban, turn around, and run smack into Kallistos. The laptop slips from my hands. He manages to catch it just before it hits the ground.

"Didn't mean to startle you," he says, handing it back to me. "I decided it would be best to clear the air. Why'd you let him do it?"

I shrug. "What is your objection? That the mark is gone or that I let Zack remove it?"

"Must I pick one?"

"Letting you that close to me is not a good idea. Not for either one of us, and you know it."

His eyes dart away. "Would it have made a difference if I'd asked permission?"

"Honestly? I don't know."

He nods. "Fair enough."

After a moment of awkward silence, I sigh. "We'll have time to work through this later. Right now, I need to know if you're going to support our plan to use Owen. He's the best chance we have to rescue these girls."

"I know this is important to you. What matters to you, matters to me."

I lean against the SUV and search his eyes. "Don't you want to try to save them just because it's the right thing to do?"

He leans against the red Mustang in the adjacent spot, mimicking my posture. "Of course, but I must weigh the potential consequences. Like Rose, I'm not anxious to place Owen in this situation. He's mine to protect."

It's a sentiment he's expressed before, but this time the tone is different. Understanding dawns. "*You're* his sire. I always thought he belonged to Rose."

"It would probably be more accurate to say they belong to each other." He shakes his head. "Rose asks for so little. They fell in love. It was the eighties. Before they met, he'd had a heroin habit. He was a talented artist. Functional, when he wasn't fucked-up. When he was diagnosed with AIDS she came to me, asking for permission to turn him. I said no."

"And Rose respected that?" It was tradition for a vampire to request the sire's permission before taking on the responsibility of a progeny. But the custom, like so many other things in the supernatural world, was changing.

"Rose respects *me*. Whether human or vampire, I figured things wouldn't end well for Owen. At best he was going to be a burden. More likely, a severe liability that would eventually have to be dealt with."

"But then you changed your mind."

"Because Rose was heartbroken. As Owen began to slip away, so did she. She stopped feeding. I relented. Took on the burden."

"You did the right thing, despite the potential conse-quences." I hug Zack's laptop to my chest and start to head back toward the entrance to the building. "You're a romantic."

Suddenly he's in front of me, blocking my path. His expression is stern, his features hardened. "I'm not a ro-mantic. I gave up that foolishness the day I died. I'm selfish. I've grown used to having Rose around. I didn't want her to leave me."

I study him, trying to gauge whether he's telling the truth or feeding me a line of bullshit. I decide it doesn't really matter, at least not right now. What matters is that we might have both a lead and an avenue to follow up on it.

"Kal, these girls have families. They are young and vulnerable. They have lives, lives that are now in jeop-ardy because they volunteered to supply *your* vampires with blood—boutique blood."

"Okay."

"Okay what?"

He turns and heads for the entrance. "I'll let you use Owen. If he agrees."

"But only because he really *wants* to do it," I say as I hurry to keep up.

"That's right. And because I have a feeling it's going to lead me to Ford and Lamont."

I shoot him a sideways glance. "And to save ten young, blond virgins," I remind him.

He shrugs. "And that."

"That was totally unnecessary. You didn't need to ask Simon to help," Zack is saying as we enter Liz's condo.

"I'm telling you, I can make it look like we were checking Craig's email from his apartment."

"I'm sure you can," agrees Rose as she slips her cell phone back into her pocket. "But Simon lives for this kind of thing. Besides, we can't afford any slip-ups and you don't want to risk associating the Federal Bureau of Investigation with something so nefarious. Now, do you?"

Her bright green eyes are fixed on those of the six-foot-plus werewolf towering over her, but her attempt to compel him into compliance is met with utter failure.

Zack smiles wryly. "I told you already, Princess, you can't put me into thrall. I'm immune."

Hands on hips, Rose stomps her foot. "How are you doing that?"

I suppress a smile. Rose has no way of knowing Zack carries a talisman to protect him from thrall, a smooth, polished stone the size of a quarter. I'm sure it's in his pocket right now.

I feel Kallistos' hand at the small of my back. "Honey, I told you we shouldn't leave the children alone."

Zack snarls something unintelligible.

I hold up his laptop. "Where do you want it?"

Liz points to the dining room table. "How about you set up over there? I could use a cup of coffee. Anyone else?"

I raise my hand. Zack asks for a glass of water. By the time Liz returns with it, he's already intently typing. I look over his shoulder. "You in?"

"Almost. Here we go." He punctuates the last statement with a jab to the keyboard and then he leans back in the chair.

A list of emails begins to load within the in-box on the screen. I don't realize I'm holding my breath until I see one pop up from sales@drinkfromthesource.com. "Bingo!" It comes out in a rush of air.

Zack clicks on it.

The message is brief: *A car will pick you up tomorrow at sunset.*

"What time is sunset tomorrow?" I ask.

"Just after seven," Kallistos answers.

"We should try to trace the email."

After a few clicks, the nicely formatted email looks like one lengthy block of nondescript code.

The doorbell rings. Liz answers.

It's Simon.

"I'm just about to run a trace," Zack tells him.

"Wait! Wait!" Simon jogs over, pulling his laptop out on the way to the table. "Let's race!"

Within seconds both men are staring at their screens, hopeful, expectant.

"Oh man!" groans Simon.

Zack shakes his head. "Whoever is behind this made sure we couldn't track the location of the computer," he explains. "The email could only be traced as far as an anonymous open proxy in Russia."

"Looks like we're back to plan B," says Owen.

We all turn to look at him. Rose gently places her hand on his arm. "Are you sure you want to do this?"

Kallistos studies Owen for a moment, then answers for him. "He feels he owes Emma. For saving his life. And he wants to prove himself. To me. To you."

Owen nods. "I can do it."

Rose turns to Liz. "Sunset falls at eight minutes after

seven. Will that be enough time for you to work your magic?"

"That depends on how quickly we can pull all of the ingredients together." Liz makes her way over toward the entry, stopping at the edge of the black-and-white area rug we'd all walked across.

She waves her hand gracefully. *"Alka awatum."*

A grimoire, huge, old, and familiar to me from when it had been her grandmother's, materializes like a wisp of smoke from under the carpet and takes form in her hands.

Rose turns to Simon. "You know how you're always complaining that your comic book collection is outgrowing your apartment? Well, there's your solution."

The leather-bound volume is now open on the table. Liz quickly turns to one of many dog-eared pages. "It's been several years since I've done this spell. I'll need some unusual ingredients."

I peer over her shoulder, curious. What I see on the pages brings a hundred questions to mind. But Liz is deep in thought, running a finger over a list that looks to me like gibberish.

"Some of these things I have," she says after a moment. "Vervain, mandrake root, almond oil, and the beeswax candles—one black and five red. I can get those from my condo. We need some of Craig's DNA. Hair would work nicely."

"Zack and I will take care of that," I say. "Evan's still at Craig's, right? We just need the address."

Liz continues absently, either ignoring or not hearing my comment. "Poplar leaves. Twenty or so should do it. I know of a nursery in Vista that's sure to carry poplars, although there might be another one closer."

Zack starts to click away on his keyboard. "Checking."

"Frankincense resin," she murmurs, looking up. "Anyone know a local priest?"

Simon raises his hand. "My brother." He pulls out his cell and begins to dial. "We're supposed to meet for breakfast tomorrow. I'll ask him to bring some. How much do you need?"

"Four or five good-sized pieces. It's the quality that's most important. They must be translucent, no black or brown impurities," adds Liz.

Simon nods. "It's rolling into voice mail. I'll leave a message."

"Maybe you should call back and speak to him in person," I suggest. "It's kind of an odd request."

Simon waves me off. "He's my brother. He's used to odd requests."

Zack's on the phone, too. Speaking in hushed tones. "They have a poplar at Anderson's Nursery. It's just a few miles from here."

"Owen and I can run and get it. I have the truck," says Rose.

Rose climbing into the cab of a pickup wearing her crinoline and taffeta? This I have to see.

Liz is looking now at Kallistos. "I'm afraid this last item is going to require someone with your special skills. And we can't wait until nightfall."

He nods. "Let's hear it."

"We need a three-horned chameleon, also referred to as a Jackson's chameleon. A male."

He crosses his arms in front of his chest, a smile tweaking the corners of his mouth. "And when I find this chameleon, just how do I substantiate it's a male?"

Liz grins back. "The ones with the three horns are male. The last time I did this spell I . . . um . . . borrowed one from the San Diego Zoo."

"So, I'm supposed to walk into the zoo in broad daylight and then walk out with a chameleon in my pocket?" he asks.

"Or you could just ask your pal Paul to do it," Zack interjects with more than a touch of sarcasm. "I hear he's been unexpectedly freed up from his last assignment."

I elbow him in the ribs. Thankfully, Kallistos doesn't rise to the bait and everyone else ignores the gibe.

"No. That won't work." Liz grabs her jacket off the back of one of the dining room chairs and starts to slip it on.

"No?" Kallistos' arms are still crossed. "And why not?"

"It's going to be too big to slip into your pocket."

Kallistos is frowning now, which makes us all smile. Suddenly I realize Liz is heading for the door.

"Where are *you* going?" I ask.

"To pick up a fifth of Ketel One."

I glance down at the list of ingredients. "You need *vodka* for the spell?"

She shakes her head. "No. The vodka's for me. I have a feeling I'm going to need it. Come on." She claps her hands like a schoolteacher rounding up errant students. "You all have your assignments." She checks her watch. "Let's get moving."

CHAPTER 19

Craig's place is in the downtown area, not far from Evan's condo. It happens to be around the corner from the former site of Barbara Pierce's lab. Zack is driving, so I have the opportunity to scrutinize the building's exterior as we go by. No outward sign of the blast that destroyed it remains.

"Looks like a brand-new building."

Zack frowns. His shoulders tighten. His grasp on the wheel becomes firmer. I know what he's thinking, that if it weren't for Kallistos, there wouldn't have been anything to repair in the first place. I focus once again on the view. The streets are dotted with Padres fans dressed in the requisite blue and orange. They're heading toward Petco Park, which is just a few blocks away.

I point to the parade. "Padres are playing this afternoon. We might have trouble parking," I say.

All I get from Zack is a "Hmm."

He makes one final right turn, then pulls into a loading zone. He shuts off the engine to the SUV, then rolls down his window. A GO-4 three-wheel scooter heads for us, a parking enforcement officer inside. Zack holds his badge out the window and waits for her approach.

"We're here on official business," he says smoothly. "We shouldn't be more than thirty minutes."

The attendant looks up. I can tell from the expression on her face it's not the badge that makes her nod and smile. It's Zack. I turn away to hide a grin. When the attendant moves on to the red pickup in front of us, I give his arm a playful jab.

"What?" he asks.

I point to the attendant who has emerged, ticket book in hand. She can't resist a glance back at us before focusing on the meter.

"The Armstrong charm wins out again."

Zack sniffs.

Our destination is across the street, but Zack makes no move to get out of the car. Instead, he turns in his seat to face me.

"Before we go in, we need to talk."

"About?"

"This mission. Your vampire. The thousands of different ways he could screw this up," he says. "Those girls are nothing more than a commodity to Kallistos. I refuse to be blindsided by him again."

"I get it. You don't trust him."

"What you don't seem to get is that neither should you. Your judgment is clouded where he's concerned. Your feelings for him—"

"I don't have *feelings* for him."

"Right, I forgot. You just let him fuck you."

The bitterness in his tone cuts me to the quick. I can't give in to the hurt. If I do, I'll unravel. "I'm a Siren, Zack.

Sex doesn't hold the same meaning for me that it does for you. It doesn't hold any meaning. It's . . ." All I have. All I'll ever have. "Never mind."

He looks away. "Lie to yourself all you want. What we share isn't about sex. And it isn't meaningless. Maybe that's what it is that terrifies you. Why you feel safer with Kallistos."

"I don't—"

"Don't bother denying it. I can smell your fear of me. It's suffocating, intoxicating . . . confusing. I don't understand it." He waits a beat. When it becomes clear I'm not going to respond, he points to my neck and asks, "How did he take it, by the way?"

I shrug, grateful for the change in subject. "Surprisingly well. You could have told me he'd sense the removal of the mark."

"I didn't know." He seems to ponder the idea. "Normally the connection goes both ways. Although not necessarily to the same degree."

"Like between Owen and Kallistos?"

"Yeah. What about when the mark was severed? Did *you* feel anything?"

I feel heat rise to my face. "Only you."

Suddenly I'm back in that bathroom with Zack, enveloped in his passion. His mouth on my neck. His fangs tentatively grazing my skin. His cock pressing into my backside.

"Nothing of him? Are you sure?"

Zack's nostrils flare. I'm certain he senses my desire— desire not for Kallistos.

"I'm sure."

I close my eyes and hope he'll let it go, as he's done so

many times in the past. Instead he reaches out, cupping my cheek in the palm of his hand. I feel my breath hitch, my heartbeat quicken. I feel him move closer. Know his mouth is hovering over mine.

"You know you are driving me completely insane." His thumb is stroking the side of my cheek.

The warmth of his breath feathers across my lips. The sound of my own blood rushes in my ears. He's waiting for something. A sign. A signal. An invitation.

It doesn't come. It can't. I keep my eyes shut tight, my shoulders rigid. If I relax, if I look into his eyes, I'll be lost.

We'll both be.

After a moment, Zack pulls away, placing distance between us. "I smell both your desire and your fear. I don't understand it. When this is over, when the girls are safe, you're going to explain it."

I release a breath, open my eyes.

He shoots me a sideways glance. "Assuming I survive."

For the first time, the gravity of what we're about to undertake begins to settle in. Kallistos is older than Lamont. It never occurred to me that Lamont might best Kallistos. That any vampire could best Kallistos. And that if Lamont does, Zack would surely be a target of his wrath.

"And if I don't," he continues, "you're going to do whatever it takes to save those girls. Can I count on you?"

I draw a breath. "Always," I reply.

Zack continues. "We aren't going to have long to prepare for what's to come. Kallistos is cooperating because he sees this as an opportunity for revenge—a chance to get rid of Ford and Lamont. Let the vampires fight one another. We go for the girls."

I touch the Glock at my waist. Then drop my hand.

Zack notices.

"These guns aren't going to cut it against a room full of vampires, are they?" I ask. "We're going to need . . . something else."

That makes Zack smile.

"You have a plan."

"Damn straight. Let's go get us some DNA. We have another stop to make."

"What for?"

"The something else."

It's then that I notice Evan across the street, leaning against the building. The ground floor contains a sandwich shop, a dry cleaner's, and a barbershop. Above the businesses are five floors of residential apartments. Zack and I exit the SUV and head across the street. Evan tosses a set of keys in our direction as we approach. Zack plucks them out of the air.

"Fourth floor, unit four hundred and six. His sire's gone," he says. "Don't know when he'll be back. Don't know *if* he'll be back. I tried to reason with him."

"But it's his call," finishes Zack. "We can't do anything for Craig." His words now are directed at me. A warning.

"It's a stupid call," I add before heading for the door. "I realize Craig's sire has the right to punish him as he sees fit. I don't have to like it."

Evan reaches out for my elbow. "But you'll abide by it?" His eyes dart from Zack to me and back again.

Zack nods, his expression grave.

"For now," I agree. "See you back at the condo."

The entryway is nothing more than a hall—mailboxes on one side, elevator at the end. I punch the call button. We don't have to wait. The doors open right away. We step inside, face front, and in short order begin our ascent.

A sign on the fourth floor directs visitors who are looking for apartments 401 through 405 to the left, 406 to 410 to the right. We head right. Music spills out from a unit down the hall. I can feel the heavy bass through the floor. At the same time, my nostrils are assailed by the smell of garlic. I sniff the air. Zack tilts his head toward the door marked 407. The offender is right across the hall from our vampire. I wonder whether the odor is what drove Evan out of Craig's apartment. And whether this is deliberate. Does the occupant know or suspect that his neighbor is a vampire?

Once Zack unlocks the door and we step inside, I realize the odor is not what drove Evan out. A wooden casket sits in the middle of the living room. At least I assume it's made of wood. It's wrapped so heavily in silver chains that I can't tell for sure. The whimpering coming from within it is faint, barely discernable. I edge closer. Zack doesn't follow. When I look back over my shoulder, his back is to the wall. Sweat is beading on his forehead. I'm reminded that Weres have just as much of an aversion to silver as vamps do.

"The proximity to the silver is weakening him," Zack says. "My guess is what's out here is meant to be a deterrent. To remind anyone inclined to execute an impulsive rescue of the fate that would await."

He's looking at me, his last words pointed as a barb. Another warning.

I move closer. It's not just one chain wrapped around the coffin. There are dozens. My eyes scan the intricate pattern, taking in the various padlocks.

"We aren't here to interfere with vampire politics. You said you'd abide by the decision for now," Zack reminds me yet again.

"Well, my now is short. I've moved on to the next moment and I'm not finding this one quite as agreeable." I pull out my cell phone. "This is barbaric. You saw how Kallistos reacted to what Barbara Pierce did. I can't believe he would condone this."

I dial the phone.

Kallistos answers on the first ring. "That took longer than I expected."

"Do you know what Craig's sire is doing to him?" I ask.

There's no hesitation. "Yes. You're not to interfere."

"But—"

I'm wasting my breath. He's already hung up.

"And you thought the news of me obliterating his mark went well," Zack says.

"Shut up."

I kneel down, lay my hands over the top layer of chains, and tug. They don't budge.

"If you free him, his sire will merely track him down and kill him."

I put my back into it and give the chain another tug. "Wouldn't that be better than this?" I feel Zack's hand on my shoulder. I shrug it off. I'm fueled by fury now. It doesn't matter that he won't help me, that Kallistos won't help me. That I'm on my own in this. In life. Tears sting my eyes. The words pour out. "Endless torture? Being trapped here . . . forever. Alone. Bound by a vindictive, unforgiving bitch!"

I feel a crackle in the air. A spark of charge as I yank once more. A wind is rising up within me. This can't happen. I know I need to contain it. Zack is too close, the potential consequences too dire. Yet I feel the push. I want to ride the sensation of my rage.

"Emma!"

Zack's strong arms wrap around me. He tilts my chin up. Blue eyes meet mine for an instant. Then Zack pulls me closer, dips his head. His nose nuzzles the place where he'd bitten me just hours before. He swipes it with his tongue. Once. Twice.

I feel the tension dissipate. Such a close call.

Then Zack is murmuring into my ear. "You aren't alone."

CHAPTER 20

Zack took care of getting the DNA sample from Craig's hairbrush. It's tucked safely into an evidence bag in my pants pocket. We're on Highway 8 heading west and an accident ahead has slowed us to a crawl. I'm a bundle of nervous energy, body taut from the frustration of having to leave the vampire trapped and in agony.

My fingers drum the dash as I crane my neck trying to see around the long line of cars.

"Damn it! Of all the times to be stuck in traffic."

"It's opening up," Zack replies, calmly.

He's right. I can see the cars beginning to move in the distance. The bottleneck has cleared. As we take the West Mission Bay Drive exit, I see three cars pulled over to the side of the road. It looks like a minor fender bender. No one injured. No need to stop to render assistance, thankfully.

Not so thankfully, I recognize where we're going.

"We're heading to your place?"

Zack nods.

"To pick up . . . ?"

"Body armor. Night-vision gear. Ammo. And Betty."

"Betty?"

"Sweetest custom tactical you'll ever see."

"You named your rifle Betty?" I can't help myself, laughter breaks through my shell of anxiety and bubbles out. "Why do men insist on naming things—cars, guns, their junk?"

Zack shakes his head. "Couldn't tell you. Although I can say that Mr. Peebles objects mightily to the term *junk*."

"Mr. Peebles?" Now I'm laughing so hard I can hardly breathe and barely see. "Mr. Peebles?"

"I'm pretty sure laughing at a guy's . . . junk . . . constitutes harassment." He's grinning from ear to ear.

I try to catch my breath. As soon as I can manage it I say, "It's just I would have thought you'd pick something more, I don't know, manly—like Conan, Thor . . . Hugh Jackman."

"Wolverine? Seriously?"

By the time we pull into Zack's driveway, we're still both in hysterics. Our moods much lighter. His sobers instantly, however, when a man dressed in low-riding black jeans and a dark hoodie emerges from the tropical landscape to the right of the driveway.

"Wait here," he says.

My hand moves to my gun. I unsnap the holster.

"He's friend, not foe," Zack assures me before popping open the door.

I sit in the car. The guy's back is to me. I can't see his face. I can't see Zack's either, for that matter. The man in the hoodie is blocking my view. He's as tall as Zack, maybe a bit taller. The conversation is brief. They shake hands. Then the stranger disappears, melting back once again into the lush landscape of the tropical garden. A large black duffel bag is tossed out onto the drive. It lands at Zack's feet.

"What the — ?"

Zack gives me the thumbs-up.

I bolt from the car.

He picks up the duffel and hoists it over one shoulder. "Come on, you've got some early Christmas presents to unwrap."

I follow him into the house.

"So, Santa's gone gangsta? Who the hell was that?"

"A ghost." He drops the bag onto the dining room table and unzips it. "Take off your shirt."

"Huh?"

He pulls out a black vest and holds it up.

"You bought me body armor?"

"We need to make sure it fits."

I remove my jacket and hang it over the back of one of his dining room chairs. Next I pull my blouse free of my slacks, unfasten the cuffs, and start on the buttons.

"This is the best," he begins to explain as he pulls apart the various Velcro fasteners. "It weighs less than our FBI-issue Kevlar. Provides almost sixty percent more coverage than the traditional ten-by-twelve hard plate. Plus, it's flexible. So you'll be able to move easier. Best of all, it's kick-ass effective. I unloaded a magazine from an AK-47 into it from under twenty feet. Not a dent."

I slip off my blouse and turn around. He helps me slide on the vest, then spends a minute adjusting the straps. The neckline is higher than normal, the coverage between neck and shoulder more substantial. He runs his hands across my back, down the sides.

"Turn around?"

I do, then hold out my arms. "How do I look?"

Zack reaches back into the bag and pulls out a black knit turtleneck sweater and watch cap. "To complete the ensemble. Does the size for the sweater look right?"

"Yeah." I slip it on over my head. It gets hung up on a hairpin. "Crap. Help?"

"Be still," he says, sliding his hand in through the neck opening.

Zack finds the offending hairpin and removes it. The sweater slides on smoothly. It fits perfectly. My hair, however, is now a disaster.

I fish out the remaining pins, pocket them, run my fingers through my hair to smooth out the tangles, then draw it into a knot at the top of my head.

Zack picks up the duffel. "The other stuff we need is upstairs."

"There's more?" Curious, I follow him up the stairs, running my hands over the breastplate of my new body armor through the thin sweater. "Can a vamp's fangs penetrate this?"

He doesn't bother to look back. "In a combat situation, you don't want to let a vamp close enough to find out. Fangs are the least of our worry. A vampire can pull either one of us limb from limb."

We're in his bedroom now. Or, more accurately, he's in the bedroom. I seem to be stuck at the threshold. It hasn't changed a bit. On the far side is a set of double French doors. Hanging over them are cream dupioni curtains. They're closed now, but I know from prior experience that just on the other side is a balcony that offers a breathtaking view of the ocean—a balcony we'd once made love on.

Zack's disappeared into the closet. I can hear him rummaging around. "Can you hold this bag?" he asks after a moment.

I walk around the dark walnut king-sized sleigh bed and past the fireplace. I try not to remember how smooth and cool the sheets felt. How sublime the warmth from Zack's body. I pause to examine the candles on the mantel. A layer of dust covers them, but I can still smell the vanilla and orange, cinnamon and ginger. I can still remember how the glow from the flames filled the room and danced across our naked bodies as we'd writhed in pleasure.

"Emma?"

I shake loose the image. "On my way."

I step into the closet. It's bigger than my dining room. "Holy shit." But it's not the size that takes my breath away. It's what he's got inside. He's pushed his suits to one side. A portion of the wall has opened up to reveal a metal door. It's a room, about four by five I'd say, behind the fireplace and accessed from inside the closet. It's an arms room. Stacked floor to ceiling with racks of guns and shelves stacked with assorted magazines.

"Can you put those in the duffel?" he asks, pointing to the magazines he's piled on the floor.

"Well, when the zombie apocalypse comes, I know where to take cover," I say before kneeling down. I examine one of the magazines. "I take it these aren't standard issue?"

He tosses out a vest that looks just like mine, only

much larger. "Not hardly. Hollow point, wooden nose. Upon impact it expands into a six-petal configuration releasing the silver inside. One shot to the heart. Poof."

"Poof?"

He points. "These four smaller magazines will fit our Glocks. The others are for my rifle."

Then he leans out, hands me a pair of what looks like strap-on night goggles.

I put them on, adjusting the head strap. "Resistance is futile."

Zack pulls the goggles off and tosses them into the duffel. "Personally, I find you more irresistible without the combat gear."

I frown. "It was a *Star Trek* reference."

"I know. Emma, meet Betty."

It's only then that I notice the rifle in his hand.

I reach out and run my fingertips over the long smooth barrel. "Sniper rifle?"

"McMillan TAC-50."

Once again, the enormity of the situation begins to weigh on me. "If they have ten girls, we can bet there'll be at least ten bidders. Plus Lamont, a few guards. Zack, we could be up against at least a dozen vampires."

He pulls a metal case out of the room, then closes its door and begins to put everything in the closet back into place. "That's about what I'm figuring. We won't know for sure until Owen gets in there."

I nod. I think about the odds. I think about Zack. He's strong. He's a warrior. A supernatural warrior. But he's mortal. I step forward and place my hand on his chest. The heat from his flesh is warm. I can feel it along with the pounding of his heart through the cotton of his shirt. I search his eyes.

"Tell me we're going to succeed."

"We're going to succeed." He says it with conviction. "We're going to get those girls out safely."

His reassurance isn't enough. I want to know he's going to be safe, too. For months I've sacrificed in order to ensure his safety, yet here we are.

"You weren't wrong," I say.

He looks confused. "About?"

"What we have. It isn't meaningless, and it does scare me."

For a long moment, neither of us moves.

Finally Zack nods. "Well, that's a start."

I nod, too. "If we're going to take it any further, we both need to come back from this. You hear me?"

Zack smiles. "Don't die. Check."

CHAPTER 21

Kallistos is waiting at Liz's condo when Zack and I get back. He doesn't look pleased to see the two of us together, even though he knew we would be. Perhaps he senses residual feelings from an emotional afternoon.

Zack pays him no mind. Rather, he heads straight for Simon, handing him the metal case he retrieved from his closet. "I trust you can handle communications?"

"Easily from my office." Simon throws open the latches and peers inside. He pulls out the earpieces and begins to examine them. "Awesome! Can I keep these?"

Zack takes them back. "No. My toys."

Simon smiles, snaps the case closed, and hands it back to Zack. "Can't blame a geek for trying." He heads for the door. "I'll call you once I'm in my office and we can run some tests."

Simon's enthusiasm doesn't surprise me. The fact that Kallistos didn't return alone does. A woman is with him. Human, thirtyish, brown hair and eyes, tanned skin. She's dressed in the beige uniform of a zoo worker. On the floor at her feet is a cage. Inside the cage is a crouching chameleon, tail twitching nervously. It's a big thing, about twenty inches long, each eye rotating independently as it takes in its surroundings.

I peer at the woman, see her eyes are veiled. She's in thrall.

How like Kallistos. No breaking and entering for him.

"So what did you do?" I ask Kallistos. "Walk into the zoo and ask the first keeper you came across to fetch you a chameleon?"

"Of course not," he answers peevishly. "This is Joan Arden. Head of the Reptilia Department. Did you honestly think I was going to try to steal a creature like this?"

Joan stirs at the mention of her name, but says nothing.

I shake my head. "So why does she think you needed a chameleon?"

"I told her it's for an educational program. Then I merely suggested she get me one and come along for a ride. Naturally, she complied. When this is over, she and the chameleon will be brought back to the zoo. Neither will remember a thing."

His last words are said with a hint of humor. I find myself smiling. Kallistos is nothing if not enterprising.

I look around. "Where's Liz?"

"Right here." She enters from the dining room. "Did you get the hair?"

The image of the coffin in Craig's apartment quickly erases the smile from my face. "From Craig's brush." I toss Liz the evidence bag before turning to Kallistos. "You'll be pleased to know he's suffering."

Kallistos doesn't flinch. "It pleases me to know with assurance he won't be draining another co-ed tonight.

You may not like it or understand it, but a sire chooses his children and is responsible for them, as well as their actions." His eyes drift to Owen and Rose. "And not merely for a decade or two. Doling out discipline isn't only a sire's right, it's his or her obligation."

"What's happening to Craig isn't discipline. It's torture." I expect him to rise to my ire, but he doesn't.

"We aren't human, Emma, we're vampire—capable of great violence, able to bring unspeakable death. Do you have any idea how many young women Craig has attacked? If he can't be controlled, well . . ."

The rest goes unsaid, but I understand the implication.

Rose is glaring at me. She warned me to leave this alone. Said that Kallistos wouldn't intervene. But I didn't want to believe her. I'd been picking at this scab long enough. It's an argument I can't win and maybe one I have no right to insert myself into the middle of. I don't know what my relationship with Kallistos will be like when this is over, but I know it will be changed. I knew it the moment I allowed Zack to remove Kallistos' mark. The way he's looking at me now, he feels it, too.

Finally, to break the long moment of silence between us, I turn to Liz. "What now?"

Liz gestures to the woman to bring the chameleon and to the rest of us to follow her. I hurry to catch up with Liz. She's crossed through the dining room and out a side door. I know the layout of her condo—in addition to a large patio in front, there's this smaller, more private flagstone patio in back. Usually it holds plants and a couple of comfortable reading chairs. Today, a table and a small daybed have been placed side by side.

"What will you do with the chameleon?" I ask when she's had the woman place the cage on the ground. "I trust she won't be bringing a dead reptile back to the zoo."

Liz laughs. "No. It will be returned completely intact, horns and all. The chameleon will act as a channeler between Craig and Owen. It is its nature, after all, to adapt its coloration to whatever message it receives from its brain. The spell will modify the message."

She asks Kallistos to take the woman back to the living room. When he returns, she shuts the door. Seven of us gather around the table: Kallistos, Zack, Rose, Evan, Owen, Liz, and I.

Owen looks at the items arrayed on the table. "What is all this?"

Liz touches each item in turn: "Incense to purify. Vervain weakens your natural resistance so that you can accept the spell. Mandrake root is a hypnotic. It will allow you to relax. Almond oil is an anti-hepatotoxicity, prevents organ damage. The poplar leaves and frankincense offer healing abilities."

Owen doesn't look assured. He picks up the vervain, a dense cluster of small purple petals. "Seems like a lot of things to prevent damage. How sure are you that I'll come out of this in one piece?"

Liz raises her eyebrows. "I'll be frank. I've worked this spell just once before." She looks at me. "But it's the same one I would have used on Sarah and Emma if our plan to trap Asa had worked. You know I would never do anything to put Emma in danger."

Owen nods, then brightens. "This sounds like something out of an episode of *Charmed*."

Liz waves him off. "Puh-lease. *Charmed*. Honey, stand back. You're about to see some *real* magic."

Owen takes Rose's hand and lifts it to his lips before sighing. "Okay, let's do this."

Liz tells Owen to lie down on the daybed. Rose starts to sit beside him, but Liz waves her off.

"You cannot touch him," she says kindly. "It might interfere with the transference. You must join the others near the door."

Owen gives her a reassuring smile and Rose moves with a swish of long skirts to stand beside me.

I've seen many spells cast over my long existence — magic both black and white. I trust Liz with every fiber of my being. Still, something about using powerful magic makes me uneasy. We're about to reorder nature. Change Owen at the very core of his being.

Liz has a small hot plate on the table. Steam rises from an iron pan. She lights an incense stick, waves it around the area, and places it still burning in a holder. She takes the beeswax candles, the five red ones, and places them around the daybed. The black one she puts near the chameleon's cage. She anoints Owen's forehead with the almond oil, drips a drop onto the chameleon's back. The lizard snaps up at her through the wire of the cage. Its tongue springing with lightning speed.

One by one she adds bits of the herbs and leaves into the simmering pan. She's murmuring in a language I recognize as early Greek. This is truly an ancient spell. With a start, I realize it may even be one of Demeter's. She was a chthonic deity in whose shrine people often hid tablets appealing for aid. But she was also capable of working powerful magic. My presence here proves that.

At the same time these thoughts wash over me, I'm hit by the fragrance of jasmine. Demeter's favorite. I look around to see whether anyone else is affected. All eyes are still on Owen and Liz. Is this a message to me? Is Demeter granting her blessing? Is she pleased that her magic is still being used and for this purpose?

I don't know whether to be reassured or frightened but it's too late to stop the spell now.

Liz is stirring the mixture in the pan with the poplar twig. The last ingredient she adds is the bit of Craig's hair.

A hiss emanates from the simmering brew. Steam rises, becoming a dense fog that seeps over the pan and onto the floor. It surrounds Owen and the chameleon. Owen's eyes are closed, his body relaxed. The chameleon becomes agitated, twitching in the cage, its tail whipping from side to side. It turns bright red, from snout to tail. Then the fog encloses it and it's hidden from view. Owen, too, as the fog seems to solidify, encasing him in a rigid cocoon.

I gasp. We all do, but Liz continues to intone her ritual, still stirring, still focused on the fog as it settles over both Owen and the chameleon. It seems like an eternity before slowly, the haze melts away. First from the chameleon, whose color has returned to normal. Once again, he snaps at his cage.

Then, gradually, the image of the daybed and the still figure on it becomes clearer.

Liz is silent now. We press forward.

I hear Zack's breath hitch.

No longer is it Owen lying motionless before us. It's another man, red haired and thin mouthed. The jeans he's dressed in, Owen's jeans, ride up his ankles. They are short by a good three inches.

We are looking at the young man we left in a casket at Craig's apartment. We are looking at Craig. At first I think something must have gone terribly wrong. The prone figure before us displays no evidence of life. But maybe it's not supposed to just yet. I think about what Kallistos is like when he goes into stasis, or sleep. He's still, unmoving. I wait for Owen to wake, to stir. He doesn't. I look up at Liz, her lips pressed together in a thin line. She's concentrating. Worried.

"Liz? Is he—?" I ask haltingly.

Rose beats me to Owen's side. She takes his hand. "Why isn't he waking up?"

But before Liz can answer, Owen's chest heaves. He sits straight up. "Did it work?" He looks around at us. "I guess from the looks on your faces, it did."

Rose flings her arms around his neck. "This is a good look for you," she says, laughing. "I like you as a red-head."

Owen grins. "Anybody got a mirror? I'd like to check myself out."

Kallistos steps between them. "Okay. Enough. We've got work to do. Owen, we need to get you to Craig's apartment in time for the car to pick you up."

"I can drive him," Rose says.

"No."

Both Kallistos and Owen answer in unison.

"Zack can take him," Kallistos continues in a tone that brooks no argument.

I register the fleeting look of surprise on Zack's face. He checks the time, palms his keys. "Actually, that's a good idea. We should get going," says Zack. "Especially if we're going to get back here in time to suit up and test the communication setup. We still have a lot to do yet."

"I could go tonight, too," says Rose. "With you, Zack, and Emma."

Kallistos softens when he sees the concern on her face. He reaches for her hand. "Don't worry. We will be fine, and in constant contact. You are my eldest living child, my Queen Regent. You must be kept safe. You'll stay here with Liz and Evan."

Owen stands, takes Rose in his arms, and kisses her. A deep kiss full of promise. "I'll be back." He glances down. "Maybe we can try out this new body."

Rose grins. "I'll be waiting."

CHAPTER 22

Zack has been on the phone with Simon ever since he returned from dropping Owen a few blocks from Craig's apartment.

"Testing. Testing. One. Two. Three."

Suddenly, I can hear him through the earpiece I'm wearing.

"You're coming across loud and clear," says Simon. "Emma?"

"Yes?"

"Say something. How about: *Kallistos is nothing more than a plaything to me, Simon. It's you I really want.* Do it in a low, breathy voice," he says.

"I can hear you," replies Kallistos, his tone a blend of amusement and annoyance.

Simon claps his hands and then drums on the table. "Well, all righty, then. Nonmystical communications are up and functioning. What about the connection between you and Owen?"

Kallistos, who's sitting at Liz's dining room table, has traded in his suit for a pair of black jeans, a long-sleeved black shirt, and a leather jacket. "He's in the apartment. He's anxious and wondering if maybe he should wait outside instead."

"I think that's fine," I tell him. "Let's do what we can to help him manage his anxiety.

Kallistos nods.

My earpiece goes silent. Simon and Zack exchange a few more words over the phone; then Zack hangs up. He's commandeered the large flat-screen on the living room wall and has his computer hooked up to it. A map of downtown San Diego is displayed with a bright red blinking dot over Craig's apartment building.

"You put tracking on him before dropping him off?" I ask.

Zack shakes his head. "No. I thought that would be too risky. If I were Lamont, I'd have all of the bidders screened and blindfolded. I prepared Owen for that, blindfolded him and practiced on the way over to Craig's. He's a natural. Kallistos just has to relate what Owen is experiencing."

Liz places a tray of sandwiches on the table. Next to them are half a dozen bags of blood and a pitcher of iced tea. "I don't understand. If he's blindfolded, what will he be able to relate?" she asks.

Zack selects a ham and cheese. "Turns, stops, variations in speed. It won't be exact, but it will be close. You and Rose will be able to watch from here. We have another monitor in the van." He takes a bite of the sandwich and pours himself a glass of tea.

I'm too nervous to eat. I check the time on my cell. "Shouldn't the van be here by now?"

Zack puts down his sandwich and walks over to me. "He'll be here. Malcolm's a pro. Come here." He circles around me, lifts up the side of my sweater.

Kallistos watches, his eyes dark and dangerous.

Zack continues as if he is unaware of Kallistos' glare. "I want to tighten this strap."

He does. The sweater drops back into place over the vest. "That's better." He pulls what looks like a custom-made tactical double-draw shoulder holster from the bottom of the bag and holds it out to me like he would a jacket. "Slip this on. I'll help you adjust it." It crosses comfortably in back. Another strap snaps around my torso, keeping the weapons securely in place.

Zack hands me his Glock. "I'll have enough with my rifle."

"Thanks." I slip his gun into the left holster. Mine I slip into the right.

"No problem."

Zack takes another bite of his sandwich. He doesn't look at Kallistos, but he gives me a surreptitious wink. He's wearing a black T-shirt and cargo pants. Between bites of the ham and cheese he slips on his own vest and checks his weapon once again. His phone chimes. He glances at it. "Showtime."

Zack, Kallistos, and I are sitting in the back of an unmarked white panel van that's decked out with the latest in high-tech surveillance equipment. Malcolm is driving, the man who delivered my early Christmas present. He's yet to say a word. He's yet to look at us. He's focused on the road, on following orders, on otherwise being invisible—the perfect soldier. We've just pulled onto the 163 and are heading north. The space seems unbearably small. Zack is positioned in front of a console that contains a monitor. Kallistos is standing behind him, looking over his shoulder. The expression on his face is intent.

"They're curving to the right," he says.

Zack taps the screen. "They're going east on Highway 8. Have him tell you when he notices a change of speed and whether he can sense the direction."

Kallistos nods.

It's strange, watching Zack and Kallistos work together like this.

Seconds stretch into minutes.

"You were right about the mask. Right to prepare him," Kallistos says. Giving Zack the deserved compliment seems to cost him something.

"We could be in for a long drive," I say.

But Kallistos shakes his head. "No, they are slowing down. Owen thinks it's an exit, but he can't tell if they are going left or right. Feels like they're going straight. Maybe traffic just slowed down?"

"My bet is they took the Fairmont exit. It runs parallel to the highway. Let's see if he comes to a stop." Zack touches his earpiece. "Simon, can you start to pull up all of the nearby properties that contain hallowed ground?"

Kallistos holds up a hand. "Wait. He's come to a stop. They're turning left. I know where they're going." He pauses, takes a seat, points to a spot on the map. "The Mission Basilica San Diego de Alcala."

"How can you be sure?" Zack asks.

Before Kallistos can answer, Simon's voice echoes in our earpieces. "Yep. That's a good guess. It's the biggest piece of hallowed ground in the area and Kallistos knows it well."

Zack and I both turn to Kallistos. "Lamont must have heard about the tunnel system. He's using it to store the girls, avoid detection."

"A tunnel system?" I ask. "Under the mission?"

Kallistos nods. "The knowledge has been lost to most, but there's a network of tunnels underneath the church grounds. They were built after a night raid by the local Indians in 1775. Father Palou put me in charge of the planning. I know them like the back of my hand. Although it's been many decades since I've used them for anything."

I don't know who is the more surprised—Zack or me. "A priest put a vampire in charge of protecting the mission?" Zack finally asks.

Kallistos waves him off. "Long story."

One I'll have to remember to ask about.

"Point is, it's the perfect place to hide. Originally we built one entrance within the mission and an exit about a thousand feet away." Kallistos points to a spot on the map that looks to be deep in a nearby canyon. "The mission has since been rebuilt. The original access to the tunnels, here, in the canyon, was closed off."

Simon has been monitoring our conversation. Architectural drawings, photos of the mission's interior and exterior, and the most recent surveying plans are now popping up on the computer screen.

"So the entry point is gone?" Zack asks.

Kallistos shakes his head. "No. I built another. I used the tunnels during Prohibition, to stash booze. It's blocked by a sizable rock. Between the two of us, we should be able to move it. Perhaps I could now do it by myself. It's been many years. In any case, the entry is about two hundred and fifty feet from the circle."

"The circle?" I ask.

We've exited the highway, turned left onto Fairmont, and are now on Mission Road. Kallistos points to an apartment complex on the left. "Pull into that lot," he tells Malcolm. "We can go the rest of the way on foot." Then he turns to me. "The tunnels were built to be a fail-safe. A place the mission inhabitants could take refuge should another raid occur. Food and water were stored there. Midway between the mission and the exit, we carved out a half dozen or so rooms that opened onto a central circular space. My bet is they're holding the girls in one or more of those rooms."

We come to a stop. Kallistos wastes no time opening the door to the van. He jumps to the ground.

Zack follows.

Malcolm douses the van's lights. It's pitch-black. It's a waxing crescent moon and high, thin clouds dot the sky. I slip the night-vision goggles on. I don't have the biological advantage that Kallistos and Zack both have.

"You lead," Zack says to Kallistos. "Emma can follow. I'll take the rear."

Kallistos grows still. He holds up his hand. "Owen's mask has been removed. He is, as I suspected, in the circle. They've erected a staging area on one side that's about six feet above the ground. A long, narrow table has been set up. Seating for ten. White tablecloths, crystal glasses at each spot. Three vampires are already seated. Owen makes four." He pauses. "One of the three is unknown to him. The others are a pair of brothers who have been a pain in my ass for years. Lamont is there. So is Ford, along with a handful of other vampires who are talking with Lamont. Owen counts four. Guards, he suspects. Plus a human he doesn't recognize."

"A human?" I ask. "One of the girls?"

"No. A man. They are calling him Cheng. It's a common name among the Chinese, yes?"

"Yes," I agree.

"Are the vampires armed?" asks Zack.

Kallistos grows quiet again. Seconds later he answers. "Owen doesn't think so. I'm sure Lamont is confident he could handle any bidder who might get out of control. When we show ourselves, some of them might ally with Lamont against us. We must be prepared for that."

With that he's off, heading across the street with purpose, his long legs allowing him to quickly cover the ground. I'm a runner and in good physical shape, but I possess neither the speed nor coordination of a vampire or Were. My predatory powers exploit other physical attributes and, unfortunately, they'll be of little use over the next few minutes.

Kallistos disappears behind a clump of palms surrounded by lush underbrush. I try to keep up, but trip on a tangle of roots. Zack catches me and sets me right without breaking stride. We use the cover of the landscape to progress up the long drive that curves up to the mission and the supporting buildings behind and adjacent. It's uphill. I know I'm slowing them down and wonder, for the first time, whether they'd be better off without me. I push the thought aside.

I've thought long and hard about Zack's request. If it falls apart, if he and Kallistos don't survive, it will be up to me to get the girls out. The last time I released my powers within a group this large, the consequences were terrible because it's impossible to control the desires and needs of dozens. I know if I have to resort to using my gift to interrupt violence, emotions will be high, the results brutal. It would be easy to redirect the attentions of the humans. But the vampires, and especially Lamont, would pose a challenge. I've survived such an assault before. I would undoubtedly survive again. And I would heal, eventually.

Kallistos has stopped. I peek around him. Ahead of us is an expanse of manicured lawn surrounded by a fence. He points to the far side. "We want to reach the canyon on the other side of the fence. See any security cameras?"

"I'm not seeing anything," I answer.

"We're good," Zack agrees. "But stick to the fence line."

Kallistos wraps his arm around my waist. "Hold on," he says, softly.

Next thing I know, I am weightless. My feet have left the ground. For the briefest of moments I remember what it's like, to launch myself into the air. To take flight. Kallistos clears the fence with ease. He lands firmly on his feet, then gently sets me down on mine.

"You okay?" he asks.

I nod.

Zack lands next to me in a crouch, the strap of his gun across his chest, rifle on his back. His eyes glow in the dark, the silver-blue matching the color surrounding the sliver of moon now visible through the clouds. In an instant, he's on his feet, weapon back in his hands, ready for action.

We move, quickly and quietly along the chain-link fence. We don't have to jump this time, and for that I'm grateful. The terrain on the other side appears to be steep. We come to a gate, secured with a chain. Kallistos pulls on it, separating and breaking the steel links as easily as rotted thread. Then, a drop-off. Kallistos leaps down. The drop is twelve, maybe fifteen feet. He holds his arms up, as if he's prepared to catch me. I hesitate.

"Jump," Zack whispers in my ear. "Kallistos will catch you."

I do. Kallistos catches me in his arms, swings me to the ground.

My partner ties one end of a cable around the fence post, then takes the leap himself. This time his landing isn't quite as soft as mine. He lands, rolls. Momentum causes him to slide down the side of the canyon's ravine another twenty, maybe twenty-five feet.

"Use the cable," Zack says to me. "Ease yourself down the rest of the way to the bottom." The command is heard through the earpiece. It's as clear as when he was standing alongside me.

Now I understand why he insisted I wear gloves. I move swiftly, rappelling down hand over hand. Kallistos moves faster. Ignoring the cable, he propels himself past me, reaching the base before I've progressed more than a few feet.

"Four more of the bidders have arrived," he's saying. "A vampire from Los Angeles who has little sense and large political aspirations. A fairly young one from Mexico, sired by their current King. An older female vampire he recognizes from the San Francisco area. I'd considered hiring her once to create blends for the Emporiums. And . . . Moira."

"Moira? Who's Moira?" I ask when I reach the bottom.

"We have a history," he replies.

His answer tells me nothing. It piques my curiosity. Do I want to know her story? I shake my head to clear it. It's not important. Nothing is as important as rescuing those girls.

Kallistos heads for the San Diego River. It runs along the perimeter of the mission property and we begin to follow it.

Kallistos continues. "Owen has yet to see the girls. Lamont has explained each of the bidders will have the opportunity to sample the units before bidding commences."

Units? The word appalls me.

"That's what the glasses are for," Zack says. "He's conducting a blind tasting."

A shiver runs up my spine. I suppose the glasses mean the blood has already been extracted. At least the vampires won't be feeding directly from the girls. Perhaps Lamont's way to assure none of the vampires go rogue and drain a prize before paying for it first?

Kallistos stops abruptly and I almost walk into him.

"Do we wait for the others?" I ask.

"Lamont has informed the group that the other two are en route and fifteen minutes away. If we move now, we could have this wrapped up before they arrive." His gaze shifts from me to Zack. "I say we move now."

"How much farther is it to the entrance?" I ask.

Kallistos places his hand on a nearby boulder. It's waist-high on me and at least four feet wide.

My mouth gapes open. "That's it? When you said rock—"

"I told you it was sizable. Come." He motions toward Zack. "On three. One. Two. Three."

The boulder lifts. Rolls. Comes to rest. The two men stand back, casually brushing dirt from their hands as if they haven't just moved a boulder that must weigh a ton.

I step close to the opening. As Kallistos promised, he's given us direct access to the tunnels. It's a deep, dark hole. Kallistos passes me and descends, feetfirst, landing as lightly as a ballet dancer and motioning for me to follow. I look down. It's about ten feet to the ground and I don't trust if I jumped, I'd land nearly as gracefully.

Zack understands my hesitancy. He takes my hands and lowers me down. Kallistos' arms snake around my waist and he eases me the rest of the way. Zack follows with an agile leap of his own. The supernatural do have physical abilities to be admired.

It's dark and the air dense and stale. We set off, Kallistos using hand signals to point the way. If his recollection is correct, and I have no doubt it is, we have two hundred and fifty feet to go before reaching the circle. About thirteen minutes before the arrival of the two remaining vampires and whatever escorts will be coming with them.

CHAPTER 23

Kallistos moves with the silent grace of a panther through the tunnel. I follow. Zack brings up the rear. Suddenly Kallistos pauses, passing a hand over his face.

I fear Owen is saying something about the girls being harmed. "What is it?" I ask, my voice the barest of whispers.

Kallistos turns to face me. His eyes meet mine. With the help of the night-vision goggles, I see his lips move. I hear him through my earpiece. "They are preparing for the tasting. Carafes of blood are being brought out. Ten of them. The mood in the room is becoming frenzied. The two brothers and the prince from Mexico want to drink straight from the source, from the girls." A pause. Then, "Owen fears he might have to participate."

"Craig certainly would," Zack says. "If Owen doesn't, Lamont and his crew may get suspicious."

I sense Kallistos' hesitation and I understand it. Owen is in recovery. He's come so far. Encouraging Owen to drink straight from the source is like giving a heroin addict permission to shoot up just this once. I want to tell him that we'll all help Owen get through this. That it will be all right. That Owen can easily get back on track. But I can't give those assurances or make those promises. I can't guarantee Owen will come through unscathed, and we all know it.

I say the only thing I can. "We can't risk the operation."

Kallistos bows his head. "I already told him to go ahead."

"Has Owen seen the girls yet?" Zack asks.

Kallistos shakes his head.

My stomach clutches. We're once again on the move. At a slight fork in the tunnel, Kallistos bears right. He pauses for a moment at the base of a short flight of stairs. He's listening intently.

Zack reaches past me and grasps Kallistos' shoulder. He holds up one finger, tilts his head toward the route we've just abandoned. A guard is coming. The sounds of his footsteps drift through the tunnels. He's carrying a radio. Amid the intermittent static, a command comes across loud and clear. He's been ordered to open the entryway from within the mission itself. He'll be called again when the last of the bidders are five minutes out. Apparently Kallistos is wrong about it no longer being accessible.

Zack motions for us to stay back. I unsnap the catch on my holster and wrap my hand around the butt of my gun. Zack draws a wicked-looking wooden knife from a sheath at his thigh.

Kallistos wraps his arm around my waist, pulling me deeper into the stairwell. He continues climbing upward. I'm torn between staying to back up Zack and pressing forward to search for the girls. I close my eyes. Zack is capable. Saving the girls is my priority. Decision made, I follow Kallistos, my weapon now drawn.

Before I reach the top of the stairs, I hear the distant sound of a brief scuffle, followed by the brittle rustle of disintegrating flesh and bone—vampires turning to ash. Zack rounds the corner. He takes the stairs two at a time and catches up with us, a pile of clothing and the guard's radio in his arms. I heave a sigh of relief.

We've reached the top. Zack and I follow Kallistos into a chamber lit with torches. My skin crawls as I take in the surroundings. I remove the goggles and secure them to my utility belt. The room has been outfitted with ten cages. Small cages. Certainly not big enough for a woman or girl to stand. I touch the bars of one. My stomach turns, sickened by what the girls have endured and by the animals who have conspired to imprison them. This is where they've been kept. The cages are set on blocks. Each one has a water bottle inside. A bucket underneath. The smell of urine and human waste overcomes my senses. Nearby is a hose connected to a water supply and generator. Water drips from the end of it. Sections of the floor are wet. Did they use it to hose down the ground? The girls? In a corner, a heap of clothes lies abandoned along with purses and schoolbooks. A tennis racket leans against the wall.

Zack crouches down next to the assortment of skirts and blouses, jeans and sweaters. He buries his face in the pile, then scents the air. How he could possibly discern anything over the stench of filth, I'll never know. With haste, he sweeps the bundle of clothes from the dead vampire into the bottom of the pile.

An open door in the far corner of the room draws

Zack's attention. He moves toward it, his rifle in his hands and at the ready. The air is fresher here, and moving, indicating that either a door to the outside is somewhere close or that this area opens up onto the larger space Kallistos mentioned, the one where the tasting is set to take place. Either way, it's clear Zack's following a trail. He's following the girls' scents.

Zack crouches down low and moves through the doorway. An instant later, Kallistos follows. This time I bring up the rear. The vampire and the Were are waiting in the shadows, hunkered down behind a small outcropping of rock. I see a stairway to the right but I can't tell where it goes. For the moment, it's unoccupied. I take a slow, deep breath to clear my head, then cover the few remaining feet as quickly as I can. Voices drift up from below. I strain to listen. Something is said that causes a wave of laughter. Zack slides his cell phone from his pocket along with a USB cord. He plugs one end into the phone, pops what looks like a tiny cap on the other end. It's not a cap. It's a camera. The three of us huddle around the screen. We have a bird's-eye view of the room below.

The scene is much as Owen described to Kallistos. I can see now that the stairway to our right leads down to the bottom of a pit, the room Kallistos had called the circle. A stage has been erected. It's eight, maybe ten feet directly below us, six feet above the ground. A long table is in the middle, ten chairs on one side. Ten places. Each set with crystal goblets that sparkle in the light of dozens of torches.

If the time on Zack's phone is correct, we now have eight minutes remaining.

Of the eight vampires seated at the table, I recognize only Owen—or *Craig*—none of the others. When I glance at Kallistos, his eyes seem to be focusing primarily on one. A woman. Moira, I suspect.

Zack moves the camera ever so slightly, providing us a wider perspective. Four vampires stand at attention at the foot of the dais. In front of them, carafes of blood are set on a side table. Each carafe is labeled with a number.

The sound of someone clapping echoes through the chamber. "Our remaining guests should be arriving shortly. Soon, we'll begin pouring. Please refrain from sampling until everyone has arrived. Until then, we have a treat for you."

From around the back of the dais, the vampire speaking steps into view. He makes a dramatic entrance, face beaming. He's holding a large carafe in one hand, a glass filled with blood in the other. His appearance is greeted with a standing ovation from those at the table. I shiver in disgust.

"Lamont." Kallistos hisses the name.

"Welcome, my friends." Lamont's accent is softly Southern, his voice low and throaty. "You have been singled out among all our brethren to partake in a unique opportunity. After all, how often is it you find ten virgins gathered together in one spot? Especially here in Southern California?"

The bidders laugh.

Lamont moves to the head of the table. His gait is smooth, his gestures grand. Like Kallistos, he's tall and lanky. That, however, is where the similarities end. Lamont's hair is close-cropped and white-blond. In fact, he's dressed all in white—suit, shirt, tie. His skin is pale, drawn tight as if shrink-wrapped over prominent cheek-bones. But it's his eyes, heavy lidded, reptilian, and his lips, too full and colorless, that make his face appear more animal than human.

"I have fasted for a week," he proclaims, raising his glass. "Tonight we will feast!"

One of the vampires who have been standing at attention appears by his side. He takes the carafe from Lamont and begins to pour.

"A little something from my private stock to get the party going!"

Several of the vampires seated at the table lick their lips in anticipation as a generous pour is splashed into the goblets in front of them. Once the glasses are all filled, the server steps down off the dais and resumes his prior position.

Zack hands me the camera, moves onto his knees. He raises the rifle. Lamont is in his sight. Quick as lightning, Kallistos wraps his hand around the barrel. Zack glares at him. He'd had a clear shot. He could have taken Lamont out. Why didn't Kallistos let him? Is Zack right? Does Kallistos want Lamont for himself?

Something is happening below. It draws our attention.

A door opens. Ford and another man—I imagine the one they call Cheng—usher in the ten missing girls. They are barefoot, dressed in white robes, their hair wet and dripping, though none of them seems to notice. They have no idea where they are or what is going on around them. They don't even realize they've just been hosed down like horses after a race. Each and every one of their faces is completely blank, stamped with the thousand-mile stare of being in thrall as they line up in front of the stage, then kneel in the dirt. Julie, Sylvia, and Hannah are among them.

Lamont describes the *product* he is offering as if introducing a new kind of breakfast drink. The vampires around the table burst into applause, coos, and whistles. Several of the bidders stand in order to get a better look at the merchandise.

"I share my bounty with you now. I trust you will share yours with me later." He raises his glass. "Now, I know some of you may be uneasy. It could very well be your . . . first time with a virgin." He smiles down at the captives before turning his attention back to the bidders. "This is Kallistos' territory, after all, and he has strict rules about partaking from an unwilling source."

I feel Kallistos tense.

Lamont continues. "But we are vampire, are we not? Not even your rulers should prohibit an act that is as natural to us as—well—not breathing."

This time, the ripple of laughter is a little more subdued. For a brief moment, I hold out hope that mentioning their sovereign reminds these vampires of what they will face if Kallistos finds out what they're doing. But then I look at the faces around the table, and I realize they are too far gone. Drowning in lust and hunger. And not only for blood.

Lamont drains his glass, then dramatically throws it across the room. Shards rain down and ricochet off the wall behind the girls. They don't move or flinch even as the other vampires follow suit. Owen included. Whether he's playing a role or succumbed to the barbarism, I can't tell. Maybe I don't want to know. What I do know is that he's probably just tasted the most exquisite blood he's ever had and the battle raging inside must be tearing him apart.

I take advantage of the uproar. I'm watching the girls, immobile, unblinking as stone. In this state, they will be powerless to help themselves. We need a plan. I know of only two ways to break thrall. The vampire responsible can voluntarily release his victim. Or the victim is released upon the final death of the initiating vampire.

"Who's controlling the girls?" I ask Kallistos.

Kallistos answers through fangs. His expression hard. His body tense with rage. "Lamont."

"Then we take him out first," Zack says, handing me the camera. He brings his rifle once again to his shoulder.

"No. He's mine," Kallistos hisses.

Then he's gone. One second he's standing beside me. The next, he's launched himself over the wall.

CHAPTER 24

I drop the phone and camera, then draw both Glocks, mine and Zack's. They are loaded with bullets meant to take out vampires—hollow wooden points, with silver inside. Zack has already made short order of bringing down the four servers. I train my sight on covering Kallistos, who has landed squarely on top of Lamont.

The two vampires roll, then separate.

When Kallistos stands, he has something in his hands. Something he's pulled from the pocket of his jacket, a braided silver chain. It's about three feet long and half an inch thick. He unfurls it with a flick of a wrist. Like a whip, it wraps around Lamont's throat. Blood drips down the Southern King's neck, seeping into the collar of his pristine shirt.

The two brothers abandon their seats at the table. They leap toward Kallistos. I pick them off, first one, then the other. Their bodies explode in ash. The Prince from Mexico takes advantage and dives for the girls. Zack, however, has him in his sights. I blink and watch as a fine dusting of red powder falls on the heads of the captives.

They remain undisturbed, completely oblivious to the hell breaking out around them.

"I'll cover you. Protect the girls. As soon as the thrall is broken, get them out of here," shouts Zack.

I'm already on my way, racing down the steps. Cheng tackles me at the base of the stairs. We're close to the wall. Zack can't see us. Cheng is human, and unarmed. But he's several inches taller and a good fifty pounds heavier. I hear the sound of my guns as they skitter across the floor. The wall breaks my fall. I don't have time to think about the inevitable bruises. I push off and take aim. The steel toe of my boot connects with Cheng's balls.

He doubles over in pain.

I follow up with a roundhouse kick to the side of his head. The momentum carries him backward. He falls hard. Tries to get up. Can't. Probably because my boot is crushing his windpipe.

A distinctive scar runs the length of his left cheek. I have the feeling I've seen him before.

"Emma!"

I turn. Zack tosses me back my gun. He didn't come down the stairs. Like Kallistos, he must have jumped. And he's managed to subdue Ford, who is handcuffed to the bars of the door the girls passed through.

"Cuff them to one another," he shouts, pointing to Cheng.

As I drag the still-stunned Cheng across the floor, I see one of the remaining vamps dive toward Zack.

With barely a glance, he points and shoots. "Anyone else want to die? Again?" He jumps onto the dais where Lamont has fallen to his knees.

Owen is beside him, on his knees, as well. He holds out his hands to Kallistos. "Please, forgive us, Your Majesty."

"Yes!" cries the other male vampire. "Lamont tricked us. Lured us here under false pretenses."

"Liar!" Lamont's hands are at the chain around his neck; his feet scrabble on the floor seeking purchase. He struggles toward the vampires. "You came of your own free will!"

"No! He's wrong, Majesty," one of the females grovels, grasping at Kallistos' feet. "We would never—"

Kallistos shakes her loose. His voice bellows across the chamber. "Get out. I want the four of you out of my sight."

The female grasps the arm of the male vampire closest to her and they back away.

But Kallistos isn't finished. "Do not mistake that this is over. I promise you. It is not. Next time I lay eyes on you, you will wish I had ended it here."

Three are gone in a heartbeat. Only Owen hesitates, looking to Kallistos. Whatever message his sire sends, Owen nods in acknowledgment and obeys, following the others toward the tunnel.

Zack makes his way over to Lamont and Kallistos. "Don't think I've seen one of these before." He tilts his head toward the silver lariat. "Let me guess—the hooks on the inside are releasing silver into his system?"

Kallistos nods. "Along with a strong paralytic." He draws the chain tighter again.

As I approach the stage, I see the smoke rising up from Kallistos' hands, see that his skin is raw and blistering. Kallistos doesn't seem to notice. His gaze is fixed on Lamont. "It's over. Release the girls," he commands.

Smoke is rising up from Lamont's neck wounds. The silver hooks are biting into and burning his flesh. His movements are slowing. His breathing becoming calmer. His eyes, however, are still alert. They dart about the room, searching for allies. The two he has are chained and human. But a vampire doesn't live as long as Lamont has by giving up easily.

I check my watch. "Let's finish this and get out of here."

"Release the girls!" Kallistos demands. "I will not ask you again."

Lamont shakes his head, slowly. The defiance in his tone cuts like ice. "Why would I do that? Released from thrall, they will remember the details of their abductions. They might even be able to identify Cheng. We have been seen together. I have no desire to be drawn into a kidnapping conspiracy." His eyes narrow. His fingers pull ineffectively at the silver noose. "Of course, I could be persuaded. If you let me go."

"You have come into my territory and put my entire operation in jeopardy and I should let you go?" Kallistos' eyes flash in anger. "You have to make restitution for this outrage. You must be punished."

"You can't punish me," Lamont snarls. "Even you won't risk an all-out war."

Zack has Lamont covered with his rifle. I eject the magazine of supernatural specials from my Glock and replace it with regulation bullets. I'll need to do the same for Zack's before we call for backup and the troops arrive.

"We've only got about five minutes before the others arrive," I remind Kallistos, inching closer to the stage.

As if on cue, a phone buzzes in Lamont's jacket pocket. He glances down at it.

"That must be the last of them." Kallistos leans toward him, his expression fiercer than I've ever seen. "You're wrong if you think I will let you go." He looks up, his eyes meeting my own. "Emma, get the phone. Tell whoever's on the other end that the Southern King has fallen."

"No!" Ford cries out.

I make the mistake of turning toward him.

I feel a rush of air. From behind me, Lamont's hands wrap around my neck and squeeze, choking the breath out of me. The metallic smell of his blood and the acrid odor of cooked flesh assail my nostrils. I know I can't be killed. Yet in the moment, the instinct to fight, to live, overcomes all else. Because I know if I die, when I return things will be different. I'll have to go somewhere else. Be someone else. It's Demeter's way of assuring I don't get too comfortable or too attached to a particular life. And I'm not done with this one yet. Not nearly.

I am slipping away but feel no panic. Blackness descends in a rush to block everything from my sight. I hear a voice, Zack's voice, in the background. He's calling my name over and over.

And Kallistos' voice, too.

"I'll find you, Emma," he's saying. "I'll never stop looking."

And then, nothing.

A blast shatters the silence.

I jerk free.

I rub at my eyes, swallow, and gasp at the sharp pain that rips at my throat like barbed wire.

Two men are kneeling in front of me. I shake my head,

try to focus on them, focus on something other than the impulse to scream every time I try to swallow.

Slowly, my head clears. Rational thinking returns. Zack has my right hand, Kallistos my left. I'm sitting on a chair.

Ford's cries are more insistent now.

The phone is no longer buzzing. The chain that Kallistos had been holding is now on the floor at my feet, covered in gore. It lies atop Lamont's clothes, under a blanket of red ash.

I look at Kallistos' damaged hands, torn and bloody from the chains. I can see clear to the bone.

Instinctively, I pull off my gloves and offer him my wrist. "Drink. It will help you heal."

Zack pushes my hand down. "Emma."

I shake my head at him and again offer Kallistos my wrist. Fangs gently pierce my flesh. Tongue circling, lapping, sucking. His arm wraps around my waist, he pulls me closer.

After a moment, Zack says roughly, "Stop. You've taken enough!"

Surprisingly, Kallistos releases me. "Not nearly," he whispers, licking the wound. "It will never be enough."

Zack nods toward the table holding the carafes. "You've probably got a gallon of fresh YBV going to waste. If you need more, drink that."

Kallistos does. He downs one, two, three of the small carafes in the space of a heartbeat. He's reaching for the fourth when Lamont's phone buzzes again.

I pick up the coat, red ash falling like a fine powder when I pull the cell from the pocket.

Kallistos snatches it from my hands. "This is Kallistos

Kouros." The words echo in the chamber. "Your King is dead."

Suddenly, I become aware of the girls—released from thrall by the death of Lamont.

The fog has cleared and they are screaming and crying, some huddled together, a few making a run for the staircase. Zack blocks their path. He's holding his badge out in front of him. "We're with the FBI."

Kallistos steps to them, and in the blink of an eye, the girls fall silent again. Their minds are restored for one fleeting moment, taken in the next.

Kallistos is next to me.

Then he's not.

He's in front of Ford and Cheng.

My gun is missing from the holster. Kallistos has it.

"Long live the King," he says.

"No!" I run to him.

A rose blossoms on Cheng's chest and he drops. Blood like a red mist splashes my face.

I grab his arm. "You shot Cheng! Why?"

But Kallistos has bent his head to Ford's neck and is breathing in his scent. "Fear." He bares his fangs. "It's been centuries since I had a blood slave. What is it they say? To the victor goes the spoils. I want to see what makes his blood so special."

I want to believe Kallistos is putting on a show. But it's not a show. It's real. Cheng is dead on the floor. Ford is howling in pain as Kallistos' fangs ravage his neck. Kallistos sucks, hungrily, at the gaping wound. Blood drips down the front of Ford's shirt.

"Kallistos. No." I grab his arm. "Ford is human."

When Kallistos looks at me, I hardly recognize him.

His features have become feral. His eyes shine with un-restrained lust. A low rumbling emanates from some-where deep in his chest. "You forget yourself, Emma," he says. "I warned you. I told you I would do whatever it takes to protect what's mine. This is who I am."

I refuse to be intimidated. To give up. "This is not all you are," I say softly. "Or we wouldn't be here right now."

He considers my words. Nods. His fangs retract. He gives Ford's neck a tentative lick, then another, and an-other. The wound begins to close and heal.

I breathe a sigh of relief.

Zack unlocks Ford's cuffs.

Weakened, Ford slumps against the door.

Zack kneels down on the floor and releases the catch on Cheng's cuffs. He turns Cheng's face to the side. "Does he look familiar to you?"

Recognition hits. "The last picture I saw of this guy was on a poster. He's wanted for human trafficking."

CHAPTER 25

"So that's how they did it?" Zack asks Ford. "Lamont used Cheng to kidnap the girls? What did he promise him?"

Ford replies without hesitation, the wound on his neck now all but erased. "What do you think? Wealth. Immortality, of course."

Just what the world needs. More immortal sleaze-bags.

"What part did Asa Wade play in your plan?" I ask.

"None," replies Ford. "As far as I know, Asa came of his own accord. He had a score he wanted to settle. With Zack and his bitch." He raises his hands in supplication. "Not my words. Not my fight. None of this is. Was." He turns to Kallistos. "Please, let me go."

Kallistos appears to give it consideration, but is soon shaking his head. "You sound like your pansy-assed monarch. You think you deserve no punishment."

"I'm just as much a victim as they are," Ford replies, gesturing to the girls.

"Victim?" Kallistos snarls. "You were Lamont's blood

slave for how long? No. You voluntarily bound yourself to Lamont. You did it because you enjoyed the power and prestige the title awarded you. Don't speak to me of being a victim. You want to see what a victim looks like?"

Kallistos turns his back on Ford and gestures toward the girls.

"Can you create some . . . reasonable memories to explain all of this so you can bring them out of it?" I ask, rubbing at my throat. The pain has eased and talking is no longer agony, but my voice is still rough.

Kallistos wipes Ford's blood from his mouth on the sleeve of his jacket. "Of course." He smiles at me. "But first—"

He raises my gun once again and shoots Ford square in the chest. The act is so abrupt, so unexpected, I'm frozen in place. Zack isn't. He's poised to protect himself. To protect the girls. To protect me.

Kallistos drops his arm. The barrel points toward the floor. "Relax," he says to Zack. "It had to be done."

Ford is bleeding out in front of me. The red stain covering his shirt is getting larger and larger. I fall to my knees beside him and put pressure on the wound.

"Undo this!" I beg.

Kallistos shakes his head. "Ford was a witness."

"A witness to what?"

"Zack killing his King. To save you."

Blood bubbles up from Ford's mouth. He tries to speak.

Kallistos kneels down beside me. "Cheng was a trafficker. I can fix it with the girls." He sweeps a hand around the chamber. "I'll plant the story that this was an attempt to auction them off. I'll have Simon hack into the FBI hotline. Plant an anonymous tip. You and Zack caught it, followed Cheng from his hotel. He and Ford resisted arrest. I'll get rid of the . . ." He searches for the word. "Unusual evidence. It will be as if Lamont was never here."

I'm too stunned to comment.

Suddenly, Zack nods. "We can also use that angle to explain the money they've been earning from the Emporium in exchange for their blood. Chalk it up to Cheng's attempt to groom the girls."

"Explain," Kallistos says.

They're ignoring Ford, already writing him off as someone who can't be saved. They're right. I watch as he takes his last breath. A wave of nausea washes over me, but I have to push revulsion aside and focus on the matter at hand. We have two bodies and the clock is ticking.

"It's something traffickers do. They use different strategies, different techniques, but basically they increase dependency while at the same time assessing how compliant and malleable their victims might be. I say we stick closely to the story you told the girls. They were approached about participating in a medical research program. They had to show up when and where they were told for their weekly blood donations, a different place each week, no questions asked. And they had to maintain strict confidentiality. In exchange, they were paid. Once Cheng was convinced they would be a good prospect, he nabbed them."

I climb to my feet, wipe the sweat from my brow. "But Julie was earning far longer than the others," I say.

Zack doesn't miss a beat. It's unnerving how easily he

weaves together the story. "He left her alone so that she could unwittingly help him recruit others. Again, it's not an unusual strategy. We'll say they used a bloodmobile. They would park it somewhere for a short period of time along the bus or trolley route so it would be easily accessible. Simon, you catching all this?"

Simon's voice comes across on my headset loud and clear. "I have the MTS bus and trolley schedules up for San Diego already. I'll get my hands on some prepaid cells we can plant. If Kallistos can confirm the names of all the girls and the addresses for their schools, I can work it out. We'll plant text messages. But I'm going to need backup to accomplish this quickly—two, maybe three hours. I have a couple buddies I can call."

"Do whatever you need to do," Kallistos says. "As soon as the job is finished, we'll dispatch someone to wipe their memories. And your memory when this is done. We can't have any loose ends."

"Understood," Simon replies without hesitation.

Zack chimes in. "We can easily buy you the necessary time. If you can get the cell phones here, we'll plant them in the room where the girls were held. They'll be discovered. Forensics probably won't start pulling phone records until tomorrow. Speaking of records, we could also use a bank account showing matching withdrawals that could also eventually be tied to Cheng."

"Simon?" Kallistos asks.

"Got it," he says.

Kallistos looks up, his gaze on Zack. "Now we need to come to an agreement on how to clean up *your* mess."

"Zack's mess?" I ask.

Zack picks up the remains of Lamont's clothes, holding them up with two fingers. "Yeah. It's after Labor Day. I'm going to have a hell of a time getting rid of this white suit." He gives the dirt floor a swipe with his boot, scattering the remnants of ash.

"Do the two of you understand what's happened here? Zack killed a sovereign."

"I also saved Emma's ass," Zack interjects.

Kallistos ignores him. "A *Were* killed a vampire King."

"And saved Emma's ass," Zack says again, this time louder.

Kallistos rounds on him. "Emma would have lived and you damn well know it. You were thinking with your dick, or your heart. Certainly not your head. If this becomes known, we risk a war that will affect more than the supernatural community. The violence will spill over to the mortal world, too. No one will be safe." He turns back to speak to me, voice softer. "Lamont was in *my* territory. He'd taken *my* people. Waged war on *my* Kingdom. And he died by *my* hands. No one can know it was Zack, not ever."

"Agreed." I glance over at Zack. "Except for the three of us."

I hold my breath, wait for Zack to say something. Finally, he does.

"Agreed."

Kallistos nods and moves off, hand at his ear, speaking into his earpiece. It's a conversation we aren't privy to. I catch the name Tony before joining Zack. We don't have much time. Once Kallistos sets the wheels in motion, his "cleanup" crew will be here in minutes. I flash back to last year and another crime scene that he offered to clean up. That one involved blowing up a building.

I heave a sigh. "Should we get the girls out of here? It would make it easier to clean up."

"No fucking way am I leaving Kallistos and his clowns here to do this by themselves. We need two large plastic barrels, rubber gloves, Dustbuster, rags." He calls out the latter loud enough so Kallistos can hear.

His request is acknowledged with a curt nod.

Only Zack isn't quite finished. "And have Evan bring the SUV here. I need the black duffel in the back of the van. . . ."

I look around. Most of the "unusual evidence" left to clean up can be dispatched quickly by Kallistos' men. But Zack isn't going to relinquish control again and I can't blame him.

I glance at Kallistos. He's with the girls now, in a corner. I listen as he speaks to them in a hushed tone, spinning the tale they'll remember as truth. In actuality, it's not far from it. Cheng evidently *was* behind the kidnappings. And he was wanted for human trafficking. They'll remember being abducted and brought here, kept in the cages until Ford arrived, then being brought out to be sold. Only the part about being bled and, of course, that any vampires were here, that vampires exist at all, will be scrubbed—just as simply and easily as he scrubs away the evidence of puncture wounds on their skin with his tongue.

"When you're ready," Kallistos is saying, "you and Zack can take the girls down the tunnel to the opening under the mission. Have them sit inside. The thrall will lift within a few minutes. They will remember as commanded." Kallistos' phone rings. He answers. "All is well. I will be home soon." He tucks his phone back into his jacket. "Owen," he says, by way of explanation. Kallistos cocks his head to the left. "Tony's here."

The sound of approaching footsteps snaps our attention. Tony, the same vampire who helped Kallistos "clean up" Barbara Pierce's lab, smiles when he sees us. He has two others with him.

"We need to hurry," Zack says, checking his watch. "This needs to be called in soon."

Tony turns to Kallistos to get his instructions.

Kallistos directs him back to Zack.

"Simon said to give you these." Tony hands him a clear ziplock bag filled with cell phones.

"Gloves on. Collect all of the glasses, the carafes, the tablecloths. Vacuum up the shards. Dump them in one of the barrels along with Lamont's phone, any radios, the earpieces on the floor, and the vampire clothing. I need to collect some clothes from upstairs and plant the cells you brought. As soon as that's done, we wipe down the stage area and all of the walls. Got it?"

The vampires nod in unison, then go to work.

Kallistos looks me up and down. "You're a mess."

I'm soaked in Ford's and Cheng's blood, my clothes painted in macabre splotches. "It's been a long night."

He reaches for my hand and tilts his head toward the girls, who are still in thrall, still waiting patiently for their next command. "You did what you set out to do. You saved them."

I step back. My hand slips from his. I fold my arms protectively across my chest. I can't quite look him in the eye. "And did you do what you set out to do?" My gaze falls, instead, on the bodies of Ford and Cheng, crumpled, bloodied, dead. "You killed them."

He smiles wryly. "Not all of them. I let a few go."

"So they would tell the story. You shouldn't have killed the humans. It wasn't right." My voice seems distant to my own ears.

He reaches out to cup my cheek, tipping my face up and searching my eyes. For what? Understanding? Forgiveness? He finds neither.

"What is right?" Kallistos asks. "You think your form of justice is better? Would you rather see them imprisoned, stuffed in cages like animals? Like those girls? Would you rather risk having it all unravel?" He leans down, his voice tight, strained. "Cheng was a monster. Your own FBI has made him one of its most wanted. And Ford? Do you really think he was any better? That he was innocent in all of this? I made the tough decision. It's what sovereigns do."

I push his hand away, match my tone to his. "Trouble is, I don't believe the decision was all that tough for you."

"Emma, time to take the girls out of here. I'm calling this in!" Zack shouts out.

He may be acting like he didn't hear every word Kallistos and I have just spoken, but I'm confident he did. They all did.

An awkward silence descends on the room. But it lasts only a moment. Soon the buzz of work resumes. Tony and his cronies move with lightning speed, disposing of the table, chairs, and blood evidence by transporting it down the same tunnel we entered through. All that remain are the bodies of Cheng and Ford, the staging area where the auction was to take place, and the area where the girls had been kept. In less than ten minutes they've "scrubbed" the entire crime scene.

Kallistos wipes his prints from my gun and hands it back to me.

Mechanically, I take it.

"Your gun. Your call," he says. "What happens next is up to you."

With that, he walks away.

I lead the girls through the passageway to the entry point under the chapel. A short flight of steps leads to a bolted door. I push through to find it's a false wall within the priest's compartment of what I recognize as a confessional. We step out into the chapel. The girls file past the statue of the Virgin Mary surrounded by the flickering of hundreds of votives and into the rear pews. I know they will come out of thrall shortly. They will remember what Kallistos told them to remember. I, however, will remember the way it really happened.

I stroll down the aisle and stand in front of the ornate altar. Iron stands line both sides, filled with candles. The smell of polished wood and incense permeates the air.

"Agent Monroe?"

I turn around. It's Julie Simmons. Barefoot and bruised. Her hair matted. Her eyes are hollow from lack of sustenance and loss of blood, but real awareness shines through. She's back. She wraps her arms around me. "Thank you," she whispers.

Tears cloud my vision. I squeeze my eyes shut. When I open them again, I see that the other girls have gathered near. They should be peppering us with questions. Instead, they are eerily quiet. Kallistos has programmed them with all the answers they need, all the answers they'll repeat to the police, their parents, one another.

Zack catches my eye. He is standing behind them.

He's changed clothes, back to his suit. Only the cuffs are soaked in blood. His hands are, too.

I make my way over to him.

"Suit's a little worse for wear," I say.

He smiles. "Right back at you. When we're ready to leave, Evan parked the SUV in the west corner of the lot. He left with Malcolm and our equipment."

I hear the sound of sirens approaching.

"How are they?" he asks, motioning to the girls.

"Better than one would expect after what they've been through," I say.

"How are you?"

I have to sift through a dozen cascading emotions. Zack waits for me to answer. But I can't. Not now. "I need to get some air," I tell him.

"The forensic team will be here shortly," he says. "Johnson's on his way, too."

"I'll just be outside. I need a moment to collect my thoughts."

Zack nods. He holds open the door to the courtyard for me. Then closes it again, giving me privacy.

I sit on the steps leading to the small garden between the chapel and the school and look up. Light from the sliver of moon glints off of the bells in the tower. The sirens are getting closer. I pull my knees up and rest my head on my arms and take a deep breath. The perfumed night air fills my lungs, jasmine and honeysuckle, rose and lavender. It does nothing to soothe my wounded heart.

What happens next is up to you.

Kallistos' final words ring in my ear.

In the distance, the drone of a helicopter draws close.

The troops are about to arrive.

I stand up. Time to put on my game face and finish the job.

My job. It's fortunate I'm good at it. Because, really, it's all I have.

CHAPTER 26

My legs feel like lead as I emerge from the chapel. It's well after midnight, but you wouldn't know it from the looks of things. The entire area is lit up. Three helicopters are buzzing overhead. The parking lot behind the mission is filled with news vans. Our SUV is, as Evan promised, parked in the west corner. I'm sure when he left it there, it seemed like a good idea. That was before the sea of reporters with cameras and microphones descended. A particularly perky blonde swoops down on us.

"Agent Monroe, may we have a word? We're hearing it was your weapon that killed two men, one of which was on the FBI's most wanted list."

I hold up my hand and do my best to keep moving. "Deputy Director Johnson will be making an official statement." The vultures move with me. There are more of them now.

"Agent Armstrong," one begins.

I don't hear the rest of his question. The cacophony around us has turned into a dull roar, an indiscriminate hum punctuated by flashes of light. I spare a glance in Zack's direction. He's talking with Johnson, who has my gun in an evidence bag. Routine procedure, I know, for an agent-involved shooting. But nothing about this is routine.

Bits and pieces of the reporters' conversations float to the top. The word *hero* is bantered about over and over. Some are asking about Cheng. Others want to know the names of the girls. I'm exhausted, physically and emotionally. I just want to get to the SUV. To shower. To scream. To cry. When I glance again at Zack, he catches my eye and motions toward the SUV. Johnson is giving me the go-ahead to leave. Tomorrow, though, begins the long slog through endless paperwork. I "killed" two people tonight.

Zack meets me at the car and opens the passenger door. I climb inside.

He has to push through the gaggle of reporters who followed him. Finally he makes it inside and slams the door.

The flashes continue. I raise my arm up to shield my eyes. "Let's get out of here."

Zack doesn't have to be told again. He's as anxious to leave as I am. With a brisk nod he fires up the engine. The media throng parts like the Red Sea. In seconds we're through the gate and navigating around the side of the mission, then down the long drive. I lean my head against the cool window. We've saved ten girls. Ten. I should be elated. But the deaths of Ford and Cheng are weighing on me. Zack's silence is weighing on me.

We're on Highway 8, heading west. It's coming up on two and the traffic is light.

"You okay?" he finally asks.

I shake my head. I'm so far from okay I don't even know where to begin. "I have blood on my hands."

"And vampire King in you hair," he adds. "I hear that's tough to get out."

I can't help myself. Despite my dark mood, I feel the corners of my mouth curve up. "You sent one of the most powerful vampires in the world to his final death with a single shot." Then the reality of the situation, the implications, come back. "The political ramifications—"

He meets my eyes for the briefest of moments. "Lamont wasn't quite as affected by the paralytic as Kallistos thought. In part, he was biding time, waiting for Kallistos' grip to loosen. He could have killed you. When you're in a situation like that . . ." Finally he settles on, "I made the right call. I'd do it again."

He sounds like Kallistos, though mentioning that would only break the mood. "But you knew I would eventually heal. That I wouldn't die."

Zack's hand slides over to mine. He covers it, gives it a squeeze. "That's what you tell me."

The warmth from his skin penetrates mine. It radiates up my arm, into my chest, and wraps around my heart.

"Before you go down what's come to be a predicable path," he continues, "don't believe for a second that Kallistos' claim of killing Lamont is for my benefit. Or the benefit of the Weres. He's doing it to send a message. He went in fully intending to take Lamont out. My stepping in when I did interfered with his plan. In his mind, I'm sure he's merely taking back control of the scenario, setting things right in order to pave the way."

"Pave the way for what?" I ask.

"His taking over the South. Merging the two Kingdoms under his rule. Ending the unrest."

"You think he plans on taking over the Southern Kingdom?" My head is spinning.

"Absolutely. And he'll be met with significant opposition. The unrest is likely to get worse before it gets better."

We drive past the turnoff to the 163, the road that would lead us to my place. For the first time I realize Zack isn't taking me home. I look back, over my shoulder.

"Don't be afraid," Zack says, softly. The statement is punctuated with another squeeze of my hand. "I don't expect anything from you."

The words I uttered when we were together in his closet come back to haunt me.

What we have. It isn't meaningless and it does scare me.

We pass Interstate 5. I feel my anxiety mounting. I try to tamp it down, but I can't. I roll down the passenger's window. The wind rushes in; it's bracing. I turn my face into it and close my eyes. *I don't expect anything from you.* "Trouble is, you deserve everything," I mutter, brushing the wetness from my cheeks.

I know he hears me. But he doesn't respond.

We take the West Mission Bay Drive exit. I can smell the salt in the air. Taste it in my tears. My face is numb.

Zack pulls into his driveway. Kills the engine. Rolls up the windows.

I step out of the Suburban. My body aches from head to toe. I look up at the night sky and remember the words Demeter spoke to me in this very driveway, not six months ago.

I will be watching you, watching you with this man. He's different. You and I both know it.

I feel Zack's hand at the small of my back. "It's late."

I turn to face him. "Why am I here?"

He guides me to the door and unlocks it. "Because you don't want to be alone. Because you don't want to be with him. Because you're tired and confused."

All true.

He goes to the fridge, grabs two beers, and twists off the tops. "Come on. I'll get you some fresh towels. Sheets on the guest bed are clean."

I follow Zack up the stairs, past his room and into another. The walls are a soft yellow, the bedding a light sage. He goes into the attached bathroom, comes out with a stack of cream-colored towels.

"Need anything else?"

I shake my head, tilt the bottle to my lips, and take several long pulls. The beer is ice-cold and it soothes my throat. Unlike just about everything that's happened in the last few hours, it goes down easy.

Zack turns to go.

"Wait."

He's halfway out the door and pauses midstep.

"Maybe a shirt or something to sleep in?"

"I'll leave it on the bed," he says without looking back.

Then I'm alone. I walk stiffly into the bathroom, shed my clothes, then step into the shower. It's stocked with body wash, shampoo, and conditioner. I lean into the hot spray and let it wash over me. The shampoo smells like citrus, clean and fresh. I mechanically work it into my hair. Lather. Rinse. Repeat. When I reach for the conditioner, my hand begins to shake. Gooseflesh covers my backside. I hear crackling and popping. My toes curl as the water on the floor beneath my feet turns to ice. Snow falls from the showerhead, assaulting my bare skin. It's like being hit with thousands of needles. Within seconds my body is covered in a dusting of fine white powder that burns. Icicles form in my hair. I know what this means.

She's here.

Demeter.

I fumble with the taps, trying to turn off the water. It does me no good. The faucets are frozen in place.

"Oh, this is just fucking perfect."

I struggle with the glass door of the shower. It, too, is frozen in place. With a loud shattering sound that makes me fear I've broken the glass, it finally lets go. I toss one frost-covered towel on the floor, wrap the other around me, and, fueled by the anger and resentment of scores of lifetimes, I round on perhaps the most powerful goddess in the pantheon.

"What?" It comes out as a hiss.

A slow, satisfied smile forms on her mouth. It does nothing to soften the chill in her cobalt blue eyes. Everything about her is cold. The sheer fabric of her long gown is woven from frozen crystals. Her translucent alabaster skin is covered in a web of ice, sparkling like hardened diamonds. Her stark white hair flows past her waist and hangs over her breasts.

"You did well tonight, Ligea."

Her declaration almost knocks me off my feet. Is she here to take me back? To release me? It's the moment I've been working toward, dreaming about—for thousands of years. But am I ready?

"I've come to grant you a reprieve. You need it. More

importantly, you've earned it." Demeter holds her hands out, palms up, and gestures toward the doorway. "Go to him."

I can't believe my ears. I wrap the towel tighter around my body. "Right. And risk—"

"Nothing. No repercussions. Not from me. Not tonight."

"And after tonight?"

"Speak plainly, Ligea. I have little time and another Siren to torment. How long has it been since you've seen Leucosia?"

Her voice is cold and calculating. She knows exactly how long it's been since my sisters and I separated. She doesn't bother waiting for a reply.

"She still pines for your vampire, you know," she says with a smile.

Leucosia is the reason Kallistos is a vampire. Although, to be fair, it was more that she was the catalyst. Demeter the cause. My sister and Kallistos were once in love and, presumably, happy. Something Demeter wouldn't tolerate. Like so many before him, he fell victim to the curse. Only his death wasn't final—not yet.

"I would hardly call him mine," I say.

She leans forward and does something she hasn't done in centuries. She touches me. Her palm caresses my cheek. Despite the burn, I stand my ground.

"You want to call the Were yours. Yet you resist. You deny yourself. Go to him. As long as it lasts between the two of you, I'll allow it. You didn't just save ten girls tonight, Ligea. With this new venture, who knows how many more would have suffered in the future?"

"You'll allow me tonight?" I ask. "No harm will come to Zack?"

Demeter's said what she's come to say. Her image is fading. "I'll allow it for as long as it lasts." Her final words hang in the air. Water begins to once again flow from the shower. I reach in and turn off the taps. I look at my reflection in the mirror. My skin is red from the cold.

Go to him.

I rush across the guest room floor, down the hall, and into the master suite. Everything feels surreal. The carpet beneath my feet is lush and warm. Tears fall, unbidden, and roll down my cheeks. I reach out and brush my fingertips across the duvet covering Zack's bed. The door to his bathroom is open. Steam is rolling out. The shower is running.

Zack's back is to me as I step into the room, but I have no doubt he knows I'm here. I let the towel fall. He waits, still, silent, giving me every chance to leave. I don't. Instead I take a step forward, then another, and another. My hand is on the door. I pull it open. Step inside. My arms slide around his waist. My body molds to the back of his. I want to melt into him. To get lost in his flesh.

He turns to face me. "Your skin is like ice." He runs his hands over my arms. "Let me warm you. You're in shock. Not thinking clearly . . ."

I move underneath the spray. Let the water run through my hair and cascade down my body. I place my hand on his chest. "I've never been so clear, so certain of anything. And I'm no longer afraid. I want this." My hand slides down over his stomach and wraps around his cock. "I want you."

Zack's mouth crashes down on mine.

I'm lost.

His sense of urgency, of need, takes my breath away.

I gasp and his tongue slides boldly inside my open mouth, plundering it with a sweet and desperate abandon that makes me ache even more. My hands grasp his biceps. I pull him closer, relishing his feel, his taste, his smell.

He pulls back. Takes a moment to run his hands over my face and neck. "Are you sure?"

"About nothing in this world but you, this moment."

He reaches for my hand, raises it to his lips, kisses it tenderly. Then he turns off the taps.

I take advantage and let my gaze run over his body. Fully clothed, Zack is an imposing man. He's tall and broad shouldered. His muscles are well defined. His body chiseled to perfection from years of hard training. Strangely, it's not his body that I want most right now. It's to hear the words. Words that I've avoided hearing for centuries. Words that I thought I'd never be able to welcome and repeat again.

Kallistos has been my lover for the past five months. But deep down inside I've known on some level that for each and every one of those days, Zack has loved me.

I reach out and place my hand on his shoulder, let it slide down his back.

The spell of the tender moment is broken as he spins around and with a primitive and playful growl tosses me over his shoulder. Wet and dripping, I'm whisked out of the shower, through the bathroom, and into Zack's bedroom. A squeal erupts from within me followed by laughter, bubbling up and escaping as I'm tossed onto the bed. I feel so light I could float. If it weren't for the fact that Zack's body is now covering mine, I'm certain I would be.

"I love hearing you laugh," he says, pushing a strand of hair off of my face.

"I love seeing you naked."

His expression turns suddenly serious. He rests his forehead against mine. "This isn't casual for me, Emma. If it is for you, I need to know. I need for you to be honest with me. I need to know where I stand." He pauses, pulls back, and searches my eyes. "This bed isn't big enough for three."

He's referring to Kallistos. I open my mouth to say something but he silences me, placing his fingertips over my mouth.

"It's a metaphor."

I wrap my hand around his wrist. "I know," I assure him. "It's just you and me. With us, that's all it's ever been."

He kisses me softly on the lips. Again and again, before moving down to my neck. His hands are on the move, fingertips dancing across the canvas of my skin. His already-warm skin becomes even warmer with each passing breath. His hand glides over a breast. I arch up, my body wantonly begging for more of his touch.

I want him. Inside me. Now. Yet I resist the urge to take control. Zack feels it, too. His cock long, hard, and poised between my legs, is a testament to that fact. But neither of us wants to break the tenderness of the moment. It's filled with possibilities I never thought I'd realize.

I wrap my legs around him, tilt my hips up.

He's poised at my entrance.

"I want you so much, it terrifies me," he confesses.

"I know." Tears leak from the corners of my eyes. My heart feels close to bursting. "It terrified me, too."

His brows furrow. "Not anymore?"

"Not anymore. Now, shut up and kiss me."

"Yes, ma'am," he says with a wink before moving away.

He licks his way down the valley between my breasts, pauses briefly to dip his tongue into my belly button, then nibbles his way over my hip bone and across to my inner thigh.

I feel the brush of his hair. The scrape of his beard. Fingertips gently separate my folds. Then the kiss comes. Openmouthed. Controlled tongue. I feel a vibration. A low, deep rumbling emanates from deep within Zack's chest. I reach down with one hand and lace my fingers through his hair. The other is searching for purchase, clawing at the duvet. His finger slides inside as his mouth continues to work. I'm on the brink. Approaching the precipice. He adds a second finger. I'm writhing with want, wet beyond all imagination. And then I fall.

But I don't come down.

No.

I'm soaring. Higher and higher.

"Christ, you feel so good," Zack, inside me now, whispers into my ear. "I want this to last forever."

We roll. I ride him. Knees on the bed. Hands splayed across his rippling abs. His are on my breasts. Then suddenly, he sits up. His arm wraps around my waist. His mouth covers my nipple.

I can't breathe. I can't climb any higher.

My fingers tangle in Zack's hair. He looks up at me. His eyes possess the blue of the wolf. I kiss him, deeply, tasting myself on his lips and tongue. All the while we're rocking, his cock thrusts into me, slow and deep. When the kiss ends Zack places his hand on the back of my head and pulls me closer still, until I feel his cheek against mine. The pulse of his breath on my ear.

"I love you," he says.

Then he thrusts once, twice more.

I shatter. Rocked by an orgasm so intense, nothing can contain it. Nothing can contain me, not in this world or the last. Overcome with joy. I'm undone. Secure in the fact that Demeter promised no repercussions, I let the walls melt away. I let the light of my power shine through. I let him see my true self. The surge of energy warms the room. A wind rises up, dousing the fire, fanning the curtains, and instantly drying my hair. The combined scents of burning firewood and ocean are overshadowed by a delicate yet complex blend of white florals layered atop citrus.

Zack's nostils flare.

The scent.

It's the last thing I remember before succumbing to the light.

CHAPTER 27

Day Five: Friday, September 6

When I open my eyes, dawn is breaking. Zack is standing at the foot of the bed. He's fully clothed. I'm completely naked. He tosses me one of his shirts. Only it's not a toss. He flings the shirt at me, and the instant my eyes meet his, I know that something is wrong.

Very, very wrong.

His eyes are cold, calculating, hardened.

Mine dart about the room, scanning the floor looking for evidence of Demeter's presence, patches of ice, pools of water. I can barely form thoughts, hardly speak. But I feel her. "What have you done?" I shout.

I see nothing. Nothing but Zack, his glare skewering me.

"Does that look familiar?" Zack asks, pointing to the shirt I have clutched in my hands.

I glance down at it. Then back up at him. It doesn't, but I have a horrible feeling that it should.

"I was changing the sheets up here a week after we closed the Patterson case. I found it under the bed."

Bile rushes up and burns the back of my throat. My head is spinning.

"The scent on it wasn't mine," he continues. "It was faint, but distinctive. One that for the life of me, I couldn't place. Until last night. It was yours."

"You kept it all this time," I say, hugging it to my breast. Knowing that Zack is slipping away, that Demeter has won again.

"In an evidence bag. You used magic on me, didn't you, to make me forget. To manipulate me."

"To protect you!" Tears begin to roll down my cheeks. "The spell was very specific. It only erased the intimate moments between us."

"A convenient way to cast aside lovers you've grown tired of?" He shakes his head. "If you're planning on using it again, you needn't bother."

He walks over to the chair in the corner of the room, picks up his suit coat, and slips it on.

I rush over, positioning myself between Zack and the door. "Let me explain. We have a chance here. I know you're hurt and . . . and confused."

"I *trusted* you." He's towering over me, reeking of sadness and fury. "I declared my love for you. And all the time you were playing me. This little deception of yours . . . If you think I can just let it go . . . Well, then you're the one who's confused. Now, get out of my way or I'm going to pick you up and move you."

I step aside. "Where are you going?"

"To ask Johnson for a transfer. I'll be back in an hour. I want you gone."

I hear him pad down the stairs. I hear the front door slam. I hear the engine turn over on the SUV. Zack and

I came here together. What I was wearing last night is covered in blood. I have no clothes, no car. I crumple to the floor.

She knew.

She's watching. Always watching. She knew about the shirt in the evidence bag. Knew Zack would put it together, feel betrayed.

For as long as it lasts.

With a burst of energy I climb to my feet, pick up the bottle of beer on the nightstand, and whip around, intent on throwing it into the mirror. Arm cocked back, I'm frozen in place. There's no sign of the glamour I rely on. The reflection that stares back at me is the true one.

"The magic's gone."

"Apparently where Zack is concerned," comes the ice-cold voice.

"How could you?" I whirl around. With every ounce of strength I have in me, I throw the bottle. With a wave of her hand, Demeter makes it explode. Its pieces embed deep in my face, neck, and stomach. The pain is excruciating. But it doesn't begin to mask that of my broken heart.

I lie on Zack's bedroom floor, bleeding. Knowing I'll bleed more if I begin to pull out the shards of glass. A particularly large shard is stuck in my forehead over my right eye. My vision is clouded. I fear the one in my neck has nicked an artery. I don't care.

"Not your best look." The words are spoken so quietly from the door, I'm not sure I've really heard them. I try to turn my head toward them, but the wound in my neck is gushing now. I haven't got the strength.

He comes to me. Kneels down next to my body. The carpet squishes under the pressure of his knee. He doesn't wince. The blood doesn't bother him.

"How?" I manage to get out.

"Seems Armstrong didn't *entirely* sever our connection." He plucks the shard of glass from my throat, then bends close and gives it a pull, followed by a lick, then another. The section over my eye gets treated next. Kallistos moves deliberately and carefully over my body, tending to the most severe wounds first. Once the bleeding is stayed, he bites his wrist and holds it over my mouth. "Open up. Just a few drops. It will help you heal."

And it does. Kallistos' blood is warm, sweet, slightly salty with only the slightest hint of copper. I close my eyes and, with effort, swallow.

"Demeter?" he asks.

I open my eyes, try to sit up.

Kallistos places his hand on my shoulder. "Give yourself a few more minutes." His gaze sweeps the room. "Is he dead?" It's asked with a hint of hopefulness.

I shake my head. Hot tears continue to leak from the corners of my eyes.

He wipes them away. "Can you tell me what happened?"

"She told me there would be no repercussions. She granted me a reprieve. But it was a trap."

"Where's Zack?"

"Gone. Probably in Johnson's office by now, asking for a transfer."

Kallistos offers me a hand and helps me to my feet. "I don't understand."

I'm shaky, but able to stand. "Liz provided me with a

spell to alter Zack's memory. I used it. He found out. He hates me."

"And he hasn't even seen the carpet."

"He's never going to forgive me."

"You used this spell in an effort to protect him."

"Zack doesn't see it that way."

Kallistos slides off the leather coat he's wearing and holds it out for me. "Armstrong's an idiot. I don't know what you see in him."

The coat falls midthigh on Kallistos. It's midcalf on me. "Take me home?"

He nods, wraps his arm around my shoulder. "Where are your things?"

I run down the list of what I came with. "Everything is in the guest room bath."

"I'll take care of it." He gestures toward the blood-stained carpet. "This, too."

Before I can respond, he's off and back. He's clutching my ruined clothes and cell phone.

"Looks like you have a text from Johnson." He holds up the cell. It came in five minutes ago.

And I thought my day couldn't possibly get any worse.

CHAPTER 28

I step off the elevator. The office is quiet. It's barely eight. The first place my eyes go to is Zack's desk. His chair is empty. The second is our boss' office. Bingo.

Jimmy Johnson comes out of the break room, coffee cup in hand.

"Emma?" he says. "A word?"

I follow him back into the break room. He pours a cup of coffee and hands it to me. "How are you?"

I take a sip, knowing I can't answer the question honestly. I raise my eyes to his. "I'm fine."

He's studying me. "From all the preliminary reports, it was a good shooting. I'm giving you your gun back, although when you return, there'll be the requisite bullshit visit to the department shrink."

I start to nod, then stop. "When I get back?"

"Go join your partner, Monroe," he says, tilting his head toward Zack. "I'll be in shortly." He takes a sip of coffee, eyes watching me over the rim of the cup.

I give him a curt nod before weaving my way through the maze of indistinct gray cubicles to the office in the back. I knock before entering. "Jimmy asked me to join you."

I sit in the empty chair next to Zack's. He doesn't look at me. I catch my reflection in a picture behind Johnson's desk. Thanks to Liz, my glamour is once again securely in place. My hair is pulled back, wound into a tight bun at the nape of my neck. I'm wearing a new black suit, courtesy of Kallistos. It's paired with a simple white silk blouse. I want to speak, but can't find the words.

Zack breaks the silence. "You smell like him."

He's yet to look at me.

"I needed clothes. And a ride." I swallow. Thanks to Kallistos' blood, my throat's no longer sore from Lamont's attack, but words are still slow to come. "Kallistos sensed that I was in need of help and showed up in your bedroom." That gets Zack's attention. "The mark may be gone, but something remains of the connection."

"That didn't take long. Hope you didn't fuck him on my bed."

His sarcasm is caustic, but underneath is anger tempered with sadness.

"I didn't fuck him at all," I manage to whisper.

Before Zack has a chance to respond, Johnson walks in and closes the door.

I sit up straighter. Wait, hands clasped together in my lap as he takes his seat.

Johnson leans forward, elbows on his desk. "The two of you are going to New York."

It isn't the announcement I was expecting. "Sir?"

"New York. The Big Apple." He tosses a file in our direction.

Zack shifts nervously in his chair. "About my request —"

"Denied," says Johnson.

"Our reports?" I ask.

"Work on them on the plane." His finger moves between the two of us. "You think I don't see what's happened here? I don't know how long it's been going on. I don't know what's happened to end it. And I don't give a shit. I don't care about that any more than I care whether you floss, believe in God, or vote. Wanna know why? Because it's personal." He taps the top of the file and pushes it closer to Zack. "This is business. Your job. You're good at it. They need you in New York. You leave this afternoon."

Zack slowly reaches out for the file.

I hold my breath.

"It's a kid," Johnson says. "A seven-year-old. The son of Roger Maitlan."

"The real estate mogul?" Zack asks.

Johnson nods. "One and the same." He stands up, pulling open his desk drawer. He hands my gun to me. "Your flight leaves at noon. You can pick up your boarding passes at Southwest's counter. You'll have plenty of time to review the file on the plane. I suggest you get packing."

It's our cue to go. Zack and I rise in unison and head for the door.

"Agents?"

I turn back. "Sir?"

"Eyes on the ball," says Johnson.

"Yes, sir," I say.

More agents have arrived in the office. All eyes are on us. Some call out "Good job" and "Way to go," even clap us on our backs as we pass. My skin crawls at the hypocrisy but I have no choice but to smile and accept their congratulations. The girls are home and safe. The secrets of the supernaturals have been protected. My relationship with Zack is the only casualty of a case that to our fellow agents was a roaring success.

Zack stops at his desk. He opens a drawer, shuffles some papers around. He's taking his time, as if avoiding having to get into the elevator with me. I wish I could say something to make this right. I realize bitterly I never can. I push the call button and the doors instantly open. I step inside. Turn around.

Just as the doors begin to slide shut, Zack steps in. "As soon as the case is over, I'm going to ask Johnson for that transfer again. And I'm going to keep asking until I get it."

I turn to him and blurt out what's true. "I don't want you to leave." I reach out, my fingertips brush his. "We're good together."

He pulls back, folds his arms across his chest, shakes his head. "I don't know how to work with a partner I can't trust."

"I'm sorry. I know you don't understand. I wish I could explain."

"But you can't," he says.

I've gone over this in my head a thousand times. My conclusion is always the same. I know Zack, and I know Demeter. Her threats wouldn't scare him. But they should. This is a fight Zack won't win.

"It's not safe. It's better this way." I try for a smile.

"Is it?"

I nod. "I'd say trust me but—"

The doors open. We step out, then head for the parking lot. Zack pulls a pair of sunglasses from his inside breast pocket and slips them on. I can no longer see his eyes.

"Johnson's right. We have a job to do," he says. "Nothing you say now is going to make a difference. What you did can't be undone."

"But maybe in time . . ."

He's not looking at me. He's looking out at the parking lot.

"Maybe in time," I repeat, then step off the curb.

"Emma?" His voice is brusque. "I shouldn't have left you high and dry. I'm sorry for that."

I check the time. I wonder whether the carpet in Zack's apartment has been replaced. "I understand."

"Want a ride to your place?" he asks. "I can drop you off."

"Thanks."

Zack hands me the folder. We climb into the SUV.

It's all so familiar, and all so different.

I open the file.

We have another case. I have another chance.

Zack pulls out onto Aero Drive and starts to head south on the 15.

My eyes are on the picture of a missing seven-year-old boy but silently I'm reciting the words I do every time I go out on a new case.

Redemption could be one rescue away.

ABOUT THE AUTHORS

S. J. Harper is the pen name for the writing team of **Samantha Sommersby** and **Jeanne C. Stein**, two friends who met at Comic-Con in San Diego and quickly bonded over a mutual love of good wine, edgy urban fantasy, and everything Joss Whedon.

Samantha Sommersby left what she used to call her "real-life" day job in the psychiatric field to pursue writing full-time in 2007. She is the author of more than ten novels and novellas, including the critically acclaimed Forbidden series. She currently lives with her husband and cocker spaniel, Buck, in a century-old Southern California Craftsman. Sam happily spends her days immersed in a world where vampires, werewolves, and demons are real, myths and legends are revered, magic is possible, and love still conquers all.

Jeanne C. Stein is the national bestselling author of the Anna Strong Vampire Chronicles. She also has numerous short story credits, including most recently the novella *Blood Debt* from the *New York Times* bestselling anthology *Hexed*. Her series has been picked up in three foreign countries and her short stories published in collections here in the U.S. and the U.K. She lives in Denver, Colorado, where she finds gardening a challenge more daunting than navigating the world of mythical creatures.